D0983507

TROUBLES

TROUBLES

A Novel by

NAOMI MAY

John Calder

LONDON

PR 6063
A 93 T 7

First published in Great Britain in 1976 by
John Calder (Publishers) Ltd.
18 Brewer Street, London W1R 4AS

© Naomi May 1976

ISBN 0 7145 3555 9 cloth edition

No part of this publication may be reproduced, stored
in a retrieval system, or transmitted in any form, by any
means, electronic, mechanical, photocopying, recording or
otherwise except brief extracts for the purpose of review,
without the prior written permission of the copyright owner
and publisher.
Any paperback edition of this book whether published
simultaneously with, or subsequent to the casebound edition
is sold subject to the condition that it shall not, by way of
trade, be lent, resold, hired out or otherwise disposed of
without the publisher's consent, in any form of binding or
cover other than that in which it is published.

Set in 11pt Plantin solid by Woolaston Parker
Printed in Scotland by M. & A. Thomson Litho Ltd. East Kilbride

To my Mother and Father

1967

'John Patrick!' Indignant at the name given to her first grandchild, Mrs Thomas Mulholland clicked the receiver and ran her finger round the dial for traces of dust. The polished surface of a squat mahogony table mirrored perfectly the telephone into which she had been complaining about a request for flowers for the christening; her garden had already been half-stripped through her generosity to the Unionist fete. 'But Thomas says I must!' she had declared. 'And so,' here she mimicked the County Down accent of her daily woman, 'there's an end on it.'

The room smelled of polish and vegetation, the north-facing bay window, with its view of Belfast Lough, being filled with pot-plants whose leaves and blooms further cut down the light into an interior congested with furniture that had been accumulated by the family over three generations. She had spent the early years of her married life in the great mansion built by Thomas's father; but, when this had been given away and they had moved to a residential suburb above the lough, Alicia had found herself unable to pack off her surplus possessions to a sales-room where they would have fetched a poor price for their value. Her friends had teased her for hoarding, but her reply had been that she was storing up good pieces for her three sons. However, although John, the eldest, was now married, his young wife had different tastes.

Certainly the things made the house difficult to clean. Lingering, putting off the moment when she must take hold of her secateurs to cut down her garden, she inspected for smears the glass facets of a china cabinet and thought of her daughter-in-law's ineptitude with staff. Her own Hannah had been with her for eighteen years—and not because of the pay. Young Catherine's trouble was that she spoiled them; how often had she reminded the girl that these things have to be kept in proportion—one must be sensible! But then Catherine employed Catholics by preference . . . Impatiently her glance travelled the room, pausing at the mantel-piece where there was a crested invitation to a function at Government House. At least, she congratulated herself, she had seen to it that Catherine had made her way up to Hillsborough to sign the Governor's book before the baby was born and she had an excuse to sidle out of her obligations.

Drawing herself up, Alicia Mulholland smoothed away imaginary creases in her beige skirt with a hand calloused on the mounts of the palm; the wedding ring was embedded behind an arthritic joint, and the finger-tips whitish because so much grit had to be scrubbed from the nails. Although she did not feel the cold, goose-flesh showed on her bare arms (the house would not be heated until late in the autumn). Energetic, if rather stout, the authoritative curve of her nose contrasted with her fleshy cheeks and the small chin that receded into a sturdy neck. She stiffened when she heard a clock on the mantel chiming twelve—Nathaniel's dinner hour—followed by a deeper chime from the grandfather clock in the hall; then a wasp buzzed in the silence. She crossed the room and searched among her plants for the angry insect. There was a nest in the garden and the house was swarming with them—she must talk to Nathaniel: they could be smoked out, or perhaps boiling water would be more effective. . . .

Anxious not to miss him, she hurried from the cold, dark house, with its smell of objects that are being preserved, into the warmth and fragrance of the summer day outside. The garden sloped downhill, a suburban oblong, which she had cleverly designed with an illusion of space and mystery. Near the house there was a rockery with rare alpine plants and else-where, among trees and shrubs from exotic parts of the world, two palms flourished in the tepid climate. Every few years the garden was opened to the public. Looking out over the lough, she had to shield her eyes against the dazzle from a ship gliding through a strip of water, blue as the Aegean, towards the open sea. Behind her, in spite of the brilliance of the day, the hills were vague with sunny haze and the sky-line was softened. From where she stood Alicia could just see, shadowed by misty trees, the towering neo-gothic residence that had housed the Mulhollands at the height of their prosperity. The family had made their money during the ship-building boom towards the end of the nineteenth century, a period when the city of Belfast was confidently expanding, though agrarian Ireland was in decline; her father-in-law had belonged to the generation that had launched the Titanic. But it was impossible, these days, to maintain the merchant's palace he had built for himself. When Thomas had bequeathed it to the Government as a home for spastics, he had been praised for public spirit, though in private there had been envious comments on a fortune so secure that a valuable site could be painlessly thrown away.

Through the delphiniums Alicia spotted her gardener hurriedly buttoning his shirt sleeves in the hope that he was unobserved. 'Nathaniel!' she sang out to him as she marched down the path, 'I can see you!'

He was a hard, sinewy man, very weather-beaten. Making a gesture of it, he removed his cap to mop his reddened forehead: 'I was just away for my dinner.' The accent, not unlike a Scottish voice, would have marked him as a Protestant. They eyed one another.

She cleared her throat: 'I wanted to talk to you about flowers for the christening. . . . '

At this his thin lips pursed into a smile: 'Ah, the babe!' To Nathaniel the birth of a grandson was a sign of divine approval. Restless in his pursuit of the Lord, he had moved from the Church of Ireland to the Baptists and on again to join the following of a self-ordained priest, who had not yet become famous and was little known other than as a common rabble-rouser. On the Sabbath his family would eat a joint cooked by his wife on the previous day and his children were not allowed to watch television unless the programme was religious. When his sister's only daughter had been run over in a road accident he had been convinced that this was a judgement on her for having spoiled the child.

'Well,' doubtfully he examined the steaming dial of his watch, 'in that case . . . '

'Those delphiniums, they're such a splendid show,' Mrs Mulholland wrung her hands, 'it does seem rather a shame . . . '

'They're past their best,' he said bluntly, but there was a knowing gleam in his eye. Now he was in alliance with his employer and together they paced their garden, taking it in turn to find a reason why this or that prized bloom should remain untouched. They paused before the peonies, which were at their most luscious, their petals, fully expanded under the sun, yielding up paradisial scents into the humid air.

She said: 'I suppose. . . . '

Nathaniel glared at the flowers, unable to find fault with them.

'We could come back to these,' she suggested, 'If the worst came to the worst.' Absently she turned from her peonies and bent down to inspect a shrub she had removed from Catherine's garden, which, being open to the winds from Strangford Lough, was too exposed to shelter such a delicate plant. Her habit of removing unhealthy plants to give them a better home often annoyed her friends. As she turned over the leaves looking for greenfly, she thought how odd it was that there should be this new fashion for building expensive houses down at Strangford, miles from the city—all right for John, perhaps, but she wondered if his sociable young wife might not find herself too isolated.

'What about those?' Nathaniel was pointing at a clump of orange lilies.

. 'Very festive.'

'And seasonal,' he reminded her, the orange lily and sweet williams being political flowers in Northern Ireland.

Mrs Mulholland smiled, remembering the day when she had lent her gardener to Catherine to advise her about planting and his indignation when she had asked him if it would be possible to grow madonna lilies.

'Yes, why not?' She took out the secateurs, her hand poised: she had been reminded of the name!

It was Catherine's background that was at fault. She came from a Plantation family, landlords in Fermanagh for over three hundred years, but for all the arrogant exclusiveness of the self-styled gentry they were unbalanced, and the line was suspect: the widowed father had caused a scandal when he had 'turned' Catholic on marrying his housekeeper, a homely creature called—of all things—Teresa! Not that Alicia or any of her friends had had personal dealings with the Hardwickes, whom she had known only by sight at garden parties given by the Governor. It had been a shock when her stolid John had produced a nineteen-year-old with the affectations of a debutante. John, who had waited until the sensible age of twenty-nine before marrying, was so enraptured that he had been quite taken in by her. The old man's debts were shameful and Catherine gave signs of having inherited his extravagance; but John would not be warned. During the three years when they built their house, furnishing it with every luxury, she had dragged him to parties all over the countryside and it had come to such a point, that one Monday morning when he failed to turn up for work his father had had to speak to him.

'They're calling the child John Patrick!'

Nathaniel watched her, wary.

'Oh, I suppose the Patrick bit is some sentimental business about Ireland. . . . '

'You don't mean,' a slight froth had collected at the edge of his lips, 'a united Ireland?'

'Her head is a-whirl with romantic nonsense,' busily she snipped at the orange lilies, 'but after all—naturally I'm devoted to the child—she is so very young, very giddy. . . . Perhaps now that she has a baby she'll settle down. Certainly she'll have her hands full. . . . ' However, the image of a maternal Catherine was not comforting as she envisaged her in her lonely house flustered and incompetent. She had been prepared to pay for a nurse, but the offer was refused.

The lilies looked like weeds in the basket. She turned to her herbaceous border, too preoccupied to observe that her husband had entered the garden and was descending towards them across the lawn, leaving dew marks although it was past midday, his shoes sighing as he lifted his feet off the spongy ground. Very masculine in appearance, he was tall with heavy bones and bushy eyebrows. Although the skin of his face was roughened and leathery, there were freckles on the backs of his hands and on the pink surface of his balding head. His eyes, which looked out on the world as if expecting the worst, were much the same colour as his faded sandy hair and there were mean lines around the mouth; he had a reputation for closeness. The owner of a firm of marine engineers, in which two of his sons and other relatives were employed, he was a tyrant on the job—although when he returned home it was to a dominant wife. Scrupulous and hard-working, intolerant with others of any lapse in the standards he set himself, he was, if not particularly liked, at least respected by his employees and he had few labour troubles. Although his workers complained of stingy wages, they stayed with the firm because the pensions were good and widows, or those who had to retire early through sickness, were usually treated with generosity. When boasting that he never had to deal with a strike, Mr Mulholland would explain that his recipe was quite simple: he employed no Catholics and so avoided the religious issue. Although this attitude was becoming unfashionable and his sons' generation might laugh at 'the old bigot', he would answer that, remembering the firm's link with the shipyards during the twenties, he had seen too much.

'Why, Thomas!' Alicia turned to her husband, a hand over her heart expressing fright. She raised her basket and shook the flowers, irritated by his benign expression: 'This confounded christening!'

Her husband's eyes glared out at her under his eyebrows, whose shaggy fronds had retained the reddish colour of youth. While she complained at first with vehemence, then querulously about the decimation of her garden, he watched her, angered. John, the eldest son, was his favourite; although he was still at times rather gauche, boisterous when enjoying himself, his shrewd father had perceived in him a depth and latent force that might not be apparent to strangers. When he married the old man had been pleased; he had told his son marriage gave a background to a man's life—it rounded it off. He had had little interest in the girl other than to ask himself whether she would make John a good wife. But she had played her part—she had given him a boy.

'You will pick the best flowers.' He pointed at the peonies: 'What about those?' Alicia shrugged, sourly accepting defeat. Having for once successfully exerted his authority in the home, Tom Mulholland turned with a smile of unusual pleasantness to his gardener: 'And how's . . . ' He could not remember the child's name; Nathaniel's wife had given him two daughters, but in later life he had found himself blessed with a son. 'How's your wee laddie?'

'Oh, he's doing fine, Mr Mulholland, he's one of the best.' Suddenly garrulous, he began a tale, explaining that the child was a comic: it was a Sunday and the car had broken down when they had been due to attend an important rally. . . . Tom Mulholland, who had lived long enough to be made uneasy by the mixture of politics and religion, conveyed his disapproval by allowing his eyes to stray to where the sun was reflected as a glassy sheen on the damp cobwebs on the lawn.

'But we did get her started,' Nathaniel was saying, 'and we went. . . . But here, listen to this! Young Nat he says to the wife, "Oh, I knew it would be all right—you see, Mother, I'd had a word with the Lord!"'

The empty building, whose outer doors had just been bolted, was of red brick and had high windows topped by ornamental motifs that were protected at ground level by iron grilles. As it was one of many such factories built in Belfast towards the end of the last century, its owners, who could see merely that it was in need of renovation, were puzzled that it should be considered of interest to the city's conservationists. A complex of keys glinted in John Mulholland's freckled hand as he checked them over, then dropped them into his pocket with a sense of satisfaction that the day was done. Tall and big-boned, with sandy hair, a reddish complexion and pale eyelashes, he resembled early photographs of his father. His features were strongly moulded but rather plain and he looked honest, reliable, loyal. Although the expression in his brown eyes was usually kind and he was not easily aroused, once angered he could show signs of the violent temper commonly attributed to people with red hair. At this moment, however, he was smiling ('How's the proud father?' the night-watchman had greeted him when coming on duty) and he ran down the steps into the hot street and on round to the car park, whistling to himself. Although it was past seven, there were still several hours of daylight ahead when he would have time to finish the shelves for the nursery or, as the evening was so fine, he might persuade Catherine to come for a sail.

On approaching the car his fingers searched absently for the keys. Fast cars had been his one extravagance and the Aston Martin, which Catherine was not allowed to drive, was the reminder of his bachelor freedom. The keys were missing. He scrutinized the ground, thinking he had dropped them, and was about to turn back to his office when he realized that he had left them throughout the day in the car itself. The hood was down and he vaulted over the door into the driving seat, then noisily revved up the engine. In what other city could one leave a car unlocked ready for any thief to drive off? He thought of the English buyer he had entertained over lunch and the man's astonishment when he told him that even in the centre of Belfast people left their houses open and the car parked at the front door with the keys inside. Northern Ireland was fifty years behind the times: there were few divorces, the suicide rate was the lowest in Europe, and there was practically no serious crime. It was boring to be a policeman because the Ulsterman, John had insisted, was naturally law-abiding—it was a dull little country!

There was little traffic because most people were at home having their tea. Under a mild summer sky the Victorian buildings looked rosy and pleasant and, when he entered the main square to circle the City Hall, he slowed down to admire that late imperial extravagance with its vast dome and white encrusted pillars. The lavish architecture boasted the wealth and success of a city which, a hundred years earlier, had been an insignificant little town in a country that elsewhere remained impoverished.

On the route home the pavements in Protestant areas were painted red, white and blue in preparation for the Twelfth of July and the streets hung with bunting, while Union Jacks fluttered from houses where flag-poles were permanently fitted to the upper windows. The Twelfth was the start of the national holidays and for several weeks before, with the beginning of the preparations, there had been a sense of mounting gaiety, a latent excitement. The English visitor had been perplexed, thinking it rather primitive. But John had retorted that England would be a jollier place with a summer festival where people danced in the streets. Besides, if all quirks and local customs were removed, the region would lose its savour.

Halted at traffic lights, his eye was caught by a wall painting, very dashing and colourful, of King Billy on his white charger ('Rem. 1690'). Should he walk with the Orangemen this year— or, more correctly, whom should he not offend, his father or his wife? Though Catherine laughed at his orthodoxy, her teasing concealed disapproval and even on his own account he felt uncomfortable in bowler hat and Orange sash as it was no longer fashionable to take such things seriously. But there was something obstinate and conservative in his nature which made him reluctant to jeer at the organization that had meant so much to his father and grandfather—although he belonged to the generation that knew nothing of the troubled twenties whose mob violence and sordid yahoo antics, were barely chronicled and best forgotten. The Ulster crisis of 1912, well documented in all the history books, was another matter. His grandfather had once entertained 'King' Carson, who had sailed down Belfast Lough, while crowds on the docks sang hymns and bonfires blazed on the hills, and the English Army prepared to mutiny because 'Ulster was Right'. Loyalists had filled the entire length of Donegall Place, surging towards the City Hall to sign the Covenant (some in their own blood) because the issue was freedom, economic and political, freedom of thought, freedom of religion. . . .

He was now out in the country and glimpsed beneath him, in a wide curve around the bay, the city which had once been so turbulent and whose sober prosperity was this evening half-obscured by pinkish haze. His Englishman would be sitting in his hotel now, eating an expensive and indifferent meal and wondering what he could possibly do to entertain himself, for as far as John knew there was no night-life whatsoever in Belfast. 'The place is dead', Catherine had often complained (she would not have permitted him to bring home a customer). Provincial, utterly respectable, Northern Ireland in her opinion was all right for family life—but there it stopped! Once she had hurt him by saying that she wished she had seen more of the world before settling down.

The narrow, winding lanes with their overgrown hedgerows were almost empty and he travelled fast, exhilerated by the wind on his face. At a cross-roads he swerved to avoid a black Volkswagon in which, incongruously, four nuns sat bolt upright, the driver gripping the wheel and glaring as if his sports car was an instrument of the devil. The sight amused him—nuns motorized, Women's Lib in the convent!—and he laughed to himself. But in reality he found the idea of a convent existence abhorrent: femininity cloistered, mumbled prayers, intrigues, a wastage of life, the black habits morbidly repulsive (would their heads be shaved under their cowls?). The whole ethos was alien; he had been brought up to mistrust the Catholic Church with its power and its deviousness, the bland faces of prelates fattened on the superstitions of primitive people. If history was authoritarian and cruel and it seemed to him that the spirit of the Inquisition had never died. The priests would meddle, as in the South, in temporal matters ('Home Rule is Rome Rule'). In so far as he was interested in politics at all, he would have voted Unionist on this issue alone.

And yet he had married a girl whose father had 'turned' and who was, herself, half way gone over. But Catherine's views were irrational and full of whimsy, typically feminine, and he could humour her without taking her seriously. She had told him his puritan condemnation of 'dark' religion had nothing to do with reason: it was instinctive like a horror of spiders, and what he was afraid of was the female principle, the embrace of Mother Church. Whereas Protestants lived by the masculine virtues of energy and integrity, the 'work ethic', and the Jehovah whose wrath they feared was nothing more than a punitive father-figure. Indulgently, he listened to her exercising her fey sensibility, her nonsense, though sometimes she would go too far and he became irritated, remembering her unstable background: it was not surprising that she had inherited an irresponsible approach.

She was already orphaned when he first met her at her brother's house in Fermanagh. He had a rod in Desmond's fishing syndicate and had felt himself very much a client, not a guest. The recent development of Lough Erne as a tourist spot was yet another example of Desmond's arbitrary good luck. Though on the verge of bankruptcy, he was still boasting about his debts, having lost thousands gambling. John had heard too often the story about the night when the bailiffs arrived (at the back door) during a dinner party and helped with the washing-up before delivering their summons. Desmond's charm was not apparent to his future brother-in-law, who saw only idiocy and fecklessness, though the devil, he was obliged to conclude, looked after his own. When all had seemed lost, and Desmond was faced for the first time in his life with having to do a job of work, Lough Erne had been opened up to holiday-makers with motor launches and water-skiing and the large run-down estate had become profitable overnight.

When John first went to fish at Castle Hardwicke, Catherine was seventeen and had just left school. Her father had died the previous year. There was another brother, but he had emigrated to New Zealand; Desmond had bluntly informed him that there was just not enough to go round—luckily it was not their own mother who had been the Catholic! During a somewhat parsimonious lunch given to the members of the syndicate, John, listening to these family revelations and wiping his fingers disdainfully on his napkin, had felt ill at ease, as conscious as an adolescent of his clumsy wrists. The Hardwickes had lived in this house for over three hundred years but the origins of his own family were untraceable. There were Mulhollands in Maghera and it was possible he had French blood through a marriage with one of the Huguenots who had settled in Lisburn, banished by Louis XIV. And a Presbyterian farmer had been hanged during the rebellion of the United Irishmen in 1798. John liked to think that this man was his ancestor and imagined him a dour radical, sturdily self-reliant, qualities which distinguished the Ulsterman from other inhabitants of the unfortunate island.

Fidgetting, wiping his mouth too often, he became conscious of being watched by the girl presiding at his end of the table, her manner half-shy, half-arrogant. Offhand, she had informed him that the beautiful young woman with dark slanted eyes on Desmond's right was at present living with him: 'But he'll probably marry her. . . . and then she'll sit here.' 'And what will you do?' She had shrugged. She was going to France. There had not been enough money to send her to school in England, so she was to be finished off abroad, where—here she smiled—they could economize yet again as she could learn French as an au pair. 'Still, the family is extremely OK.' She had tossed back her head, rejecting sympathy, 'I don't see myself as having to drudge.'

Later, when showing him round the luxuriant but entangled gardens, she had told him how much she loathed her Irish boarding school, and he had felt protective towards her. After she left he continued to come up to Lough Erne, not so much for the fishing as to be reminded of her and, when her image began to fade, it seemed to him that her spirit had become diffused through the romantic, neglected house with its long memories and its view of misted waters, and touched with poetry in her absence, he discovered that he had fallen in love.

It was easy for John to dissociate her from the other young women he had known. The daughters of his parents' friends were too familiar, too predictable, and their mothers, who eagerly invited him home to watch television with the family, had made him aware that in his own society he was a 'catch'. So any interest in the opposite sex had been quickly followed by caution, then ennui, and amorous forays in the backs of parked cars would suddenly pall and he would lose his nerve through fear of being trapped into a forced marriage. Sometimes, when in London with friends, he had gone in a group to strip-shows and on two occasions he had been introduced to call-girls. But what he remembered most from these experiences was his drunkenness and a vague sense of relief when it was all over, so that when he met Catherine, if not technically, he was emotionally still a virgin, which he had not regretted as he firmly believed that innocence made marriage more special. When Catherine returned from France to find the Polish countess officially installed as lady of the house, he had reappeared too, and after a brief courtship married her; it had seemed the natural thing to happen.

As he drove through the green landscape with its blurred outlines and distance vapourous with humidity, he was trying to decide whether he should congratulate himself on his good judgement or be grateful for his luck: in marrying Catherine, a stranger, at that time almost a child, he had abandoned himself to an impulse—but the gamble had paid off. If anyone were to ask him: 'Are you happy?' he would have replied without hesitation: 'Yes, I am a happy man!'

He passed through villages a-flutter with bunting, under

painted horsemen on their triumphal arches, and it seemed that the festivity of the countryside was reflecting his own euphoria back to him; he saw drummers outside a farm-house and his car roared past a line of old men solemnly blowing flutes. But it was when he came in sight of the sea—a triangle of vivid blue between green hills—and a race of yachts with their spinnakers blown out, that he literally caught his breath and his eyes clouded. Then the spasm passed, and he was able to breathe again, telling himself calmly: 'Now I am home!'

He thought of his own boat and the regatta he would miss because of the christening; he took his sport seriously, was keen to win. Before his marriage he had spent his weekends sailing in summer, or fishing, in winter golfing or shooting. This year, because of the baby, Catherine had been unable to crew for him and he had felt guilty leaving her at home. His mother had hinted that it was unwise to leave a young girl so much by her-self—but then she had opposed his building a house at such a distance from her own.

He had laid the foundations of the house while Catherine was in France. His brothers had laughed at his nesting prepar-ations (he had bought an entire island off the shores of Strang-ford Lough) as there appeared to be no bride in view. When the house was almost completed, they were introduced to Catherine and again had laughed, but this time behind his back: he was as canny as their father.

The island was approached by a causeway, very narrow and inadequately walled in, which his friends complained made for dangerous driving after a party. To enhance their fears a warn-ing had been painted in huge, white letters across a rock at the sea's edge: 'Prepare to meet Thy God!' This had angered John, but he felt uneasy about obliterating it. The rock passed, he drove carefully over to the island—a green mound with stunted trees, a ruined cattle-shed, a few sheep grazing—then faster round the final bend and up through the wood that he had planted. Set among the young trees was a pleasant modern house, Scandinavian in influence and timbered throughout; in winter the windows that faced the view were coated with salt blown up from the lough.

He parked and went inside where it was very warm. Cather-ine, who had spent her life in damp houses, now pampered herself and the heating was kept on throughout the summer. Oriental rugs covered the wooden floors and everywhere there were flowers. His mother had said that the high temperature was damaging to the furniture. Having grown up surrounded by beautiful things, Catherine had an eye for fine pieces—an 'expensive eye' his mother had added, as if warning him that heredity was showing itself (Desmond's debts were too disgraceful to be mentioned openly).

He walked from room to room, inhaling the aroma of his house (the smell of the baby had added a new flavour, oversweetened, alien) moving quietly, listening for her. He found her in the kitchen at the sink. Her prettily curved shoulders were sagging and he caught a glimpse of her white skin through a tear in her sleeve. She was thoroughly untidy, sluttish almost, with her auburn hair loose and straggling across her back, endearingly unlike his mother! When she turned to him he saw from the hollows under her striking violet-blue eyes that she was exhausted, but he was unable to repress the uprush of sentimental pleasure at finding her there, utterly domesticated, his wife, his Catherine!

'Well, where's my tea?' He was standing in the doorway, his arms folded. Although he had been educated at an English public school, he had stubbornly retained his Ulster accent.

The baby had been sick. While she was washing out his clothes she noticed strands of her own hair in the suds. Her hair was her most remarkable feature, thick and springy, russet-coloured with golden lights; she had stopped brushing it because it was falling—she was moulting like a dog! Bent over the sink with its smell of infant nausea (since the birth of the baby her sense of smell had been heightened) while her husband watched her with pride, Catherine was thinking that at no point in her upbringing had she been in any way prepared for the monotony and drudgery of domestic life. But then her background had been a preparation for nothing whatsoever. When she returned from France, she had taken singing lessons, to pass the time; it had never been suggested that she should train for a career. If she had been obliged to earn her own living she could have only been a waitress or a factory hand—she could not even type.

Although she spoke fluent French and was, somewhat emotionally, inclined towards the arts, the education she had received at
her detested school had left her with abysses of ignorance in
common knowledge: she knew no geography, for instance, and
could not have named the great rivers of the world, nor the
capital cities, and her grammar and spelling were so erratic
that when she had to write a letter (she wrote copious letters
on large sheets of paper) she was forced to resort to a form of
literary impressionism. Quite simply, she had removed from
under her father's roof into the establishment of her husband
and when she heard him booming at her in his deep voice,
'Where's my tea?' she felt her inadequacy and that she was
being reproved: she was still the daughter of the house.

'Well, where is it?'

She had turned to him when he came in, but now her eyes
were again staring at her reddened hands in the sink. No one
had warned her she would feel morbid and she could not
understand why childbirth should have made her so conscious
of death. When the baby was asleep she thought him dead; a
fear of death would come over her at odd moments in the day
and for no reason, often when she was happiest. At last she
said: 'Patrick's been sick.'

'You must have over-fed him.' John was strolling across to
her, unprepared for the savagery with which she shouted:

'Must everything I do be wrong?'

'Why, darling!' He tried to tilt up her face to see what was the
matter, but she pushed him angrily away. Her own violence
astonished her; before the baby she had been easy-tempered.
When she saw his hurt look she wept, in the grip of a destructive
urge she could not control. She was weeping through dread that
she was driving him away, she would lose all, she was suspended
over a black gulf and the sensation was terrible.

'Now, then! He guided her over to a kitchen chair and sat
her on his knees. His mother had warned him to be understanding: he might find his wife rather 'trying' at this point.
'You're tired, that's all.' He stroked her hair. 'And I'm very
late—I should have come home earlier.'

She leaned against him while he rocked her protectively, like a
little girl, and felt soothed by his warmth. Her brother had been
astounded at her marrying a dull fellow like John and had

23

assumed it was for the money: 'My sister's marrying a Belfast magnate!' The phrase had enraged Catherine. 'We, the gentry,' Desmond was fond of saying, 'of course, there are only about fifty of us left, we're a dying race. . . .' He had mocked his little sister's emulation of bourgeois values, not understanding that she had had enough of carelessness and waste and her family's selfishness; at their father's funeral Desmond had talked quite openly about the problem of disembarrassing himself of Teresa. John by comparison was considerate and sincere and she had sought security in marrying a man she could respect. When he had written to her in France (the envelope addressed in firm, legible handwriting) she had been touched by the seriousness of his concern for her: he had wanted to know if her French was improving, if she was seeing places of interest, and had asked her to reassure him she was not being made to drudge. From Desmond she received only one post-card, casually expressing a hope that she was having fun.

John mopped her face with his handkerchief: 'How's herself?'

She took the handkerchief, blew her nose, got up and caressed his neck, but with her face still turned away from him. Then she went back to the sink where she wrung out the baby clothes. She raised her eyes to the window, cried out in alarm: 'The pram!'

He stood behind her, looking over her shoulder: 'What about it?'

'I forgot to bring it in.' He said nothing. Her voice rose: 'It'll get damp!'

'Well, bring it in then.' There was a moment of opposition between them.

'You wouldn't. . . . ?' He looked irritated. 'And while you're at it could you hang these on the line?' She handed him the dripping suit. Holding it by his fingertips he went out, grumbling, and she smiled to herself: he had been brought up on the theory that there was man's work and woman's work.

She went to the window and gazed at the pram. The baby had been born in the spring and he had slept under the apple tree when it was in blossom. On sunny days when there had been no sound but the larks she had wheeled him round the garden and down on to the causeway, abandoned in happiness, her hair wildly flowing. She had put him in a sling and had walked over the fields, cuddling him (her mother-in-law had been horrified) exploring her haven, her island.

John was jerking the pram, which had stuck; she could see him muttering, then he was kicking at the brake. Her anxiety returned. She ran through the house, certain she had heard a cry, but there was no sound. The furniture had been polished in preparation for the christening. She adjusted cushions, calming herself, straightened books on their shelves. During this early period in her married life she had become obsessively house-proud. The curtains she had made herself, not through necessity, but because she had wanted to demonstrate to her husband that she was not completely unskilled. The furnishings reflected her sentiment for the country, Irish linens and tweeds, pottery bought from local craftsmen, modern, semi-abstract paintings of bogland in the rain. 'Why the bad weather?' John would ask, who would have preferred a conventional picture of the purple hills of Donegal with the sea bright blue and the grass emerald green. Catherine unnerved him when she talked romantically about the future when Ireland would again be united. Sometimes in the evening, while he tried not to let her see that he was dozing by the fire, she would read aloud to him from the Irish poets. She had cajoled him into taking her to the theatre in Dublin, the opera in Wexford, and they were forever visiting her many friends in the South. 'I like a quiet life,' he told her when she had shown him round the gardens at Castle Hardwicke, and she had had the novel experience of seeing another human being regarding her with sympathy.

She was unable to resist peeping into the nursery to make sure that the baby was still asleep. Movement in the room disturbed him and he opened his eyes to stare, unfocussing, at his mother. He resembled Desmond and had a cap of yellow hair that was beginning to curl. His tiny, damp hand clutched her finger and she felt anguished at the thought of time passing, when the bliss would fade and the baby grow up. As she gazed at him in his cot, she was awed by the intensity of her maternal passion, as if her spirit was over-flowing its limits in a love that could not be satisfied, for if she were to express it she would crush the life out of his little body. She lifted him, fondled his moist, milky flesh and thought how delicious it would be if a

25

grown man were to retain that infantile allure. She sniffed his downy head and pressed her cheek against him, altering her breathing so that they inhaled in unison as if still one flesh. When his father entered, the child cried.

'I expect he's hungry,' said John, 'like me.'

Returned to his cot, the baby wailed, panic-stricken. So Catherine picked him up again and nursed him until he was quiet: it continually amazed her that peace could be transmitted physically.

'Look, John, see what happens when I kiss him—he closes his eyes and holds his breath, then he smiles!'

'Lucky Patrick!' Darkened, John's large frame was silhouetted against the window.

'What's that?'

'They're drumming on the beach.'

'Lambeg drums!' Little Patrick whimpered, sensing at once his mother's agitation. 'How dare they! You must tell them to stop!'

'Not our beach—it's carrying from across the water.'

'Oh, I do hate it!' If her hands had been free she would have blocked her ears. 'How long will this go on?'

'You know perfectly well,' tired and unfed, ousted by the baby, he had lost patience with her: 'They'll go on until their wrists bleed!'

Patrick howled. 'I must feed him—at once!' Catherine was looking around for somewhere to sit; she believed in demand-feeding. 'He's always hungry when he wakes up.'

'And who woke the little bugger?' John did not normally swear, particularly in front of women. She ignored the signs of anger. 'Oh, come on then—get down to it if you must! But not in here.' He placed a hand between her shoulder-blades and gently propelled her back through the house to the kitchen where he rolled up his sleeves, resigning himself to cooking their evening meal. 'Tomorrow I'll wash out the nappies for you.'

His jibe had misfired. Catherine had unbuttoned her dress (it slightly shocked him that she should do this, on a whim, wherever she happened to be) and was suckling their child, her lips slightly parted as she gazed, enraptured, at the infant's closed eyes with their waxy lids and delicately separated lashes.

He laid the kitchen table, busied himself at the stove, was

26

cheered by the smell of bacon filling the room, the sound of it sizzling in the pan. But behind this sound, from a distance and eerily, stopping for a while then starting up again, came the insistent drumming. Catherine's hair had fallen over her face; now she looked like a gypsy with her breast bared and the child tugging.

'It's primitive,' her voice was hoarse, whispering, prophetic: 'That feeling—it's still there. . . .'

'What feeling?' It was just a few old boys amusing themselves of an evening. He cracked eggs into the pan. 'You don't know what you're talking about—that's all a thing of the past!'

It rained in the morning and Catherine fussed, thinking he might catch cold, while she was dressing her baby in the long family christening robe she had borrowed from Desmond. But by the afternoon a wind blown up from the sea had scattered the clouds and, although the ladies had to cling to their hats as they picked their way between the tombstones and the elderly shivered in the ill-heated church, brilliant light, flecked with shadows from the rustling trees outside, cheered the waiting congregation. The parish church had been built near the ruins of an old abbey that was now protected as a bird sanctuary, and swans nested in the rushes at the water's edge. Although, since his marriage John had become slack in his church-going, he had an affection for the quiet graveyard where the old family vaults bore Latin inscriptions. He had sometimes thought, on mild mornings when a white mist was lifting off the sea, that to be laid to rest there would be satisfactory.

John's parents arrived early with their youngest son Peter, and his fiancée Carol, who was wearing a green coat with a lemon hat and gloves and matching lemon shoes. Self-consciously dressed up, she sat with her hands folded beside her future mother-in-law, who disapproved of her son marrying at twenty-four when he could not afford a house; it was a mistake to start married life in a flat. In the pew behind were Tom's sisters, the widowed Maude, turbaned and immensely stout, furtively popping sweets into her mouth, Sadie, who had never married, and his younger brother, Arthur, an amiable, garrulous character, white-haired and rosy-cheeked with a boy's innocent

27

blue eyes. Due to the astuteness of her stock-brokers, Sadie's investments had grown vastly during her solitary lifetime and she was much concerned with her will, fearing lest her money pass to an unworthy recipient. An expensive mauve costume did little to enhance her ashen features as she sat, blinking in a shaft of sunlight, fidgetting with her gloves or with the ropes of pearls around her meagre neck, then tapping Arthur on the knee because he was chattering to Judge McTaggart, husband of Alicia's cousin Brenda, who was huddled into her mink coat at the end of the pew.

John entered with Catherine and the baby and smiled at his parents. His brother, George, who was to be one of the god-fathers followed after, surreptitiously eyeing Catherine's profile as she bent over the child, her hair escaping untidily from under her hat. Somewhat rough-hewn, like the other men in the family, George, who wore a loud tie and was too often to be seen combing his hair, was more flamboyant. He had left his father's firm to work in the motor industry; the high point of the year for him was the Circuit of Ireland rally.

The vicar swayed in his robes, apologetically turning over the pages of the baptism service so as to avoid looking reproachful. To pass the time, Catherine walked down the aisle and the great-aunts craned forward to glimpse the pink face in the shawl with murmurs of: 'Dear love him! Isn't he good?' When it had been decided that they would have to proceed without him, the second godfather appeared, quite unabashed and at the head of a large group of people that included a couple of his own house-guests not invited to the christening. Catherine was pleased: they would make it more of a party.

To Judge McTaggart Arthur whispered: 'Have you heard about the Irishman and the Spaniard? The Spanish chap was explaining the word *mañana*. . . .'

'Ssh!' Sadie poked him with the corner of her prayer book.

There was a movement of hats, a sound of ruffled propriety, while the Hardwickes filed noisily down the aisle and Desmond took his place at the altar. His wife, Sonia, wearing a black cloak and an immensely tall black hat, stood in for the absent English godmother.

The service began and the Mulhollands, fluttering their prayer books, sneaked glances at the late-comers, affronted by their bohemian clothes and irreverent manners. Their curiosity was not returned, apart from old Uncle Hugo, who was quite dapper today in a high winged collar and his old Etonian tie (and had been persuaded to leave behind his greasy paddy hat), who stared back at them rudely, as if asking himself: 'Who the devil are they?' He had brought along his fifteen-year-old grandson, Guy (another unexpected guest) because he enjoyed the company of the lad.

While the vicar rapidly mumbled the prayers, Desmond whispered in his sister's ear to cheer her up. Straw-haired and ruddy, looking more like a country bumpkin than an important landowner, he had an animal warmth and an allure which came from a simple gift for enjoying himself. When he bent over her, Catherine flushed. She was still unable to get into her other clothes, and in a dreadful hat and shapeless tweed suit she felt stodgy and plain; added to her misery was a fear that she might leak milk as she had mis-timed the feeds. She had produced a boy, an heir, and was now accepted by her in-laws—she had been their incubator.

When the vicar made the sign of the Cross over Patrick's forehead, he whimpered slightly, but did not cry out as he should. The devil, Sadie was to remark later, noticing the resemblance to his spendthrift uncle, had not been allowed to escape. Which gave Desmond the hope that his godson had not been born without a sense of humour.

Tom Mulholland strolled through his son's garden, refreshed by the salt breeze, well-satisfied (he could just see a fleet of swans on the water, drifting past) while his wife frowned at a camellia: 'They'll never grow that here!' and stooped to pluck out a weed.

'Who's she?' Puzzled, he jerked his head towards the porch where Catherine was talking to a middle-aged countrywoman: 'The new help?'

'No, no, dear!' Alicia hushed him. 'It's Teresa. Presumably,' her own voice was lowered, 'she didn't want to join us for the service.'

'Ah,' he said vaguely, 'ah, yes. . . .' He waited till she had gone in before entering the house himself, followed by Alicia who was indignant that her peonies, which had been intended for the church, were in a vase in the hall.

The others had gone into the drawing-room and they could hear John's voice above the din, boisterously hospitable. His parents stiffened at the sound of champagne corks. Tom peeped into the dining-room, surprised, as he did not think of Catherine as a housewife, by the excellent buffet (a little too extravagant of course, was it necessary to have bought a whole smoked salmon?); the very lavishness suggested to him that his daughter-in-law was somehow morally suspect.

She came out into the hall, and kissed them in turn on the cheek. Meeting his stern gaze, her hand instinctively went to the back of her neck to make sure that her hair had not come unpinned, thinking that her meddling mother-in-law was in some ways easier than this silent man because more direct. Still smiling, she asked: 'Can't I take your hat?'

He grunted, handed it over. Tom Mulholland was not a man with an interest in the opposite sex; conventionally nice girls left him indifferent, but if he scented sex appeal he became hostile. Catherine seemed the type of young woman who can only approach a man through flattery and coquettishness, wiles (lies!). Proud of being the man he was, he was not impressed by her smart background and despised her relations for their arrogance and idleness. But he was being too harsh, she was the mother of his grandson. With some reserve, not showing his teeth, he smiled at her:

'Well done!' he laid a heavy hand on her shoulder: 'Well done you!' And he followed her into the drawing-room where members of Ulster's Protestant ascendancy were discreetly enjoying themselves.

Depressed by the company, Desmond murmured to his sister: 'You sure there'll be enough to drink?'

Overhearing this, John exclaimed at the top of his voice: 'Let it never be said that there is not enough of the right stuff in this house!' and shocked his aunts: some of the guests were teetotal.

The party had already split up, the older men grouped in the centre of the floor, their ladies, like wall-flowers at a ball, round the edge, while Desmond and his wife were talking to their own friends, Davina and Julian. Julian's beautifully-cut black hair drooped over his collar and Davina was wearing an enormous hat and a dress so long that it trailed on the ground behind her.

'I must say,' Davina was looking around in astonishment, 'it really is rather nice here! Irish Chippendale,' she picked at a piece of loose varnish on a handsomely-carved side-table. 'One can always tell by that sturdy look—I suppose they were made that way to survive being kicked about by drunks?'

'Your house looks super—absolutely super!' said Carol with envy to her future sister-in-law. 'It will be a long time before Peter and I can manage anything like this. But it's been a lovely party, Catherine, really it has! The crack's been wonderful!'

The 'crack' was languishing. Teresa was sitting alone, her knees and her plainly-shod feet pressed together. John talked gadgets with Peter. Desmond's twins, dressed prettily in velvet with lace ruffles, were chasing each other round the room. One of them had caught hold of Judge McTaggart's legs and his wife was looking at him in alarm as the Judge, being prone to melancholy, was particularly susceptible on festive occasions. George was making up to his rich aunt Sadie, who in her fidgetting had dropped her bag.

'Allow me!' gallantly he picked it up. 'My word, auntie, you're fairly dressed to kill!' But his compliment was not appreciated. Sadie snatched back the bag as if it contained her entire fortune, and stared stonily ahead.

'I say, dear,' Aunt Maude had grabbed a twin, 'would you fetch me one of those little cakes I saw in the other room—you know, one of those whirly things with cream inside?'

Watery reflections rippled on the ceiling; the ennui was stupefying.

'Oh, dear!' Catherine wrung her hands over Maude. 'You're famished!' She raised her voice to suggest to the other occupants of the room: 'I'm sure you're all famished?'

So they trooped into the dining-room and in silence attacked the food.

'Caviare?' The bushy eyebrows were raised accusingly, while the hand stretched out for more.

'Oh, no, Mr Mulholland!' Catherine touched his arm, then quickly drew back: 'No, it's only lumpfish.'

'Hi, mum!' George, with his mouth full, taking advantage of

31

his special position as godfather/brother-in-law, put his arm round her, digging his fingers into her expanded waist: 'Sexy eats!'

She escaped from him and joined her female relatives, who had again segregated from their menfolk and were huddled in a group at the far end of the table.

'What you need here,' said her mother-in-law, 'is a deep freeze.'

Carol was astounded: 'Haven't you got one?'

'Not a bit of it! She's a clever girl, our Catherine. Seems to manage without any help whatsoever.' Mrs Mulholland bit into a vol-au-vent, murmuring, 'delicious, my dear, full marks!'

They discussed domestics, a dark topic with Sadie whose elderly cook brawled with the arthritic housemaid. The subject was tactfully changed to furnishings and decor; then 'good works'. Brenda McTaggart, an active committee member of the Save the Children Fund, set about recruiting Carol.

Catherine, whose feet were aching, sat down beside Teresa. 'I've been neglecting you. How are you, darling?' Catherine tried to think of something further to say to her, then remembered the shawl she had knitted for Patrick. Teresa brightened, suddenly in her element. She leaned forward to whisper: 'And how's baby? Does he feed well? What do you give him?'

At this all the women turned: for three years they had been studying Catherine's figure before they had been satisfied.

'They say,' Carol blushed, being daring, 'that a woman is never really,' she hesitated, '*fulfilled* until she has had a son.'

'Now this interests me,' said Mrs Mulholland, 'I mean, John Patrick. On what exactly do you feed him—that is, apart from—' she coughed; in her opinion Catherine had made too much of a fetish of breast-feeding. 'You've introduced him to solids, I take it?'

'We just call him Patrick,' said Catherine, but did not answer the question. She had heard a cry—though no cry could have been audible through the noise—and wondered how long she would remain in this animal condition.

Sonia, bored by the men's conversation, was drifting towards them, still in her cloak and black chef's hat.

'Ah, Sonia!' Alicia thrust herself towards her. 'You're the very person I've been wanting to speak to. Well, it's this

32

question of the raffle—you know, the coffee morning in aid of the Unionist party—and I was wondering if there wasn't a little something you could contribute. . . .'

She was received by a stare, haughty, blank. She was not to know that this strange woman, who had a passion for horses and wrote incomprehensible poetry, had also a Slav's capacity for alcohol and was now drunk. Dabbing her lips with extreme fastidiousness, Sonia turned to Catherine:

'Perhaps you could give me some tea? I haven't had any.' So Catherine poured out (the silver tea-service had been the wedding present of her parents-in-law) and held on to the cup until she was sure that Sonia's long, ringed fingers had grasped it firmly. 'Milk or lemon? I take it you don't want this?' She held out a jug of cream; it had been an astonishment to her to discover that the women in her mother-in-law's circle enjoyed their tea laced with cream.

There were little pockets of silence, dominated by the sound of tea-cups replaced on the ravaged table and a faint sighing as napkins were crumpled up and discarded. The view of a sea brightly wrinkled under a freshening breeze drew the men over to the window. It was the day of the Strangford regatta and they watched, speculating on the competing boats.

'Bet you wish you were out there?' said Desmond to his brother-in-law, yawning. Sometimes Desmond came down at the weekend to sail and use the swimming pool, often casually accompanied by people that John had never met.

Old Arthur had found an unlikely companion in Uncle Hugo, who now towered over him, disproportionately tall and thin, twitching up his wisp of a moustache:

'It was a disaster my dear fellow—an utter disaster!—old Desmond Hardwicke turning R.C. My cousin—did you know that? First cousin, on my father's side, of course. So naturally in our part of the country he was a somebody—ah, indeed, yes! —but he lost the place,' with its remaining tufts of hair, its gravemarks, the bald head was shaking: 'lost it completely, I'm very sorry to say.' His grandson, who was standing behind him, an unusually graceful youth with moody eyes, was pale with boredom. 'And such a waste when he went and died a year later! Suppose he's in Purgatory now, what?' The genial Arthur beamed at him. It did not seem to trouble Hugo that Teresa

33

was within earshot. He caught sight of her: 'Ah, there she is—poor old thing! That damned boy over there—' his hand rasped the white stubble on his chin as he glared at Desmond, 'the young scoundrel would have kept her on as a house-keeper given the chance.'

Davina, who had persistently declined to join the females, insinuated herself between the two men. 'But surely, Mr Hardwicke, it can't have been such a disaster? I mean—' she licked her lip, 'well, what I was really meaning to say is that two of my friends have married Catholics.' She laughed, drawing in her breath with little gasps, her eyes widening. The boy, seeing his grandfather distracted by a pretty girl, slipped out of the room. 'In our village there are plenty of mixed marriages—the Catholics are helping the Prods to string up the bunting at this minute and they'll all get boozed together round the bonfires the night before the Twelfth.'

'You must forgive me, my dear young lady, if I tell you you're talking rot? In this country you are either a sheep or a goat—and that's all there is to it!'

'But you're so out of date!' she smiled at him with her mouth open, her tongue moving between her teeth: 'Things have changed.'

'You think things can change in Ireland! *Plus ça change*, eh?'

'Which puts me in mind,' said Arthur 'of the one about the Pope knocking at the gates of heaven—oh, dear,' he scratched his head, 'no, I've got it wrong. . . . But have you heard about the Ecumenical Council where the Cardinal was seated at dinner beside the Presbyterian Moderator? The waiter gives a glass of sherry to the Cardinal and then he offers one to the Moderator. "God forbid!" says he, "I'd sooner commit adultery!" "Wait a minute," says the Cardinal to the waiter, "I hadn't realized there was a choice." '

'Arthur!' Sadie rapped him on the shoulder: 'Time we went!' Her skinny fingers fastened on his wrist. She had brought him to the party (Arthur, the baby of the family, had never quite grown up) and was now taking him home again in her chauffeur-driven Rover.

Then Maude went, and the McTaggarts. A woman in a filthy apron came in to clear the table.

'Where's Guy?' Hugo's purple lips were trembling. 'Drat

34

the boy! He'll be up to some mischief. . . .' But the old man, in his distress, was ignored.

Catherine was in the hall being kissed. She could hear the baby. George saw his chance and stood beside her, as if he were the host, with his arm round her shoulders: 'Good-bye, Aunt Sadie,' he said, 'and Aunt Maude, good-bye, sir—very good of you to have come!'

The host had made his escape, off with the chaps for a breath of fresh air. Desmond was telling Julian that he must see the swimming pool:

'You should come for the weekend sometime. It's like a country club here—once they've made their tennis court they'll have the lot!'

Tom Mulholland raised his eyebrows questioningly at his son: 'You never told me you were intending to build a tennis court?'

The champagne had worn off and John was peeved: 'Have I your permission?' At once he regretted having said this; he respected his father.

There was a pile of clothes at the edge of the pool where Guy was swimming naked. They watched the boy, who was unaware that he was observed, crawling languidly from end to end, very sun-burned, a faun. The lining of the pool was bright blue, the water immaculately clear. In the silence the loneliness of the place became oppressive, in spite of the blandness of the evening and the festive sight of sailing boats on an ultramarine horizon returning from their race.

Guy got out, shook himself like an animal and walked towards them, a sullen expression in his eyes, not at all embarrassed. Mr Mulholland looked outraged.

Desmond was amused at this affront to the Establishment (he had a mental picture of the crabby old boy in bed in his Orange sash). He said: 'Tell me, sir, if you were ship-wrecked when the royal family was on board and it was given to you to pick one person for the life-boat, the Queen or your wife—which would you choose?'

This was so unexpected that for a moment Tom Mulholland gave serious thought to his reply; then his eyes narrowed in suspicion, a choleric flush spreading up over his bald scalp: 'That is not, young man, a fair question.'

Near midnight, after the last car had driven away (Desmond had

had to be told the party was over and that it was time to go), John walked in his garden, in which a heavy dew had brought out the smell of the grass, freshly mown for the christening. A calm sea reflected greenness in the sky where daylight lingered and, although the night was moonless, he was in no danger of stumbling as he wandered over the lawn and down to the shore. Islands on the lough and the round hills on the far bank, which in bad weather would be invisible, were clearly outlined, their detail simplified, apart from occasional lights on the far side and lone, bent trees on the islands.

It seemed to John that the landscape had altered little from the days when the Vikings had sailed into Strangford, bringing terror and fire and giving it its name. On one of the islands celtic crosses and a few stones marked the site of a monastery they had burned, where Irish culture had once flourished. It would be a good place for a picnic, he thought, making his way carefully over the stony beach (very faintly he could hear a seal bark) and his imagination was projected into the future when Patrick would be old enough to handle a boat, and there would be other children. John liked the idea of a large family.

In particular he looked forward to the things that he would do with his sons, sailing and fishing and exploring the countryside with its hints of the past: legends that give a magical dimension to places in Ireland, as suggestive and illusory as the hazy landscape. By nature John was conservative with a reverence for the traditions of his forefathers and his country, and with the birth of his little boy he felt, in a sense that was almost religious, that he was fulfilling his part in continuing a heritage. If there had been a war, he would have offered up his own and his sons' lives without question. His patriotism was naive and straightforward: to an Ulsterman the word 'loyalty' had a special meaning no longer understood elsewhere.

He turned back, picking his way between the young trees he had planted, towards the house where a single light glowed in their bedroom window. For a moment Catherine appeared within the frame, bent over a chest of drawers. Then she found what she had been looking for and vanished into the room. Her long, heavy hair had been let loose and she looked weighed down by it, fragile. At the sight of her John felt himself over-flowing with protective tenderness: as faithful in love as he was 'loyal'

36

in politics, it would not have occurred to him to look at another woman. In the fading light he walked along the edge of the flower-beds, plucked a dark rose, buried his face in its petals, then went in, where he found her seated, rocking the baby. Clumsily romantic, he presented her with the rose, then bent down to tickle the blond fluff on the infant's scalp.

Each object had a downy look, a moistness, in the dimmed room where form merged with shadow and Catherine, feeding her baby, was made giddy by the smell of his powdered skin. Beyond the undrawn curtains the sky was too intensely blue, the suggestion of space so awesome that she turned away from it and, lilting the infant, who had dozed, she thought of dark afternoons in the winter when, even at midday, the view would be restricted by spray on the windows and she would be completely enclosed, cocooned, within her warm house.

John came in with a rose. He stood before her, twirling the stem between his square-tipped fingers, murmuring: 'My pet!' and to Patrick, 'my little pet. . . .'

They settled the baby in his cot, waited until they could hear his peaceful breathing, then went to bed. Fragrance from the garden and the mown lawn was borne in through the open window. They talked about the party, John's aunts, and Uncle Hugo's reactionary views—he had played on Judge McTaggart's pessimism by lecturing him on the Yellow Peril, the Red Menace. At least Hugo was a likeable eccentric, said John; when it came to personalities he had to admit that Catherine's family were more fun. Had the food been all right? she asked anxiously, then giggled when she told him that his mother had brought a half pint of cream, thinking she might forget to serve it with the tea, and had been shocked when she had seen two large jugs, much more than would be used, already on the table.

She lay against him, in the embrace of his muscular arms, listening through the open door to the contented snuffling of the baby asleep in the next room. The large, sheltering man had become fused with the damp, small body of their child and she was at once excited and lulled by his caresses. His deep voice, chatting inconsequentially in the summer dark, reassured her so profoundly that it seemed as if there was nothing that could

37

go wrong and she would remain safe within his arms forever.

1969

'Down with O'Neillism!' The news-sheet held aloft in the man's mittened hand was rattled by the wind. Passersby in Donegall Place, making for home through the January darkness, turned their faces away from him, as if deaf to the bitter voice. Rigid against the cold, his eyes were alight with fanaticism: 'The traitor must go!'

Hurrying along amid the crowds, John turned up his collar, feeling spots of rain. As he approached he tried to catch a glimpse of the head-line, wondering how they had raised the money to print their own newspaper; he had no curiosity to read its contents, indeed he would have thought it shameful to be seen buying a copy and contributing a few pence to a disreputable cause. The very fact that the man was standing there in his shabby mackintosh in the principal shopping street of the city seemed to him merely a freak symptom of unquiet times. As he drew level with him, John slowed down to listen. The accent was rough, Scots-Belfast, the man's breath clouding before him as he mouthed abuse, obscene in its coarseness, mixed with biblical invective: 'Hark ye! The hour draws nigh. . . .' Under a cap sitting squarely on the centre of his head, the features were angular—a "hard-faced Prod," Catherine would have called him. The Protestant, she had said, looks self-righteous, unsympathetic to human weakness, whereas the Catholic face is genial and relaxed—did it matter that the twinkle in the eye was not entirely to be trusted?

At the thought of his wife John tucked his chin further inside his collar and his thick, reddish eyebrows contracted. They had engaged a nanny after the birth of their second son two months earlier, but Catherine had become frenzied by the girl's carelessness—she had actually rung him at the office to tell him that the baby had been left out in his pram uncovered—and he had promised that when he went home he would get rid of her.

At bus-stops people struggled against the wind with their umbrellas, while rain blackened the pavements. As he walked on up the street towards the City Hall, where the lights were being turned off one by one, he could still hear, above the traffic, the sound, if not the words, of the agitator's high-pitched ranting. Fragments came back to him, newspaper cuttings, photographs of Civil Rights marchers, of Protestant hooligans waiting in ambush; he had read accounts of corruption in Londonderry. . . . That there were areas of injustice so close to home had come to John as a surprise and he had only half-believed it. He was still not at all clear as to what had been happening. But, while he walked along trying to warm his hands in his pockets and looking around at the familiar place, foreboding weighed on him; without really thinking about it he could feel the disturbances in the country through his own misgivings, as if he were a part of the landscape, like a boulder or a tree unsettled by earth tremors.

Putting off the unpleasant moment when he would have to sack the nanny (John did not question that his wife should have asked him to do this for her) he decided, on arriving at the muddy car park, that he would visit his father who was off work with bronchitis. The detour took him well out of his way as, to reach his parents' house, he had to drive in an opposite direction from his own home in Strangford. The rain was falling steadily when he got out and sounded the bell and he listened to it hammering the panes of the glass-roofed porch that his mother kept filled with pot-plants. The door opened and she exclaimed:

'Why look who's here!' But, before he had time to kiss her, she had turned away from him to call, sing-song, into the interior: 'Thomas! You've a visitor. . . .'

John shook out his wet coat and followed her into the smallest sitting-room where his father, looking suddenly faded and old, was sunk heavily in his chair beside a smouldering fire, on the other side of which his mother's cousin, Brenda, was chatting with animation, her pink face rather flushed. Although the space in the room was cramped by too much furniture, the impression, due to the inadequate lighting, was of austerity. Parked by the door was a gilt trolley bearing the remains of an elaborate tea.

'My dear boy! This is good of you. . . .' The older man roused himself to look up at his son with real pleasure; he had been finding the female company oppressive.

'Well, Dad!' John rubbed his hands, wishing the fire were a little warmer. 'And how are we today? No, no!' as his father rose to greet him he pressed him back, protectively, into his chair: 'Sit you down!' Then he turned to the tea-trolley and helped himself to some scones, watched with satisfaction by his parents—their hungry boy had come home. There was a pause while John wiped crumbs from his lips and his mother tidied the newspapers at her husband's feet.

'How's the family?' Cousin Brenda was staring at him inquisitively through her rimless spectacles. 'And Catherine?' John looked gloomy. He explained about the nanny and his mother clicked her teeth:

'If she will employ these little girls from the Falls!'

'We could have been unlucky . . .'

'Not a bit of it! I could tell how it would end the minute I set eyes on the girl. It's a different attitude to life. . . .' She glanced at her cousin, who nodded, pursing her lips. 'If you want someone clean, honest and hard-working, you employ a Protestant. The other sort may be amiable enough, but. . . .'

Brenda leaned forward eagerly: 'But what will poor Catherine do now? Will you stay home to help?'

Tom Mulholland shifted his position, muttering to himself. He hated to hear women's gossip. John drew in a chair beside him and picked up the newspaper.

'Nothing but trouble these days,' said Alicia complacently. 'This Civil Rights nonsense—one just wonders what it will lead to.'

'Is it such nonsense?' said John.

'So you're one of those?' Brenda tapped her finger-nails on her plump knee. She was a militant Unionist of the old school.

43

'They say "tolerance" is quite the thing among you young people.'

'What they ask for is not so unreasonable—one man one vote —it's what they've had in the rest of the U.K. since the end of the War.' As he spoke John's eyes remained on the newspaper. In Northern Ireland the municipal vote was still based on property and he could not understand how the issue had become so distorted that people in England seemed to believe that the Catholics were politically—or in any other way—disenfranchised. 'I can't really see what difference it would make,' he turned over to a new page. 'After all, whoever shows up to vote in a local election?'

'Civil Rights,' said his father, 'yes, that's all very well, but what does it solve? In this country the average Catholic refuses to take part in public life—they appear to forget that there are also civil duties.' He leaned forward and brooded over the fire, which had been heaped with coal dust to make it burn more slowly. 'The Press—it's those slick English journalists who've turned the whole thing upside down—' he sucked on his teeth, ' "media-men". . . . And that!' He pointed accusingly across the room at the television set. 'There's the new gadget that makes all the difference!'

'Well, I don't care what any of you say—' Brenda was becoming tearful with emotion: 'Give them an inch and they'll take an ell!'

'What d'you mean? What else is there to take?' John threw down the paper, crumpling it. Then suddenly he was good-humoured, teasing: 'I've always said when it comes to politics it's women who are the reactionaries.'

Brenda composed herself, her flush paled. 'And Catherine— what does she think about it? I suppose that in her case—' he was being regarded slyly, 'now she I imagine would be something of a sympathizer?'

'Oh, Catherine!' John raked the fire till a bluish flame showed, and left the question unanswered; his wife's views were of no real interest—politics was a man's game. He thought of her waiting for him to come home. But when he looked up at the clock on the mantel-piece he saw it was time for the news on television and stayed on to watch.

The news was uneventful. They saw prize-winning dogs at a

44

show in Armagh, then a still photograph of the chairman of a textile company that had gained an important new contract; time was taken up by an old lady in a wheel chair being fussed over by nurses and smiling rapturously at her son, who had returned, after forty years in Australia, for her ninetieth birthday.

'Not much today,' Alicia switched off the set, 'no Paisley, no Bernadette!'

'That's it,' said Tom, 'the comedians! With television the news becomes entertainment.'

'Did you hear that Bernadette has secretly been to tea with the Paisleys and they all got on like a house on fire? Mrs P. is supposed to have said of her that she's really a nice wee girl!' Alicia was inspecting the plants in the room to see if they needed water. 'My Nathaniel's a Paisleyite.'

'Now there's a "bitter Orangeman" for you!' said John to his aunt amiably. 'What's it his house is called, Mother—Galilee?'

'Bethesda.'

'He's a lay preacher in his spare time. One of those fellows you see out with their sandwich boards,' he got up and prepared to strut in front of them,' you know the sort of thing— "What will ye do on that Solemn Day?" '

His father watched, unamused by his crude miming. 'You do wrong to laugh at these people. They may be uneducated—but they have a right to their beliefs.' Startled by the hostility in the old man's watering eyes John sat down, feeling foolish, tried to laugh it off. But his father was again staring into the grate, dabbing at his lips with his handkerchief, his breathing congested as he tried to suppress his coughing. After he had deliberated for some time, he said: 'I'm not as you know, by any means a Paisleyite—but I am with him over one thing. . . .'

'And what's that, Dad?' The tone was gentle, as if he were talking to a child.

'He's right to fear the I.R.A.'

John banged his fist down on his knee: 'But that's absurd! Where do they come into it?' He got up and stood in front of the fire with his leg astride. The I.R.A. was a myth—a bogey! It was common knowledge that the movement had fallen apart. In the fifties, when they had murdered policemen on the Border, they had lost sympathy, both North and South, and had been

45

discredited; it was a thing of the past. 'You can't seriously believe. . . .'

He was interrupted. His father had been overcome by a fit of coughing, painful to watch, with the veins bulging in his temples. When it was over he rested his head on the back of his chair, his eyes half-closed, lapsed in memories. As a child going to school in Belfast he had lain on the floor of the tram while fire was exchanged across the street. 'I never told you,' he said, 'that when I was seven years old I saw a policeman shot dead before my eyes. We were on holiday at the sea, walking along the front, when these two fellows got out of a car, shot him in the back, then drove off, leaving him lying there in his own blood.'

'No, you didn't tell me.' John paused: 'Why?'

'Why what?' The eyes under their shaggy brows glared at him.

'Why did you never mention it?'

The downward lines around his father's mouth had become sharply pronounced and his vision had closed in. 'There are some things that should be forgotten and are best not talked about.' He stifled a cough, spat into his handkerchief, then said slowly, lifting the poker and prodding the fire, as if to give emphasis to each word: 'But I would not like to see it happen again. . . .'

'Now then, Thomas!' Alicia plumped up his cushions, settling him like an invalid: 'That's enough of this gloomy talk. Perhaps John's right. It is a long time ago and—don't forget—this is a new generation.'

John was still standing in front of the fire, shifting his weight, embarrassed, from one foot to the other. Brenda plucked at his sleeve:

'Tell me, John, has she had you wheeling the pram yet?' She leaned back, with a cackle of laughter, slapping her knees. The amusement was general: no self-respecting Irishman can be seen with a pram. She removed her spectacles to wipe their steaming lenses: 'I'll bet you're a dab hand with the nappies!' The vision of John as nurserymaid caused further merriment.

Tom was chuckling to himself: 'I know what he needs. Over there, Alicia!' He flapped his hand at his wife: 'Give the boy a wee drop of whisky.'

'Oh, no' John touched his watch, 'I must be off. Really. . . .'

'Ah, now! Come on then, it'll do you good—just one for the road ?'

In measured portions Alicia poured out drinks, joining in with the conspiracy to delay him from returning to his wife.

A little later, when John was leaving, his father with some effort raised himself out of his chair and followed him into the hall. John noticed with concern his shuffling walk.

'It's cold out here, you should have stayed put.'

'Oh, I'm not so bad—I'll be right in no time.'

'That's the way!' John's laugh was too hearty. 'And when you've surfaced,' he did an imitation golf swing, 'we'll have a spot of this ?'

They shook hands. The older man clapped him on the shoulder. When he had gone he gazed after his son into the streaming darkness beyond the porch.

Catherine wakened with a sense of bliss when she saw raindrops sparkling on the window-frames. The babies were in their cots, the nanny had gone home and the house was silent; there was no noise from outside, not even the wind, nor the gulls that settled on the lawn in bad weather. The book she had been too tired to read had fallen on the floor. She felt faint, unable to raise her head; her limbs ached with weakness. And yet, when she looked up at the bright drops trembling against the sky, she experienced a thrill so acute that it was as if she had stopped breathing for a moment and her life had been suspended. . . . Then the excitement passed and she was back within herself, greyed over, puzzling as to why she should be subject to these illuminations, as if for an instant she had been permitted to see through, to glimpse at a mystical world from which, normally, she was excluded.

Catherine's dream was of a fulfilment of being. The latter part of her schooling had been in a convent where her educators, in fostering spirituality in their charges, had played on adolescent fantasy so that earthly love and a yearning for the divine had become confused. As a young girl she had imagined herself transported by romance. However, although it had seemed to her that she was in love when she had married and, on the whole, she

47

had been content, the rapture she had expected was missing. She had then thought she might be made complete by having children; but with Patrick she had been too anxious and the birth of Edward, instead of the little girl she had hoped for, was a disappointment: she felt cheated, as if where there should have been more there was now less. Although she had disliked her school and was not at all religious, her sublimated upbringing had left its mark. During the lonely hours which she spent as a housewife, mindlessly busy, what she resented was the lack of poetry in her life and her escape from routine was to abstraction, a special mood induced by listening to music, or a sentimental involvement with her country, with Ireland as an idea.

Her book lay face down on the carpet, its pages crumpled. Patrick had wakened and was bawling to be let out. Before going to him she wandered round the untidy room, pausing before the mirror where, depressed by her dulled appearance, she unpinned her hair and tried it out in a new style. Then she turned away in vexation, feeling ugly—overnight she had aged. It was because she was still unwell, she told herself, and had wanted a daughter, because she was too feeble even to cope with the slovenly girl who was supposed to have been a help. But John would manage her: he had been quite nice about it, seeming to take it for granted that the sordid job of dismissing her would have been too much for her feminine sensibility. But she felt demoralized by her cowardice in leaving the moment of harshness to the man.

By the time she went to him Patrick had resigned himself and was playing with his toys. He was a bonny infant with a rosy face and blond, curly hair. He was frowning in concentration with his lips slightly parted, the curve of the cheek still babyish and plump. She hesitated before disturbing him. The sense of ecstasy returned, of illumination. When she picked him up and cuddled him the child responded with abandon and she imagined him grown, a lover, very sensual, rather callous; the resemblance to her brother was startling.

'More!' his lips were very moist, 'kiss more!' and she buried her face in his neck, feeling the muscles under a milky softness. She had been embarrassed when Mrs Mulholland had caught her wallowing in caresses. She set him down and he trotted off, satisfied and now happy to be free; his mother had been forgotten. Naturally adventurous, he at once went outside and she ran after him with boots and a jersey. When he was dressed, she watched from a window while he gambolled about, perfectly co-ordinated, a beautiful little animal: it seemed a pity that he would one day grow up to be a gross man. Catherine was not exactly aware that she was thinking of her husband, whose boisterousness and jerky bouts of energy had begun to oppress her.

She went in to Edward, who was lying in his cot with his eyes open, and she wondered how long he had been waiting for her. His wisp of hair was carrotty and he had John's brown eyes, pale eyelashes and colourless lips. When he looked up at her, it was with an expression of trust that got on her nerves. She could not understand why she was so indifferent to him and she thought of the phrase, 'the gift of love': it seemed that it had been given to her to love one child and not the other—for however dutifully she looked after him there was no way in which she could change her feelings. She had no desire to touch him—unlike Patrick; when it came to her expectations of what she had understood by the 'pleasures of the flesh' it was her first child and not her husband that she associated with this.

Edward smiled up at her rather timidly, and she felt mean.

'Oh, dear,' she said, 'I'm sure you'll be an awfully good boy. . . .' With excessive gentleness, she lifted the little creature who depended on her so totally.

She changed and fed him, then returned him to his cot, but all the time she had been watching Patrick from the window, feeling guilty that he should be her favourite. It was not Edward's fault that things should seem so dreary—she had been told that with the second child the sense of the miraculous would not be repeated. She felt his brown eyes reproaching her. It was unfair that in his resemblance to his father she should have become conscious of the limitations of John's solid virtues. Even the house, of which she had been so proud, now seemed characterless and artificial and she thought nostalgically of her family home in Fermanagh and a way of life that was past.

She fed Patrick, bathed him, played with him, then instead of putting him to bed allowed him to run around, while she sat with her back to the fire reading John's paper. On the front page

49

there was a photograph of a dog with a rosette on its collar and inside she saw another of a Cabinet Minister bending down so that a little girl could murmur in his ear. That's Ulster, she thought—a crooked politician patting the head of an ugly child! If she had made such a remark to John he would have been irritated. . . . Her enthusiasm for Civil Rights, he said, was emotional; it was unfortunate that there was a sense of injustice—most unfortunate—but it was nothing that could not be dealt with by sensible legislation, a calm approach. When she dismissed the Protestant establishment and his parents' friends as old die-hards, he would turn away from her, his face morosely set, and she would wonder if in time his eyebrows would become as overgrown as his father's.

Catherine stoked up the fire, folded the paper very carefully and laid it on the arm of his chair (he said women left papers in a mess) without having read it very thoroughly. The girl had returned. She could hear her in the kitchen, bumping about. Catherine had hoped, when she had sent her off for the afternoon, that she would stay away until John came home. She listened, then with relief heard her retreating to her room. What would she do when she was gone ? she asked herself. But others managed—the poor—why should she be so incapable of looking after her own children ? She caught hold of Patrick, smacked him unnecessarily and put him to bed. Edward was sleeping, of course; he slept, he ate, he did everything he should—he had been born a good citizen. Catherine returned to the drawing-room and stood, wringing her hands, in front of the fire, which was now blazing up the chimney. The curtains were undrawn, the window black. There was no sound of a car. In her agitation she exclaimed aloud :

'What can have happened to him ? Why is John so late ?'

But when he did get back, instead of appearing pleased to see him, she nagged him for worrying her, because she was ashamed that she was leaving him to do the job she could not face herself.

Though summer in Ireland is a damp season, this year had been an exception with continuous stretches of fine weather where the moisture that evaporated in the morning would remain suspended as a golden haze, when the sun was at its height, throughout the long afternoon. By July it was announced on the news that the Churches were praying for rain.

Leaving Edward asleep in his pram and Ellen at the sink (she had given in, allowing her mother-in-law to find her a suitable girl) Catherine would set out with little Patrick, holding his hand or touching the back of his neck with her finger-tips, as he was now much too old to be carried. At this time of year the fields were speckled with flowering weeds and the soft, whitish moths that thrived on them, whose fluttering would entice Patrick to escape from his mother. She would watch him chasing through the long grass, her face slightly flushed by the humid sunshine, while she listened contentedly to his shouts. She had almost forgotten how lowered she had felt a few months earlier; it was her health, she told herself, she had been absurd to have thought suddenly that her life had gone hollow. She counted the successive sunny days as they increased in brightness and stillness.

They were standing one morning on top of the little hill above the house, their legs drenched. Although it was very early, the mist on the sea, which obscured the far bank of the lough, was dazzling and white. The noise of a car on the shore road that passed the island came over muffled, as if distant, and apart from the larks above their heads there was no other sound. Even the dogs, searching for rats in the bushes at the foot of the hill, had become shadowy. Patrick, restless in the tight grip of his mother's hand, slipped free and ran off after his father's labradors and she followed him, rather slowly, gazing at his blond head.

When he climbed the gate and went down to the beach, she became anxious and began to run. She was panting when she was over the gate. The dogs rushed towards her, their hackles up. A few moments had passed before she saw the two men standing in the shadow of the bushes and the glint on their gun barrels. The dogs snarled at the burly countrymen in their wellingtons and paddy hats.

'What are you doing here?' She tried to appear calm. They looked her over, said nothing. 'What d'you want?' she was staring at their guns.

After a pause one of them lit a cigarette, blew smoke towards

51

her in defiance: 'We're out for a few rabbits.'

'But you can't shoot here! Don't you know that this is private land?'

The smoker grinned. He pointed his gun at the dogs. They must be Protestants, she thought: they had that look of open aggressiveness. Earlier in the year when there had been disturbances, John had said that the difference was simple: a Prod will punch you on the nose, while a Catholic will smile amiably, waiting till you've passed before stabbing you in the back.

'Them animals, missus, is they wicked?'

'They're not guard dogs—they're trained for the gun!'

At this the intruders laughed. The second man lit up. Self-confident, quite unmoved by the pretty girl or the child on the shore, they were taking a break from their sport. She knew she should stand up to them, tell them to go—but their guns were still aimed at the dogs. While she was not exactly afraid for herself, it did occur to her that they might have no scruple about shooting the dogs, accidentally, as it were, in self-defence. A few weeks earlier after a rally in a nearby market town, a collie, chained up for the night, had been kicked to death; the incident, ugly in itself, had caused resentment when the owner had insisted that the outrage was political. It was in the air, incipient lawlessness. She had time to think: a year ago this would not have happened.

'Guns are dangerous,' she said feebly, 'and illegal.' She had not the courage to tell them that her husband owned the land. The dogs whined, licked her fingers, glanced nervously at the pointed nozzles, crouched on the grass.

The first smoker, having finished his cigarette and become restive, said to her: 'What about your kiddie? Better mind him.'

'Patrick!' She laid her hand over her mouth, shrinking from them. There was a mocking gleam in their eyes as they exploited the mother's fear and they watched her, stumbling over the rocks and embracing her child in a panic, before they moved on.

Patrick, having enjoyed his moment of freedom, was now happy to feel the warmth of her arms and nestled against her, oblivious. Above his curls she could still see them, their dim shapes, to one side of the gap of brightness above the gate. Then they were gone. A little later she heard shots. That evening, when she told John about it, she was apologetic for her timidity, but he said that this was just as well: these days the atmosphere was bizarre—it was best not to take chances.

She walked Patrick home by the shore, feeling safer in the open where the gentlest of waves was breaking in a whisper along the shingle. Was her fear over-dramatized? But, although she tried to calm her unpleasantly thumping heart-beats, she could not forget a sense of militant excitement, an expression in the men's eyes as if they were impatient, waiting. . . . Enclosed in her island she had only been vaguely aware of the events of the past few months, the rising tension. She had seen John frowning over his newspaper, or, watching an unruly scene on television, when he would shake his head, saying: 'I don't like this.' But, if she tried to question him, he would merely shift uneasily in his chair, preferring not to talk about it. There had been a rowdy election and O'Neill had fallen (he had withered away, said his enemies, like the barren fig tree). At Easter, when there had been a commemoration of the 1916 Rising, she had been astonished to see policemen in groups of three with machine guns. But nothing had happened; no one really believed it possible that shots could be fired. It was rumoured that foreign agitators had infiltrated the Civil Rights movement and occasionally the I.R.A. was mentioned. There were many rumours, manifestoes, slogans—also a certain frivolity. A recent Civil Rights demonstration had lasted for as long as three days, but, after the speeches were over, they had ended under the green midnight sky enjoying a Ceilidh, Gaelic sing-songs, fiddlers and jigs in the street.

When Catherine got home, she found the two men in the kitchen drinking tea, their guns balanced across their knees. They had come to the door, said Ellen, asking for a drink of water because the day was so warm; they had been very civil. They were civil to Catherine, thanking her with a politeness that was almost genteel for allowing them to take 'refreshments' in her house, and she felt confused. But when they were gone her fear revived: they had been inside, they had observed the lay-out of the place.

Although the heat was already enervating and she had planned to spend the afternoon by the pool with Patrick, Catherine now decided to go up to town. She must get out. She felt suddenly oppressed by her seclusion and the very quietness of the blue day made her ill at ease. So, without any particular aim other than a curiosity to see what was happening, she drove off towards Belfast through a countryside where even the beasts in the fields seemed too torpid to swish the flies off their backs and in the villages, whose streets were decorated for the Twelfth, the bunting was limp in the breezeless air.

However, there was more bunting this year, more Union Jacks—and the flags were new. In places where she had not seen it before, she noticed graffiti on the houses or across the roads: 'No Pope here!' 'Taigs beware!' Wall paintings of King Billy on his prancing horse had been freshened up. She had always liked these paintings; it pleased her to think that the country was exceptionally rich in its folk culture, with its street musicians, its ballads, the innumerable songs, political, sentimental or nostalgic, or jingles for children's games in the back streets. Catherine was surprised to see a band in a village square practising so early in the day, and there were more bands than usual. She would come across them unexpectedly at a bend in the road, marching along unsmiling and very respectable, some of the men in bowler hats. As she approached Belfast she could see Stormont far off on its elevation, that proudly neocolonial edifice, rather too imposing for its function, expressing the determination of the people of Ulster to govern the Province in their own way.

In the city the holiday atmosphere was even more noticeable. Riots were expected after the marches on the Twelfth and, as if the possibility of violence were an allure, record crowds were expected: the boats from Glasgow and Liverpool had been booked up weeks before and special flights had been chartered from Canada and the States. 'God Save the Queen!' was daubed on the walls in Protestant districts, or '— — — the Pope!' the obscene word obliterated, though the vicious sentiment remained. (The Irish, with their sensitivity to insult and their feeling for words, have also a horror of bad language.) Once or twice Catherine saw on the walls, more ominously: "Burn the — — — s out!" An extraordinary number of people appeared to be walking the pavements, jostling and smiling in the sunshine, gathering in little knots outside the pubs. Although the crowds seemeds seemed peaceful enough, there was an undercurrent, which would become more obvious at the end of the day when no one felt like going to bed during the long wait for dark. When she looked back on this period it was to seem to Catherine that there had been an expectation in the air, heady and mercurial, which had nothing to do with political causes or a sense of injustice: the streets had been over-heated and people were spoiling for a fight.

But at the time she was more concerned with finding something to do that would justify her impulse to come up to town on such a beautiful morning. She parked her car and wandered past shop windows, looking in at the indifferent wares and thinking how dull the place was; even the faces in the crowds were uninteresting. At a loss for distractions she thought of paying John a surprise visit at the factory, then felt ashamed at the contrast between his busy life and her own idle days. When, eventually, she made her way to the Arts Council's new gallery, she did so less from a desire to see the exhibition than to prove to herself that she had not become insensibly domesticated.

It was stuffy inside, although the gallery was almost deserted. At the far end of the room, invisible to her behind the screens on which the pictures were mounted, she could hear women enthusiastically praising the artist whose works were on show: melancholy water-colours of Irish houses that had been burned down during the Troubles, a wan greenness reflecting from the grass on the broken rafters. Unaware, when she came into their view, that one of the women had begun to scrutinize her, Catherine moved from canvas to canvas, in which two figures obsessively recurred: a man with a gun, sneaking off, and a corpse whose blood on the grass had been transformed into flowers. Absorbed by the morbid imagery, she gave a start when she felt a hand tapping her shoulder.

'Now I'd swear to it it's Catherine Hardwicke?' Catherine nodded, puzzled. Her questioner was a young woman in her late twenties, wearing jeans and a stained artist's smock with a grecian band round her head tying back her short, curly hair. Her face was freckled and without make-up and her large, friendly, inquisitive eyes seemed to protrude when she became animated. 'Ah, come on now! You remember me—Felicity O'Keefe?'

'But of course! How extraordinary. . . .' It was nine years

55

since they had been at school together. Felicity, three years her senior, had made a pet of Catherine, taking her over and mothering her, partly because she was the only Irish Protestant in the convent, but also because the older girl had been intrigued by Catherine's background and English manners, which had earned her the nickname, 'the Debutante'.

'Sure, it's great to see you, lovey!' The southern accent was rather genteel: 'I must give you a kiss!' When she clasped her Catherine smelled garlic on her breath and an aromatic scent that was unfamiliar to her. Felicity then held her back by the shoulders: 'Well, you've grown up very nice. . . . You should have seen her when she was thirteen, Mrs McMullan,' she glanced over he shoulder to address her companion, a talkative grey-haired lady who worked in the gallery, 'she was just the sweetest little thing—she wore her hair in ringlets, if you'll believe it!' This brought back to Catherine a disagreeable memory of the tangles in her hair being brushed out by a cross nurse. 'But you're married, aren't you? I can't remember your husband's name. . . .'

'John Mulholland.'

'Ah, now let me see,' Mrs McMullan's eyes brightened, 'that wouldn't be the family that gave their lovely home to the spastics?'

'Those Mulhollands?' Felicity drew back and looked at Catherine more guardedly: 'Pillars of the Unionist establishment, no less! How curious. . . . At school we always thought you would marry a lord.'

Catherine glanced at her with surprise: Felicity's father was a judge and in his own way was as much a member of the establishment as her in-laws. To change the subject she questioned her about herself and was informed that Felicity's marriage had been a failure. She had travelled, having spent a number of years in South Africa where she had had two children, but her husband was making it difficult to get a divorce because of his religion. This, she said, was annoying as she had stopped going to Mass. She had seen through the bourgeois system with its hypocrisy and false morals. Catherine murmured sympathetically.

'Oh, don't pity me, darling—I prefer to be free. Although much is talked of the joys of union, one was never told about the ecstasy of disunion!'

'You're a dreadful girl, so you are!' Thinking she looked shocked, Mrs McMullan took Catherine by the arm and asked her what she thought of the exhibition. 'He's an interesting young painter,' she said, 'very intense—very promising. His grandfather was a steward on some big estate in County Meath before the place was burnt down. A terrible bad time that was,' she wrung her hands, 'all those beautiful houses.'

Felicity interrupted to tell Catherine that the artist was a friend of hers: 'You must meet him—I'll introduce you.' She claimed to know most of the writers and artists working in Belfast: she would introduce Catherine to them all! 'But what are you doing now? Why don't you come home with me for a scrap of lunch? I was on my way.'

So Catherine followed her out and they drove up to the residential area off the Antrim Road where Felicity had a flat. In spite of the heat all the windows were closed and there was a smell of paint and stale food, the living-room being used as a studio. The older boy was at school, but to Catherine's surprise Felicity's four-year-old daughter, Aramanta, had been left in the house alone. The child seemed quite accustomed to strangers and hardly looked up at Catherine when they came in. She had long red hair and a pretty face, though rather pinched and delicate, and was dressed like her mother in patched jeans and a grubby smock. Felicity went through to the kitchen which was full of brushes and paint pots. She had started to paint, she told Catherine, as an escape from her monotonous life at home; later, when her marriage had begun to deteriorate, she had done a training course, gaining a diploma that enabled her to teach. Seated on a child's low chair in a corner of the narrow room, Catherine listened admiringly: she could not imagine herself taking a decision to study and make herself independent.

'But there was nothing for it, sweetheart—women are trapped in their marriages. If it goes wrong, unless you can earn your own living, or,' here Felicity glanced at her friend, 'you have a private income, there's not a thing you can do about it—the choice is between marriage or poverty.'

'It would be poverty for me. I haven't a bean—Desmond got it all.' Catherine looked around with apprehension. Then her fear vanished: the idea of a divorce between John and herself was unthinkable! Distressed by the contrast with Felicity's broken

57

life, she said: 'You must have gone through a lot?' Felicity was at the stove and Catherine could not see her eyes. It was only after some hesitation that she asked: 'What went wrong?'

'Oh, this and that. But it was partly marriage itself, the basic thing—it's an institution that's out-moded. You've got to be pretty blotto to enjoy spending your time shut up in a house as an unpaid servant. After all, if you remember,' the voice was cheerful, complacent, 'Domestic Science was for the C stream.'

'But when you were first married you must have expected. . . .' Catherine was plucking at the material of her dress, twisting it in her fingers: 'Surely to begin with you must have been fond of him?'

'Oh, yes, when I was first married—when I was too green to realize that romantic love is a social myth aimed at women to trick them into a lifetime of drudgery!'

'You take a cynical view,' Catherine had begun to look unhappy: 'It would never have occurred to me to put it like that . . . .' But, when she thought of her own life, she realized that she could hardly have described her marriage as romantic. 'I suppose if one looks at it from a different angle—perhaps there is something in what you say. Still, I can't. . . .'

'There, there!' Soothingly Felicity patted her cheek: she had resumed her mothering role. She opened a bottle of wine and handed Catherine a glass, becoming more confidential. 'I daresay it wouldn't have been so bad if Derek had been—well—keener. But then they're a sexless race. . . . D'you know the one about the Irishman being the only man in the world that will crawl over twelve naked women to get at a bottle of whiskey?' Catherine laughed; she could feel her face becoming heated with the wine. 'They make good fathers, of course. Derek was all for the cosy stuff—slippers by the fire and dozing together in front of the telly with the kids tucked up for the night. But one wants a bit more out of life than that!'

Does one? Catherine asked herself. Aloud she said: 'Don't you miss him—not at all?'

Felicity gave her a look and was about to say something, then thought better of it. 'Have some of those,' she handed her a jar of olives, 'I expect you're starving?' She busied herself making lunch. Catherine questioned her about her travels in Africa, and, listening to a description of wild places and exotic scenery, she felt that, although she would not have exchanged roles, her own experience was tame by comparison. They went through to the living-room with lunch on a tray, and finished the wine.

'Now what's the low-down on yourself? Are you happy with John? Tell me about him.' Felicity had leaned her elbows on the table and was staring into Catherine's eyes: 'What's he like?' At this Catherine blushed: the tone was too intimate, it was as if she had been asked what her husband was like in bed. 'Oh, dear, I seem to be upsetting you—you're one of those people who believe in the sanctity of marriage? Are you still in love with him?'

Catherine looked solemn: 'John is a good man.' She added, after a pause: 'Yes, I do love him.'

'But?' Felicity was smiling at her, waiting. 'Oh, don't look so worried—I was only teasing.' She pushed her plate away and offered her a gauloise, but Catherine refused. 'You don't even smoke?' She lit up, glancing at her over the flame. 'I remember seeing John Mulholland years ago when I was brought along to some do at the yacht club. Not, of course, that he would have taken any notice of me.'

'Whyever should he not?'

'He belonged to his own set. I think to people like the Mulhollands I would be regarded as somehow not quite acceptable.'

'What d'you mean? John's not like that!'

'This society is like that—it's made up of a collection of water-tight little cliques. I'm afraid you would find that your in-laws would consider me and,' she dragged on her cigarette, 'my way of life rather disreputable. . . . But to get back to your John, is he civilized or a male chauvinist?'

'I'm sorry?' Catherine had not heard this expression.

'Well, does he always do the driving? Does he take the decisions? If you go away on holiday is he the one who gets the tickets—and so on? In short, are you treated as the helpless little woman?'

'I suppose he does look after me. . . . He's very generous.'

'As I thought! Still, it would be odd if it were otherwise in this male-dominant society. I've often felt that in Ulster feminine emancipation might as well not have happened'—

'Then why did you come back here?'

'There you have me!' It was Felicity's turn to look defensive. 'Well, it's like this, don't you know—there's something about Ireland, you miss it when you're away. . . . Besides,' she reached out for Catherine's hand, 'it's an interesting time to be here. There's a new spirit, a great change is coming!' While she was squeezing her hand, the door bell rang and at once she jumped up and ran over to the window. 'Why, its Seamus Traherne!' In her excitement she again caught hold of Catherine, linking her arm: 'Now if this isn't a piece of luck! Here's a man you'll find really stimulating.' Seamus, she explained, was a Civil Rights worker; he had campaigned for Bernadette, he knew them all. 'Oh, he'll put you in the picture all right—he'll open your eyes for you!' The bell rang a second time, more insistently, and she hurried to the door of the flat. A squat man with a black bushy beard enter¿ d, carrying a sports jacket over his arm and complaining of the heat. Felicity closed the door behind him very quietly, a gratified expression in her eyes.

'Seamus, meet my old friend Catherine—Catherine Mulholland.'

He looked her over, sucking against his teeth: 'Mulholland Engineering?'

Catherine nodded. Rather coolly she held out her hand to him, but he turned away from her and seated himself with a grunt in the best chair.

'Seamus is a lecturer at Queen's University.'

'Oh, really?' Catherine was determined not to show that she had been offended. 'And what's your subject?'

'Linguistics.' He picked at his fingernails, glancing at her with hostility.

'You speak Gaelic then?'

Unexpectedly he laughed: 'No, I regret to say, I do not.' He got up, stretched himself, removed his tie, then shouted at Felicity: 'Can't you get us a bottle of beer, woman? I'm parched!' Obediently Felicity went out to the kitchen. He stood over Catherine, resting his fists on his hips. 'So you're a Mulholland, are you? A lady Unionist?'

'Not me. I've no interest in politics.'

'Then you should have! Don't you know that this country is on the verge of revolution?'

'Now then, Seamus!' Felicity had returned with a glass of

beer: 'You're not to frighten my Catherine—she's very sheltered.'

Aramanta entered. She had been playing so quietly in another room that Catherine had forgotten about her. She went up to Seamus: 'Hullo there!'

'Ah, it's my wee pet!' Suddenly benign, Seamus lifted the little girl and carried her round the room; he had the Irishman's fondness for children. Catherine realized that his beard had given him a false air of maturity and he was probably not much older than his students. While he was playing with the child, Felicity talked to Catherine about the aims of the People's Democracy movement:

'This is beyond Protestant and Catholic—it's a socialist republic they're after. Religion is an anachronism.'

'Are you in this?'

'Well, I am and I'm not—but it's worth the discussion.'

'Discussion!' Seamus bellowed at her: 'Talk! Too much talk is the thing that's wrong with this country.'

'I'm confused,' said Catherine, 'I'd thought Civil Rights was a Catholic movement? And I must add,' she tried to look Seamus in the eye, 'that I sympathize.'

'Oh, you do now? You're a fair-minded little lady?' He then sat down and harangued her, as if she were personally responsible, for the injustices in the country: housing, employment— a Catholic name or a Catholic schooling was enough to close the doors. . . . The picture was so extreme (Irish people of all types tend to be cheerful and easy-going) that Catherine began to object: John had told her discrimination went both ways and that segregated schools, which divided the population from early childhood, were due to the policy of the Catholic Church. Seamus' response was to confound her with statistics.

'I can't argue with you—I'm not very well up on all this.' John had warned her to avoid politics: women argued, he said, emotionally without a proper knowledge of the facts. 'The only thing I can say is that the Catholics I know don't appear to suffer from it, they're just like anyone else.'

'And how many Catholics do you know?'

Under his intense gaze she became flustered, feeling the contrast between his commitment to a cause she did not fully understand, whereas she was merely chattering to pass the time.

61

'Well, not many. . . .' mentally she began to count, 'no, I'm afraid. . . .'

'And those few would be like yourself?' He was gripping the arms of his chair: 'Privileged!'

'I did go to a convent,' she said lamely, and turned to Felicity for support. But Felicity, who had seemed to her so emancipated, was looking up at Seamus with worshipping attention, like any old-fashioned Irishwoman at the feet of an intellectual.

Seamus was slouched in his chair, his bearded chin sunk down on his chest. He, too, glanced at Felicity. As if at a signal from him, she whispered to Aramanta:

'It's time for you to run along, darling. You go upstairs and play with Johnny and Maria.'

The child pointed at Catherine: 'But isn't she to go too?'

'Well, perhaps,' Felicity looked embarrassed, 'yes, in a little while. . . .'

Seamus sighed, fidgetted with his watch. Catherine began to feel uncomfortable, suddenly aware that they were impatient for her to leave. It was a few moments, however, before she had really taken in the idea that Seamus must be Felicity's lover and that after she had left they would go to bed together—in the middle of the afternoon! A new world of impropriety had opened up to her.

She rose to her feet and said good-bye to Seamus, who waved at her casually but did not raise his eyes, seemingly immersed in his own thoughts. When Felicity embraced her, her cheeks were very red, her eyes rather moist, and she was effusively affectionate:

' 'Bye love, 'bye honey, 'bye-ee!' she called after her down the stairs, blowing a kiss. Before the door closed Catherine heard Seamus grumbling at her:

'Where the hell did you dig up a female like that?'

As she latched the gate to the small, bedraggled garden, Catherine looked up and was surprised to see that Felicity was watching her from the window, unsmiling, almost forlorn, her face, now much paler, half-hidden by the curtain. And she thought back to the past with a pang of wistfulness that so much had happened—it seemed to her a long, long time since the days when Felicity had led her about by the hand and they had been confined by the nuns.

'Now I wonder how many of you have heard of Londonderry?'

The radio reporter, himself unfamiliar with the name, gave the English pronounciation. 'Well—' he paused to clear his throat, 'whether we like it or not, this is still a part of the United Kingdom. . . .' There was a crackling sound and the voice fluctuated as the programme was being broadcast live. Catherine was in the kitchen preparing a picnic to take out in the boat. Ellen had left the children and had come in to hover over the radio: nowadays everybody made a point of hearing the news. 'It may seem strange to most of us,' the tone was patronizing, facetious, 'but we actually have tribal customs in our own country. And tribal is the only way to describe it!' He was covering an Orange march, the Apprentice Boys of Derry. The mike was held out to the crowd: 'Just listen to this for a primitive noise!'

When Northern Ireland had been finished with Catherine switched off and turned to Ellen, incensed by the contemptuous treatment of their country. Ellen's boyfriend was in the Army; at his barracks a notice had been pinned up saying that a dance would take place on a certain date provided 'the natives and the animals behave.'

'It's always the Orange boys that get the blame,' said Ellen, 'though it's the Taigs that are doing the damage.'

'So far!' Catherine thought of the drummers on the village squares. 'You shouldn't use the word "Taig", you know,' an obstinate look came into the girl's eyes and she tossed back her hair, 'it doesn't help.'

Ellen leaned against the table while her employer bustled round the kitchen. 'Why do they let them get away with it?' They had seen stone-throwing crowds on film and heard the terrifying howls of a mob in riot. 'From the way the reporters go on about it you would think they were on their side.'

'Oh, they are,' said Catherine, 'there's no question about that.' She, too, was bewildered that the violence should be dressed up in terms of some noble cause when everyone knew that the wreckage was common hooliganism. The English

63

Press, John had explained to her, was Catholic-biased, through sympathy for the underdog and an historic guilt about Ireland; in order to present a confused situation with clarity the Press simplify, giving a moral edge to an issue with a division between goodies and baddies, and the public is prejudiced at once. The local Press was no better: each evening he would come home with three or four newspapers to compare their viewpoints, but sometimes an account of the same incident would differ so unrecognizably that it seemed as if the reporting of fact had been abandoned for story-telling, the creation of a new folklore.

They had watched crowds in the evening on television cheering in the Bogside, to cries of 'S.S.!' and 'Gestapo!', as a petrol bomb set a policeman on fire. 'It doesn't seem to matter that the man's a human being!' John had shouted, ineffectually shaking his fist at the screen: 'It would be interesting to see the reaction if one were to pour petrol over a dear little Shetland pony and set that alight.' (By the end of the year one third of the entire police force would have been injured during riots.) They watched the spectacle, melodramatic against the night sky, of Derry's shirt factories going up in flames. What was not shown were the Catholic female employees weeping on the pavement because unemployment was so high that it was unlikely they would find other jobs: they were observing the destruction of their own city.

'Bang! Bang! You're dead!' Patrick pointed a stick at them; Catherine did not allow him to play with toy guns.

'Why do children enjoy war games?'

'It's only natural,' Ellen sneaked him a biscuit behind his mother's back.

Crossly Catherine wrapped up the sandwiches. 'Will you be going to this dance?'

'Indeed I will—that is,' the girl glanced at her slyly, 'if the animals behave.'

'You should watch it going out with soldiers,' Catherine lectured her, 'they're only here for a short time—perhaps they regard you as an "animal"? What's wrong with the local boys?'

'Oh, I wouldn't be seen with one of them, Mrs Mulholland, they don't know how to talk to a girl.'

'Well, how's it going?' John had come in, smiling and rubbing his hands in anticipation of an outing: 'Are we ready?'

'Did you know that this country was tribal?' Catherine threw at him.

He looked puzzled. Then said: 'Well, so it is! What are you going to do about it?' and glanced at Ellen, reminding her not to argue in front of the servants. He went over to the window and looked out at the unrippled sea: 'It's a good thing we decided to take the motor boat. This is no day for a sail—there's not a breath stirring.'

On the following day Peter and Carol gave a lunch party to welcome George's new wife into the family. George, more exuberant than his brothers, liked to think of himself as a bon viveur and had shown no signs of settling down, so his engagement had come as a surprise. Although he still lived with his parents, he was often away, either in the South or in England where he had met his wife, Liz, during a weekend's shooting; it was his boast that every Ulsterman who can afford it marries something from outside. On reaching thirty George had grown a moustache and was doing his best to acquire a cosmopolitan manner, having disembarrassed himself, unlike John, of his Ulster accent.

Catherine sulked at having to dress up and go out. The fine weather held and they could have spent another day on the lough drifting from island to island. John's family depressed her, particularly Carol, who was fussily suburban and a model daughter-in-law. Carol had helped the elder Mrs Mulholland with the Unionist fete and was forever running errands for her, but Alicia seemed to expect this as her due and maintained a grudge against the girl for trapping her son before he was in a position to set up a proper home. Carol and Peter lived near his parents in a rented flat. George, on the other hand, who was prospering in the motor trade, was doing a stylish conversion of a farm-house on the far side of Strangford Lough and it had been whispered during coffee mornings that they had acquired an aubusson carpet for their drawing-room.

It was Catherine's fault that they set out late, with Patrick squeezed in between them, in John's new sports car. Although he would be bored being the only little boy at the party, Catherine could not bear to leave him behind. Her uninhibited fondling of the child added to John's irritation as they drove off, dangerously fast, along the unfenced causeway that connected their island with the shore. Although there was little traffic, the lanes were so narrow and the hedgerows so overgrown that it was difficult to pass and they got trapped behind slow-moving cars with labels on the rear window: 'Seek ye the Lord!' or more grimly: 'The wages of sin is death!' John was naturally punctual and, as they crawled through the mildly steaming countryside whose colours had been bleached by the heat, his features hardened with tension. Studying his dour profile, Catherine felt that, if he were ever to become really angry and she had anything to hide, she would be afraid of him.

Although the Twelfth was long past and it was well into August, the flags were still up, even in the villages. On the outskirts of Belfast they saw a pub that had been burned. The fire must have blazed very fast as the roof had fallen in and they could see blackened timbers through the broken windows. John slowed down as they approached. All was quiet and the few passersby seemed to be looking in the opposite direction. Perhaps it had been accidental, John suggested: as far as he knew there had been little more than a certain restlessness in the city, and abruptly he changed the subject. But, though nothing had been said, the shock remained, (the charred ruin was an ugly sight) as if, in the hazy sunshine, they had imagined it.

The Twelfth had passed without incident, in spite of the fears of the authorities and the incoming planes crammed with journalists of all nationalities. It was estimated that over a hundred thousand people had marched in different parts of the Province and this did not include the huge crowds of spectators who lined every route. As a popular demonstration it had been remarkable: watching at home on television, John's aunt, Brenda McTaggart, described the effect as a 'wonderful impression of loyalty'. To please his father John had joined the marchers, but he had felt unhappy about it: the excitement was out of proportion and he thought too many of the people were there for the wrong reason. But, when Catherine told him she thought it shaming to be married to an Orangeman (since meeting Felicity she had become more militant in her support of Civil Rights) he turned on her with an uncharacteristic burst of temper, saying that it was people like himself who prevented the parades from disintegrating into a rabble. Then, as if he had surprised himself, he walked away from her, brooding over his own words.

The congregation was emerging from innumerable churches (in Northern Ireland there are sixty-three registered denominations and over two hundred sects) and the pavements were almost as busy as during the week. It was only on entering a poor Protestant area that they noticed anything abnormal, and John was forced to drive very carefully to avoid large numbers of men massing in the streets, most of them smiling cheerfully, as if enjoying the bright day. Some were wearing kilts. They had to stop while pipers strutted across the road in full regalia playing martial music, whereupon little Patrick stood up in the car and shouted, to his parents' embarrassment:

'Hello bands!'

'It's the time of year,' said John in his deep voice: 'What we need is some bad weather—a shower of rain would soon drive that lot back indoors!'

She laid her hand on his knee to silence him. They were being eyed in their expensive open car and she was nervous: they were too vulnerable with the crowd closing in on them. It was their eyes, she said later, and something about the way they held themselves, as though they were flexing their muscles. . . . Once the car was through, she made light of it—after all, the pipers had been rather colourful—and they talked about the Irish love of pageantry and parades, although Protestants dare not march in the South. 'Let's hope,' said John, 'they won't also have a chance to indulge their love of funerals.'

He drove down Belfast Lough, ignoring the speed limits: it was only in his sports car that John disobeyed the rules. On arrival at Peter's flat, standing in the entrance hall crammed with furniture, he apologized for their lateness: 'All my fault,' he insisted, 'of course!'

The drawing-room was similarly cluttered, as Carol spent her time searching antique shops in preparation for the day when they would move into their own home. Making excuses for the lack of space, she said: 'My little place is not like yours, Catherine!' Immaculately neat and crisp, wearing a turquoise blue sun-dress with a matching Alice band in her hair, she tried to keep her eyes off Catherine's peasant blouse, whose laces

67

seemed to have come undone, exposing too much of her breast.

John picked his way over to the window where George and Peter were standing with Liz, looking down into the back garden, the view of the lough being only visible from the main part of the house. Seeing them together, Catherine was struck by the resemblance between the brothers: tall and big-boned, with ruddy complexions and features that lacked refinement, John and Peter in particular might have been farmers dressed up in their best. George was more casual and more elegant. When he strolled across to Catherine, glancing down her blouse before bending to kiss her, she caught a whiff of eau de cologne as his moustache touched her cheek. He kissed her a second time, murmuring: 'And how's my favourite sister-in-law?' Then he clasped her hand and led her towards Liz, a pretty blonde with a discontented mouth, saying: 'It is my hope that you two will become friends.' He had told his wife that Catherine, with her county background, would be the member of the family with whom she would feel most at home. He now urged Catherine to pull a few strings to get him into Desmond's fishing syndicate on the pretext that Liz would be more in her element among the Fermanagh set. 'The thing that's wrong with Ulster,' he offered round cigarettes from a monogrammed case, 'is that everything here is second-rate—one needs a few trips across the water to keep up one's standards.'

'You're becoming very enlightened!' When John frowned at him, he resembled their father. He had taken a dislike to Liz, who was loud-voiced and snobbish and, in common with other 'imported' wives, was already complaining about life in the Province although she had only been living there a few weeks.

While Peter was serving drinks, Carol positioned little mats around the room in case the glasses left rings on the woodwork. Then she produced plates of decorated savouries, which she had obviously taken great trouble to prepare. The newly-weds were toasted. Then the men, quickly draining and re-filling their glasses, drew apart to discuss cars, while their wives talked recipes and decor.

They had too many drinks and Carol began to despair about her lunch as they waited for the final guest, Liz's cousin, Tony, whose regiment had been flown in to reinforce the troops in Londonderry. He arrived in a jeep. This was so unexpected that they all went downstairs to have a closer look at the real soldiers sitting behind wire netting with rifles on their knees. Patrick, miserable with boredom, rushed out, overjoyed, and was given a ride in the vehicle before it drove off.

Although Tony was an ordinary young man, scrubbed and eager, the fact that he was in uniform and had come, as it were, ready for action, caused a heightening of the atmosphere. While there had always been a garrison in Ulster, the Army until recently had lived apart, secluded in their barracks, and their social presence was a novelty. Tony's pleasure at finding himself with pretty young women put a stop to the domestic chat, while their husbands imperceptibly straightened themselves, shifting about or folding their arms, eyes alight at the prospect of adventure. Patrick tugged at him, wanting to know if his gun was loaded.

Over lunch, although Tony was the centre of attention, the state of emergency was not discussed. He was asked about his service elsewhere and his reasons for joining the Army. He was given addresses of houses to visit outside Derry. George, who had become affectedly civilized, savoured his wine, then turned his glass and sniffed at it while remarking casually that Desmond Hardwicke might invite him to stay if he wanted to fish; he, himself, would take him shooting once the pheasant season had started. The soldier made them laugh by telling them of an advertisement in the window of the Ulster tourist office in London: 'Come to Northern Ireland where the shooting is splendid!' He gratified his hostess by his hearty appetite and his compliments on the food and seemed especially delighted by the three elaborate puddings, blushing when he explained that he had a sweet tooth. It was only after the ladies had retired, taking their coffee on a separate tray, that he was questioned about the crisis.

'Well, what are you here for?' John asked him: 'Who have you come to fight?' He had heard a story in the Ulster Club that the Irish Army were drilling along the Border and had for years been preparing for this moment by sending consignments to the United Nations peace-keeping force where they had been re-equipped with modern weapons.

'The role of the modern Army is not to make war but to preserve peace—we're not here to fight anyone.' Tony then

69

described the welcome the troops had received in Derry because, unlike the police, they were non-partisan.

At this the brothers glanced at one another. John asked him if he was aware that of the two police chiefs in Derry one was a Catholic. He was about to add that they were waiting to see if the Army could do a better job in controlling the rioters. But instead he said: 'I wouldn't be too optimistic about your popularity—you could put the Papal Guard into the Bogside and they'd be stoned within a fortnight!'

Tony looked shocked. 'With due respect—' he paused, while Peter handed round cigars, 'you will surely agree that this country has been misgoverned for the last fifty years? It's a sorry state of affairs when the population can't be held down without military aid! After all, the Protestant ascendancy . . .'

Suavely—to avoid bad feeling—George side-tracked him by asking: 'Is there any evidence that the I.R.A. have a hand in this?'

'Oh, the I.R.A.!' Peter's Ulster accent was broader than John's: 'That's just hysteria, the thing's played out—finished! They're reduced to a handful of old men, there's no appeal to the young.'

'But what about the new splinter group? What's it they call themselves—Provisionals?'

'Hooligans,' Peter stated with confidence, 'no credibility!'

'But all that is by the way,' said Tony. 'The point, quite simply, is this: the people of Derry have had enough of being bullied and pushed around—they've had more than they can take. And we're here,' he smiled up at Peter, who was re-filling his brandy glass, 'to protect them.'

John said: 'No Englishman could believe that anyone would be crazy enough to burn down their own city unless they had a grievance that was intolerable. But what you're up against is a different temperament—the volatile Celt. In this country it can all be done on a whim, a fit of summer madness. . . . Have you ever heard the saying that in England things are often serious but never desperate, while in Ireland things are always desperate but never serious?'

'Fenians out! Burn the bastards out!' A hurricane of rabid

voices, two or three thousand men and youths—no one was ever to know how many—had come hurtling through the streets, armed with bricks and kitchen knives. . . . There was nothing the police could do about it. They had raided the pubs, looted the drink, then set them on fire, the fearful bacchanal taking place when the city was asleep during the brief period of darkness after midnight.

The tape of the yelling mob was followed by an interview with one of the victims, who described his terror as he had bundled his family out by the back door; when he returned in the morning his house had been gutted. A quavering voice: 'No. 83 was my home. I have lived at No. 83 for forty-five years—and now No. 83 is no more.' There was a long pause: 'It's just not there. . . .'

There were frequent news flashes, to which Catherine listened in the kitchen with Ellen, who was very excited and could not stop talking. In the village, 'Have you heard the news?' or 'Isn't it terrible!' had replaced comments on the weather as a form of greeting and a topic of conversation in the shops.

When she woke John, Catherine told him that the riots in Belfast had been the worst for two generations. He had buried his face in the pillow, not in the mood for a joke, having thought she was being facetious about the party of the night before (there had never been a summer like it for parties), from which they had returned in dazzling sunlight at six in the morning. It was true that on their way out, driving through Belfast, they had seen groups of men idling at street corners or drinking on the pavements. They had followed a warning to avoid the city coming home, imagining that there might, perhaps, have been some drunken brawling. So Catherine shook him and they almost quarrelled before she got it through to her husband that shots had been fired—and people had been killed.

At first it had not seemed credible: the event was freakish, a bad dream, a Press report exaggerated. But the riots continued night after night and all roads to Belfast were thronged with hitch-hikers, agog to see the fires. Then suddenly it was over, when natural exhaustion set in and the rioters went home to bed. Felicity rang up to say that the roads into the city were now open, her voice trembling as she told Catherine that it

71

would be an education to her to see what they had done to the place: the Protestants in Belfast had made a more thorough job of it than the Catholics in Derry. But John angrily forbade her to join the sightseers who were crowding in to gape at the wreckage.

At home she listened to the news and to Ellen's gossip. The I.R.A. had been in the thick of it, Ellen told her, gleefully adding that they had had heavy losses—though, with their usual cunning, the dead had been sneaked away. 'Fifty coffins—think of that, Mrs Mulholland!—smuggled over the Border in furniture vans.' Meanwhile, it was still said, in particular by the English Press, that anyone who expressed a fear of the I.R.A. was a 'fanatic'. There were stories from the other side, that the B Specials had joined forces with the rioters and were responsible for the shooting. On the BBC an unusually disinterested commentator spoke of the difficulty of accurate reporting in a city dominated by rumour, concluding regretfully that a rumour which is false, even absurd, if believed has more effect than the truth.

Prayers were offered up by all the Churches. The Catholic Church prayed for peace—but 'peace with justice'. This phrase was to become odious to Protestants, who saw in it a casuistic subtlety that, if anything, gave a moral gloss to the violence. The Church of Ireland prayed for the Establishment: for the safety of Her Majesty's officers in the Army and the police, for the wisdom of Her Majesty's ministers and civil servants, for the well-being of Her Representative, the Governor. The Presbyterians, as outspoken as the Cardinal was oblique, prayed for restraint because violence would lead to clashes with the police, thus confirming Catholic fears that the security forces were partisan. Only the Methodists lamented the wickedness of the riots and the damage to humanity. . . .

In the evening the news was presented as imagery: an old man wrapped in a blanket, a family of many children on one mattress in a centre for refugees, pathetic images of dreary little rooms whose contents had been smashed, a broken ornament, a toy, or, more provocatively, a holy picture that had been ripped lying upside down in a corner.

'It's not the religious trouble,' said Catherine, 'but the poverty that's shaming.' During the previous year they had seen televised riots in so many cities in Europe and the States that it seemed as if the Irish were following a fashion. She was particularly reminded of the coloured disturbances in America: 'It's the poor who do it and the poor who suffer. I'd had no idea,' she glanced around at her expensively furnished drawing-room, 'that it was quite so bad.'

'There's poverty everywhere,' said John: 'But that's only a part of it—not everyone who lives in a slum runs amuck.'

She flared up at him: 'How can you be so complacent?'

'Well, what d'you expect me to do about it?' He regarded her with animosity as she sat with her bare feet curled up under her on the sofa and her hair all over the place. 'What is there that any one individual can do about it?' On the following day he posted a cheque to a fund for the refugees, but, although the amount was generous, he felt guilty at the ease with which he had been enabled to offload his conscience and he sent it anonymously.

The new Prime Minister came on the screen with a personal appeal for sanity, for calm, stammering regrets, looking bewildered. 'Think what this would be like in colour!' said John, as they watched firemen swaying on their ladders and flames soaring against the night sky: 'I suppose in a few years' time everyone will have colour. . . .' Blood on the pavements in black and white was bad enough. Worldwide television coverage had placed a magnifying glass on Northern Ireland, enlarging and dramatizing, so that at that moment an obscure provincial city seemed the most dangerous spot on the globe.

Although John had refused to allow his wife to inspect the devastation, he did so himself, rather casually, on the pretence that he had some other reason for driving through the area. Only the main roads were open, the worst streets having been either sealed off by the Army or barricaded by the inhabitants. He gazed in astonishment at the shells of red-brick factories, built at the same period as his own. It was worse than the blitz, people said, adding that more damage had been done in a few nights than during the entire course of the war. The place looked like a rubbish dump: paving stones had been torn up for use as ammunition and monstrous piles of old junk had been heaped on the barricades, sodden mattresses, broken prams and bath tubs, burnt-out cars. The crowds on the streets, normally cheerful and bustling, now looked grim; even their clothes seemed bedraggled. The broken windows and boarded shops suggested that any prosperity there might have been was an illusion. And the Army was everywhere, hurtling through the other traffic in an extraordinary variety of vehicles, carrying soldiers with laughing faces who pointed their rifles at the populace. To John this was a private indignity and it took him a little while to realize that he was living in a country under military occupation.

In the city centre an enormous poster had been hurriedly erected, covering an entire wall: 'Love thy Neighbour!'

It was several days before John described all this to his wife. That evening when he got home he ate his meal quickly, then went out again, driving down to Newcastle for a few holes of golf before the light faded. Walking alone over the sand dunes, he was affected painfully by the beauty of the place, a placid gleaming on the sea, the gently undulating silhouette of the Mourne Mountains, tiny roses spread over the ground under his feet, the extreme stillness. He told himself: I have been there, I have seen it. But he remained astounded by what had happened. He wondered why—then felt ashamed of his naivety and of the little thought he had ever given to the society in which he occupied such a position of privilege. Life had seemed so secure, so pleasant. He had never had any reason to doubt his own intentions or to reassess his values. Was this what Catherine had meant when she had called him complacent? She had been shocked by the sight of poverty. The poor in Northern Ireland had no spokesman, as political divisions were based on religion not economics and, with no labour movement, the running of the country was paternalist. Was this what was wrong? He had prided himself on his lack of interest in politics, a dirty game no gentleman would soil his hands with or waste his time on. Besides, Stormont was nothing more than an inflated county council. . . .

He played badly, losing his balls in the gorse. Light slid away from the landscape and the darkening mountains seemed now to loom above, oppressive and melancholy.

It was possible—no, it was almost a certainty—that among his own Protestant workers there were men who had taken part in the bloodshed. Was he sheltering a murderer? In Catherine's view discriminating employers like his family were responsible for the trouble. But, then, Catherine was an unworldly little girl when it came to practicalities. . . .

It was difficult to see and he turned back. But as he tramped over the grass, already soaking with dew, he began to realise that four nights of violence might be paid for by a generation of bitterness. He felt a need to talk to his father. Although it was late to disturb the old man, he set off in his open car, travelling with impatient speed over the empty roads.

On the way to his parents' house he drove through a little town, only three miles outside Belfast, where a civic celebration had taken place, with sports and bazaars and a beauty competition, during the week when the capital had been in flames. Here, although the population was mostly Protestant, intermarriage was not uncommon and there were no 'ghettoes': at the opening ceremony they had congratulated themselves on their ecumenical relations. Community singing and dancing round the maypole had concluded the festivities—on the last night of the riots.

The baby, Edward, was left behind when they took Patrick up to Castle Hardwicke for Desmond's twins' birthday party.

While she was settling him in his cot, Edward's brown eyes looked up at his mother who felt reproached (she had never quite got over her revulsion at his white skin and pale eyelashes). 'But you really have quite a nice face,' she tried to tell him. He gave her a sweet little smile, as if grateful for her attention, and remorsefully she picked him up. 'I'm sure you'll be a kind person—you'll be just like your Daddy.' As he lay in her arms, very docile, she thought of her husband and how she could not possibly imagine him doing anything dishonest or cruel. 'We won't be away for long,' she said soothingly, 'and you really wouldn't enjoy it.'

'Why the fuss about leaving him?' John was impatient to go. 'You've got it all out of proportion—as usual. Besides he hasn't a clue what you're saying!' He could not understand why women talked to babies as if they were people.

Once in the car, his good humour returned. He sang nursery rhymes with Patrick and reminisced about his own childhood

75

and his nurse from County Kildare, who had really believed in the Little Folk and told him stories about giants and leprechauns and magic thorn trees. Did Patrick know that gate-posts in Ireland are always pointed so that the fairies can't sit on them? But Patrick had fallen asleep on his mother's lap and Catherine, too, was dozing. John thought of his in-laws in rural Fermanagh and their relaxed way of life, hardly changed since the eighteenth century, and remembered the peaceful days he had spent fishing on Lough Erne, the silence of the landscape and how easy it had been to lose oneself amid the islands. His expression was very cheerful, as if he were setting off on holiday, not admitting his relief at leaving familiar surroundings and the ruins he had seen in Belfast.

West of the river Bann the countryside became wilder and more unkempt, the hedgerows straggling, the spindly trees overgrown with ivy. This was more like the real Ireland, thought John, where the poor tending of the land reflected a careless mentality in the people. At the end of the journey, passing through Desmond's estates, there was no improvement: broken gates were held together with string, there was a stray pig on the road; John annoyed his wife when he remarked that it was surprising Desmond wasn't prosecuted for the weed seeding in his fields.

The drive leading to Castle Hardwicke, which curved along the banks of Lough Erne before ascending through woods up the hill, was so badly in need of repair that they had to go carefully to avoid pot-holes so deep that they were permanently filled with rain-water. It was raining now, very gently, almost a falling mist, and the islands on the lough were a greyish blur behind the drizzle. Castle Hardwicke was set back at some distance from the water amid grounds that had been handsomely landscaped. But, although the vistas remained and the rhododendrons still flowered in the spring, the trees, which were the finest for miles around, had had little attention and broken branches were left to rot in the undergrowth. Thistles and nettles grew waist-high all along the edge of the drive. Although Catherine seemed not to notice this, it saddened John to see a beautiful place so neglected.

To Catherine a visit to Castle Hardwicke was simply a return to where she belonged. The rambling building, which had been added to piece-meal over the centuries, with its elegant, if austere Georgian facade of grey stone, seemed to her to have more reality than her own modern comfortable home in County Down. It was said to be the third oldest house in the Province. Certainly in the early part the walls were so thick that it would appear the original building was little more than a fortified farm-house. Catherine tried to see into the hollows under the rhododendrons where she had played as a child. They passed a broken-down out-house from which chickens issued to scutter across the drive in front of the car. John hooted at them, but Catherine was trying to catch a glimpse of the stable yard with its bell tower. When they climbed the front steps, with their curved stone balustrades, and entered the hall, it angered her that he should tilt back his head to sniff the air, saying that one could smell the dry rot. She wondered what had put him in this tiresome mood: throughout the long drive he had been quite unnecessarily jocular. She now dreaded his talking business at table or behaving in some other way that her brother would consider bad form.

The main part of the house had been built at the end of the eighteenth century and the high ceilings, with their decorative mouldings, made the rooms difficult to heat. It was better to visit the Hardwickes during the summer, John had said, as it was, if anything, colder inside than out.

In the drawing-room they found Sonia reclined, statuesque, on a chaise longue, studying a volume on the culture of water plants. This room, which looked out on Lough Erne, had been furnished with great style, even if the drapes over the windows had faded, crystals were missing from the chandelier and the savonnerie carpet was stained. There were many pictures on the walls: a few dull but quite valuable Old Masters, a battle scene painted by an obscure provincial artist, and a number of charming little sketches of birds or plants or exotic places that had been produced at different times by members of the family. Sonia did not greet them. There was a decanter on a table at her elbow, but the colourless liquid it contained was gin, not water. Without bothering to pour out into a glass she took a sip from it and turned over another page, beckoning to Catherine:

'D'you know about water-lilies, darling? I'm thinking of

77

doing something with the pond below the croquet lawn—I'm rather bored with it looking like a cesspool. But what d'you think? Is there anything that could be done with it?'

Over her shoulder Catherine peered at photographs of luxuriant plants: 'I don't see why not—if one had the know-how. . . .'

'Never short of a new plan in this house!' John rubbed his hands together and strode energetically across to the window to see when the rain might lift. Whenever they came there always seemed to be some new project being discussed, either aesthetic and to do with the renovating of the place (regardless of cost), or a miracle cure for Desmond's finances. Talking about these things was a way of passing the time.

Sonia closed her book and laid it aside on the table, adding to a pile of other tomes on famous gardens, palaces, works of art. 'The trouble with all this,' her long fingers were caressing a volume on the Loire chateaux, 'is—oh, I don't know. . . .' She stared moodily at the rain. In Fermanagh there is some rain if only for a little while, during most days in the year. 'The worst thing about going abroad—quite definitely,' she frowned with an air of purpose, 'is that it's unsettling. When one comes home one feels so fed up with one's own house.'

Desmond entered the room, genially tossing back his yellow hair and spreading out his arms in a gesture of welcome. He kissed his sister, then held her back for a moment appraisingly. John he clapped on the shoulder: 'How's Brother Mulholland?' Catherine glanced from one to the other: John did not like being teased about his membership of the Orange Order. However, he laughed it off, following Desmond across the room to where the drinks were laid out.

'The others are down in the kitchen making lunch for themselves,' said Sonia. 'Want some?'

Catherine shook her head: 'We ate on the way.'

'You did?' Sonia lowered her feet to the ground and got up, arching her back to stretch herself: 'That's just as well.' She ran her fingers through her black hair trying to remember what to do next. 'Oh, by the way, Teresa's coming in to do the tea—very loyal of her.'

Already the men were talking politics. 'Had much trouble locally?' John asked his brother-in-law.

'Nothing to speak of. They've burnt the odd hay-rick, that sort of thing—peasant disturbances.' Desmond raised his glass to him: 'Can't compete with you lot in the big city!'

There was a noise of children screaming: the Punch-and-Judy man arrived. 'He looks rather like Mr Punch, himself,' said Sonia as she swept out into the hall to greet him. The hall was now crammed with children and their mothers, many of whom were so whimsically attired it might have been a fancy dress party. They were swarming around a stage that was being erected with great cunning in one corner near a stuffed grizzly bear, who was wearing the entertainer's muffler and hat. Old Coogan had a wig of coarse, wavy hair, gold teeth and a red, shiny nose and he did indeed resemble Mr Punch. He was known far and wide throughout the country, travelling by motorbike with his equipment packed into a tiny bag behind the saddle and a tattered flag waving aloft as an advertisement.

Patrick had disappeared and Catherine panicked until she saw him with Teresa, standing with a couple of farm girls who had been allowed in to peep over the edge of the crowd.

The show was performed with great verve and ferocity. When the puppet Punch leaned his cruel face over the edge of the box to snarl at his audience: 'If yous don't wheesht I'll separate yous from your breath!' a small boy in the front began to cry. The element of terror held the children enthralled. Afterwards they crowded round to see how it had been done, while Coogan, going through his repertoire of tricks, asked Sonia which would she like next: ventriloquism, magic, hypnosis? The latter had been his speciality; he had hypnotized dogs and cats, even donkeys: 'But donkeys, they're the devil—stubborn brutes! They won't come round once you've put them under.' To the delight of the children watching his wig move, he scratched his head. 'Shall I try it out on these youngsters?'

'Oh, no!' Catherine had become very agitated. She clung to Sonia in protest. Coogan flashed at her a gilded grin:

'Don't you trust me, girlie?'

There was a break for tea and the mothers retreated to the drawing-room, where they talked about jewellery and the Dublin Horse Show, while the children were dealt with by Teresa and Sonia's cleaning woman. Coogan chose to remain in the hall, munching his own sandwiches and singing hymns to himself, while he inspected the weapons on the walls.

The rain had stopped and the rest of the entertainment took place outside on the damp croquet lawn. At this point John and Desmond reappeared. When Coogan concluded his performance by making toys out of twisted balloons which he threw into the pond, Desmond laughed until his red face turned purple at the children flinging themselves into the muddy water in pursuit.

'Well that's that for another year,' Sonia turned her back on the children, preparing to re-enter the house.

'What about a head-count?' Desmond suggested. 'Better make sure they're all there?'

But Sonia was already making her way upstairs to rest for a while in her locked bedroom.

The dripping children were hustled away; the fun was over. Coogan packed up his equipment—a conjuring trick in itself—and was off again on his motorbike down the lanes into the summer twilight.

Catherine took Patrick's hand (he had remained in the kitchen, being petted by Teresa, and was still dry) and led him out to the swing in a hidden part of the garden. Standing in the dank greenery as she pushed him back and up, she gazed at the weighted curve of the child's plump cheek and the evening light glistening on his curls, and thought that there would come a time in the years ahead when she would look back at this moment with nostalgia.

Although the low, drizzling cloud had lifted and the sky had become luminous, the air was still very humid and full of midges when they set out in Desmond's motor launch across the lough to a party given by their friends, Davina and Julian. No one was quite sure whether or not they had been invited or even if this was the night. They had been joined by Uncle Hugo, who hated to miss any excitement. With him was his grandson, Guy, and a tousled young woman he had picked up at a village dance, who was so overcome by the company she was unable to answer when spoken to.

Before they set out there was an unpleasant scene when Catherine asked what was to happen to Patrick. 'Bring him with you,' said Desmond. But she hurried off, almost in tears, to leave him in the care of Teresa. On her return her brother said scornfully: 'You've become a Mulholland!'

On the boat she clung to her husband. 'If the child had drowned it would be a joke—everything in this country is a joke. . . .' She was shivering. John took off his coat and wrapped it round her. She could feel his warmth as she sheltered against him.

The noise of the engine echoed back to them as they circled island after island, the dense vegetation casting green and gloomy reflections upon the water. Desmond was pretending to be lost. Suddenly a second launch came into view, also full of people. A portly man, wearing an Orange sash draped over his paunch, was being towed behind on water skis.

'Why it's old Ambrose!' shouted Desmond. 'Then we must be heading in the right direction—no party is complete without him!' Ambrose, Desmond's closest friend, came from a family that had lived in Fermanagh almost as long as the Hardwickes and for the moment he was High Sheriff of the County. They drew alongside and Ambrose let go of the rope, took off his skis and climbed into Desmond's boat. Although he was over-weight, he was sturdily built with immense rounded shoulders. A thrusting jaw and cheeks lined with crimson veins suggested a vigorous life in the open air; he was a keen horseman. He straddled the boat, grinning at its occupants. When he saw Catherine sitting mutely in the stern beside her husband, he clambered over to her and dragged her away from John, putting his naked arm around her.

'What's the matter? Tell Uncle Ambrose all about it!' She smelled the whisky on his breath as his bloodshot eyes stared hard into her own. 'What have you been up to these past few years? Breeding away? Don't tell me you've only got two children—you haven't started!'

It was decided to race to their destination. The two boats left a curving double wake, which broke up the perfect reflections and sent up a flurry of frightened water birds.

Usually at parties in Fermanagh there was no need for intro-ductions as every face was familiar. Tonight, however there were a number of strangers and Catherine was puzzled to see people whom she would never have expected to meet in this company. George Mulholland, for instance, had managed to get himself invited and she was even more surprised to find Felicity with a group of her arty friends. They were spending the weekend in the country to escape the dreadful atmosphere in Belfast, Felicity told her; it was Ambrose, whom they had met by chance in a pub, who had told them to come along. Later, after a few drinks, she confessed to Catherine that she had been made to feel more at her ease among the gentry than in Catherine's own home. 'Not you, lovey,' Felicity patted her arm, 'it's your dreary husband. . . . Whatever did you see in him?'

Uncle Hugo's shabby hat (Guy insisted that he slept in it) could be seen bobbing above the crowd. There were one or two other elderly people and some children, who had been given toxic drinks and were chasing each other between the legs of the adults. There were far more men than women, the strangers being mostly Army officers from a local barracks that had recently been reinforced. 'We have a duty to entertain them,' Davina, the hostess, told Catherine, 'After all,' her widely-spaced eyes were very bright, 'think what they're doing for us!' The vague sense of living in a time of danger and the impact of new personalities on a closed society had a stimulating effect: the guests were in excellent spirits.

Apart from a huge log fire in the drawing-room, the house was unheated and the women put on their coats when they went into the dining-room to eat. Davina had hired a local pop group who stood in a corner singing Irish folk songs, their thin voices barely audible above the laughter and clattering plates.

'Minstrelsy!' Uncle Hugo tapped Davina on the shoulder, 'very charming my dear! Got jolly good tunes these Fenian songs!' He had been arguing with an English civil servant who was one of a team engaged in writing up the disturbances in Ulster. 'You English,' said Hugo, 'You come over here thinking you know all the answers, and yet none of you seems to have got the hang of it at all. But it doesn't stop you lecturing us about how we misgovern the place—damned impertinence!'

'If you'll excuse me. . . .' The Englishman was trying to slip away.

'You think it's a waste of time to listen to an old fogey like me? You're looking at my grave-marks?' He laughed happily, 'you think I'm an old dotard? But I'm telling you,' he had caught the man by his lapel, 'it's the I.R.A. that are at the back of all this—I've seen 'em at it before, I know their tricks! You make a mistake—mark my words—not to listen to the Protestant bigots who are warning you against them.'

'In our view,' solemnly the man cleared his throat: 'It would seem to us that the Protestants have caused the worst of the damage.'

'The rumpus in Belfast, what? That other lot of yahoos? Well, if you *allow* people to riot. . . .' Hugo broke off to chuckle to himself.

'And what would you have done?'

'I'd line a few of them against the wall and shoot 'em!'

'Oh, Uncle Hugo,' Davina caressed his arm, 'you're so amusing!'

After dinner records were played in the drawing-room and people began to dance. Ambrose switched out the lights and the great fire threw up capricious shadows on the ceiling. Beyond the windows, in spite of the lateness of the hour, daylight lingered, greenish, in the western sky.

'We appear to be seeing the start of a new English invasion,' said John. Although he did not normally enjoy dancing, he led his wife on to the floor where he nuzzled her sentimentally.

'What's got into you?' she tried to draw away from him: 'You're suffocating me!' It was a little while before she realised that her husband, like everyone else in the room, was very drunk. Catherine, herself, had drunk very little. As she listened to the music, with its repetitive themes of love and longing, she asked herself: Is this all that will ever happen to me? Will there never be anything more?

There was a commotion as the dancers edged away from a spot in the centre of the room where a gun had been dropped. Ambrose snatched it up. The soldier, to whom it belonged, came forward, red with embarrassment, and held out his hand for its return. But Ambrose was examining the weapon, opening it up to see if it were loaded. Then, as if looking for a target, he pointed it round at his friends until his eye alighted on Uncle Hugo.

'Let's see if we can shoot old Hugo's hat off! Got any ammo?' In the silence that followed, the amorous music whined monotonously.

Catherine was bored: 'Even the Troubles are a joke.'

John was tired of dancing. He left her to join a group of men who were talking among themselves in another room. There were too many men at the party. Sober and alone, she went over to the window and looked out at the shadowy landscape, reflecting on the mores of this society where drunkenness was acceptable and it was a vice to be unhappy, or complex or to complain. In Ireland anyone not cheerful becomes an outsider.

'Who is that super-looking girl? Is she really your sister?'

'You like her, do you?' Catherine turned at the sound of Desmond's drawling voice. With him was a young officer, his face half-obscured, who was staring at her intently. At once she looked away. As she did so, she caught sight of her own reflection, very palely, in the glass: she had forgotten to think of herself as pretty.

'I suppose she's not bad,' said Desmond. 'Want to be introduced?' Catherine noticed a cynical gleam in his blue eyes as he took her hand, offering her; earlier in the evening he had abused her for becoming stodgily middle class. 'Well, there you are,' he introduced them: 'Enjoy yourselves, children!'

The young man was very polite. He told her how pleased he was to be posted to Ulster with a chance of some real soldiering. He was sun-tanned with clear-cut regular features, but, although flattered by his attentiveness, Catherine wondered if she would think him quite so handsome if he had not been in uniform. When he mentioned his family left behind in England, she surprised herself by thinking: this man is here without his wife!

'I've been wanting to speak to you all evening—I noticed you as soon as you came into the room.' Catherine fidgetted, unable to think of a reply. 'Perhaps we should dance?' he suggested. They danced for a while in silence. Catherine felt guilty that she should prefer this stranger to John, who was a clumsy dancer and trod on her toes. Most of the other couples round them were embracing. 'I must say,' he tried to look into her eyes, 'you people certainly seem to let your hair down at a party!'

84

'I think it's rather tedious and adolescent,' primly, she stiffened, pulling away from him. 'It's always like this—they're all married—I just don't see the point.' It was not, she thought, as if they did anything about it afterwards, the community being extremely circumspect within its rules.

'I suppose the point about marriage is that after a while the gilt comes off the gingerbread.'

'Well, it hasn't for me.' And it won't, she determined to herself: never! But, as she was thinking this, he kissed her on the lips.

'You make a mistake—I'm very square!' Trembling a little, she disengaged herself and walked off. But at the door she glanced back and saw that he was still standing there, staring after her with a look of anger and astonishment.

She went to find John, but he was absorbed in conversation with Uncle Hugo and a couple of strangers, making it obvious he did not welcome distractions. When she returned to the drawing-room, she saw her soldier dancing with Sonia, on whose white face there was a rapturous glow as she circled the room in his arms, haughtily drunk. Catherine remembered his kiss, was bitter with jealousy, then angry with herself and suddenly felt very tired.

As nobody showed any sigh of wanting to go home, she went upstairs and lay down in one of the bedrooms. But beneath her, under the floor boards, she could still hear the throbbing of the party and the languorous music. Lying on her back, staring up at the blank ceiling, she again asked herself: is this all?

In the dining-room, amid a clutter of leftovers and dirty plates, the men were getting down to what Desmond described as 'serious' drinking. In spite of his white hairs, Uncle Hugo, in better form than his juniors, was holding the floor with a theory that the I.R.A. were setting out on a campaign for the destruction of the country. The English guests listened with bemused tolerance as he insisted, a light froth at the corner of his lips, that the answer to the problem lay in the Republic.

'So long as they can escape over the Border and get supplies of money and arms from the South you'll never get rid of them. But what's this damned Government doing about it? That's what I'd like to ask!'

'Well, it's not quite so simple,' explained a businessman

85

who had come to Ulster to check the security of his firm's Irish interests. 'After all, it wouldn't quite do to be seen bullying a little country. And we've done enough damage in Ireland as it is.'

'Typical British hypocrisy! That's all the politicians ever think about—Britain's image abroad. But one didn't see them having the same qualms about putting sanctions against Rhodesia. Why not try that one, for a start?'

There was a murmur of disapproval.

'The thing you don't seem to realise,' Hugo continued, 'is that they're niggers—white niggers! And they ought to be stopped!'

'But how?' John was embarrassed at Uncle Hugo using such language.

'How? It's not my job to know how! But I do know that right now it could be done. They're still a rabble—they haven't yet got themselves into shape. It's a question of political attitude: to you, English, the I.R.A. seem to be the representatives of some noble cause, but to us they're common criminals. How would you like it,' he pointed his finger rather too close to the businessman's face, 'if London were taken over by a Soho gang?'

'That's hardly a parallel,' the man backed away: 'There's the social factor, a question of justice. . . .'

'Aha! Now I've got you—the underdog is always right!' Hugo's elation left him and his head drooped as he muttered into his collar: 'Idiots! These no-go areas. . . .' Then he looked up. 'That's the most laughable bit of all, allowing them to have no-go areas in the two major cities, where terrorism can be organized, is sheer insanity! But then,' his eyes had begun to water, 'perhaps I've outlived my generation? It sometimes seems to me that there are so few normal people left that we shall soon be shut away in sanity bins!' He mopped his forehead with his handkerchief, then abruptly walked away, asking John: 'Where's that clever wife of yours?' He preferred the company of pretty women.

'Well!' The Englishman straightened himself: 'The old boy's quite a character in his way.'

'You see, the point is that. . . .' Desmond, no longer as articulate as his uncle, took him by the arm. 'The point is, your

86

average Ulster Protestant, he's not a bad chap—he's just a bore. A plain, dull, priggish, hard-working, self-righteous. . . .' Desmond paused to scratch his head. 'The Catholic, you see, he's got the gift of the gab, he's sympathetic, a delightful rogue and all that blarney. And the British love him. But the Prod—who can't in any case express himself—lives by a set of puritan and victorian values that the English have spent most of this century trying to get away from—so of course he's repellent.'

'Puritan?' The businessman watched Desmond staggering against the table; he seemed not to have noticed that he had overturned a glass of wine. 'Surely not here?'

'Oh, don't take me as an example. But him,' Desmond slapped John on the chest with the back of his hand, 'he's typical.'

The Englishman glanced, embarrassed, at the large sandy-haired fellow who was absorbing these insults with gloomy impassivity. Though straightforward, it was certainly not a humorous face.

John startled him by remarking: 'It could be there's something in what he says.' He despised his brother-in-law for his upper-class rudeness, but was too preoccupied with his feelings of confusion and foreboding, although it was assumed that at the end of the summer the Troubles would blow over. He was not to know that, although the main points of the Civil Rights Movement would soon be granted, the violence would continue, or that a few months later businessmen and politicians from Dublin, among them members of the Irish Cabinet, would meet secretly with the I.R.A. in Belfast to promise them money and arms provided they confined their activities to the North.

'Well, I must confess, you've got me bushed!' The Englishman was making an attempt at jollity, too polite to say that he found his companions and, indeed, the problems of the country itself, incomprehensibly bizarre.

But Desmond turned from him and put his arm round John's shoulders: 'I'm going to descend on you one of these days! What about a round of golf? I feel like stretching the old muscles.' John responded with sudden cheerfulness and the two brothers-in-law casually moved away, excluding the Englishman because, whatever their differences, the other was an outsider.

1971

On the first dry day after a week of rain Catherine took Patrick into Belfast to buy his new school uniform. When she saw him stiffly dressed in his blazer and cap, she bent down and hugged him: 'You're beginning to look such a big boy!' His blond curls were fluffed out under the rim of his cap; his father was insisting that he had a proper hair-cut before going to school. 'I suppose it's bad for them,' Catherine turned to the motherly shop assistant, 'to want to keep them as babies? They change so fast. . . .'

'Ah, it's when you've got children,' the woman sighed, amiably settling down for a chat, 'that you notice just how quickly the time goes in. Then they're grown up and they've gone—and you wonder what happened to all those years.'

While Catherine was trying to decide how many shirts she should buy and what exactly was her child's sock size, the woman, in no hurry to make a sale, reminisced about her own family; her eldest son was now married. The brightness of the morning, broken up by the dummies in the window, filtered inwards in streaks and patches, glittering a ring on Catherine's hand as she picked through a tray of socks.

'D'you know I can't even remember his shoe size?'

She had talked it over with John, whether or not it would be safe to bring Patrick into the city. She could telephone and have it sent out on appro, he had suggested, if she was really worried. Or he would go in during the lunch hour and get the things himself. But what help would that be, she had said, why should he be the one to be blown up? He assured her that no one was going to be blown up—not in the morning; there were far too many troops around for them to dare by day. It was after dark that it happened, the worst news coming in while they were eating their breakfast. But life must go on, John had added, trying to encourage her, it was giving in to them to become too frightened to carry on with the ordinary routine. That was their aim: to disrupt the community through terror. During the summer the I.R.A. had started bombing in earnest and a second Prime Minister had fallen. Replacing him, Faulkner had pledged himself to end the violence and had introduced internment; but he was now being blamed for the escalation of the Troubles.

Patrick's shoes were removed, but the size number had been worn away. The assistant then took off one of his socks, pausing before measuring it to give him a sweet out of her pocket because he looked bored.

The explosion was so loud and so close that objects shivered on the counter. No one moved. Peculiarly detached from what was happening, Catherine observed that both Patrick's and the assistant's eyes had literally started out of their heads, showing the shape of the eyeball. There was a reverberation of falling debris, then silence. Then passersby burst into the shop from the street, among them women sobbing hysterically: 'Oh, those poor people. . . . the whole building went up—it was full of people. . . .' Amid the confusion of gesticulating hands—'It was that way!' 'No, it was over there—in Bedford Street!' After the screaming sirens of a fleet of ambulances and fire engines, there was a second explosion. And a third.

The shop was in the central square and through the window they could see the green dome of the City Hall. Women and children were still streaming in through the door. 'The multistorey car park's gone up,' someone said, 'there was a man inside getting into his car.'

'I'm not staying here,' the assistant was obsessively wiping her hands on her overall: 'The management's got to send us home—they've got no right to keep us here. Look at that glass!' she pointed, her face, which had been pale with terror, now indignantly flushed: 'Just think if that window had blown in!'

The streets were full of flying glass, it was being said, there could be no escaping it.

There was now a crowd at the door, watching the ambulances. The bombs had been placed on three sides of the square, though it was not known exactly in which streets. No one dared to go out.

Patrick tugged at his mother's skirt: 'Can I put my sock on now?'

'His shoes!' The assistant rummaged among the pile of small shirts on the counter. 'I can't find his shoes. . . . Now isn't that an awful thing?' There were tears in her eyes. At the back of the shop a group of women were standing with their arms round each other. 'The poor child—how will he get home?'

'How indeed?' Catherine listened to her own laughter. Who was to know if the bombing was at an end? Around her she heard a whispered speculation on the extent of the casualties. A woman had fainted, another wept uncontrollably in lament for the dead. Telling herself to keep calm, Catherine smiled, asked for the bill, found Patrick's shoes on the floor. She took him firmly by the hand.

'Mummy, you're hurting me—you're squeezing my bones!'

'There, darling!' The assistant popped another sweet into his mouth: 'Hush, pet!' Then she parcelled up the clothes: 'Better keep busy or we'll all go out of our minds.'

Catherine left the shop and hurried away, dragging Patrick after her. There was a huge crowd of men and women on the pavements, moving along like sleep-walkers, utterly quiet, their eyes staring. The city centre had been bombed in daylight: no place was safe.

Patrick had begun to cry. The child—I must save my child! Catherine muttered to herself, as she pulled at his hand. But she was unable to find a way to get to her car. A number of entrances had been cordoned off. Down one street there was no view at all, only smoke, black as night, rising higher than the roof-tops. She stared for a moment in disbelief—the image belonged to newspaper photographs, to television. . . . The gesture was automatic and conventional when she turned Patrick's face away so that he should not see the body being lifted on a stretcher into an ambulance.

It was only when she at last had found a way through that she began to panic, because, although the street was open, the pavement was inches deep in broken glass. People had been blinded, had had their limbs sliced off by flying glass—and, horrified, she lifted the child, covering his head inside her coat, and began to run. Afterwards she was amazed that she had had the strength to carry him, for he was now quite heavy, and she thought how stupid she had been as they could both have fallen among the splinters on the road.

In the car Patrick whimpered, accusing his mother of taking him to a place where there were 'bad people'. But, once he was home, he boasted to his little brother: 'I saw bombs—you didn't! I saw a dead body. . . .'

'Mr Mulholland's been on the phone all morning,' Ellen told her: 'He's wild to know what's happened to you.'

But Catherine took her time before telephoning him. She fussed about the children's lunch, watered some plants that had been given to her by her mother-in-law.

'Catherine—darling!' At the sound of her husband's anguished voice, she twisted the receiver, unable to think of anything to say to him. Beyond the window she could see the rain starting. 'Well, are you all right?'

'Rather an anti-climax, I'm afraid—yes, we're both all right.' She held the telephone away from her ear. Her flippancy had turned his anxiety to anger and she could hear him shouting. It was then that the reality of what she had been through caught up with her and she burst into tears, remembering a newsreel of a child's funeral, the coffin so small that the father had been able to carry it in his arms through the throng of spectators.

'Oh, please don't cry!' John was now ashamed of his outburst. He asked gently: 'Would you like it if I came home?'

'No, no, I'll be better in a minute. . . . It's just that it didn't quite hit me at the time—too bad to be true, or something. . . .' But she continued to cry and he became frustrated by her inability to answer his questions.

'Calm yourself, do!' Again he had begun to sound severe, lecturing: 'You know there are people who have to live through all this. My typist comes from the Shankill—she's only a wee girl of eighteen—and quite often at night she hears shooting in the street.'

94

Catherine laid down the receiver, feeling demoralized: she had given way to hysteria, reacting like a child. She thought of ringing Felicity, then remembered that this was one of the afternoons when she would be at work. The rain was heavy now and it would be impossible for the boys to go out to play. She drifted around the house, wondering what to do with herself, making a note of a door handle that needed repairing, picture frames that had not been properly dusted. The house had been decorated and equipped with great thoroughness and for a long time, apart from maintenance, there had been nothing new that had needed to be done. With Edward three years old and Patrick at school, it was time, of course, that she had another baby. . . . When she had first married she had envisaged herself the mother of a large family in an atmosphere of affection, a closeness of personal links that had been absent from her own upbringing. But although this vision was partially realized, it seemed to her that an important element was wanting, as if she had deluded herself with an artificial picture of happiness.

She picked up a newspaper and went into the bedroom intending to read it, but, after glancing at the headlines, she let it fall from her hand and lay back, staring at the ceiling. Her life had emptied, she had told Felicity, she must find some useful occupation. Surely, with all the disturbances and so much unsettlement among the very poor, there must be something she could do? The previous time she had been in Belfast there had been a curious incident the night before: the inhabitants of a Protestant street had burned down their houses on the rumour that a Catholic gang from another part of the city was about to do it for them. (It was their Catholic neighbours who had tried to comfort them by helping to pack up their belongings.) Out shopping, Catherine had seen whole families bundled up with their possessions on carts, looking glumly bewildered as they circled the City Hall in the rain with nowhere to go; boys, who had jumped on for the ride, sat on the back, swinging their legs and grinning at passersby while the refugees huddled for shelter against their own damp bedding.

Catherine had left off what she was doing and gone to see Felicity, indignant and excited: she would do voluntary work in one of the bad areas—but only among Catholics, she insisted, just to show that she was impartial; the time had come when someone must cross the barrier! Felicity, encouraging her, at once rang up a priest and Catherine had a long talk with the man. But, after going home and telling John she was going to do meals-on-wheels in the Falls, he had laughed at her idea of a personal peace-mission: did she think that all by herself she could solve the Troubles by doing a few hours' charity work—which she would abandon as soon as it became a bore? He did not believe in her, she protested. He then cut her off, saying that it was not worth risking her life—did she remember that there might be bullets ricochetting from the walls?—for a sentimental impulse. What about the children? And who would make his tea? He concluded by warning her not to pay too much attention to Felicity and her Fenian friends. She was too easily swayed, had no sense of proportion, he said, and her daydreams were no help: dreaming, he reminded her, was the Irish national vice.

She gazed at the rain clouds shifting past the window, and bent down to switch on the radio at the side of the bed.

An emergency news broadcast: 'The I.R.A. have declared war on the civilian population. . . .'

She switched it off, buried her face in the pillow, saw again the image of the stricken father as he carried his little coffin through the streets, a seventeen month old Catholic child, shot dead, while she was playing, by a sniper. During a television interview one of the I.R.A. leaders dismissed the incident as 'one of the hazards of urban guerilla warfare'. His colleague then added that everyone in the community was to be made to 'pay dear and very dear' for the continued presence of British troops in the Province. The I.R.A. were now being televised full-face—no longer with their backs to the camera—like members of any respectable political movement.

Catherine leaned across to the telephone, dialled, asked for Felicity. But it was a man who answered, telling her that she was not yet back.

'There's no point in even talking about it,' said Felicity. 'It's the Government who are to blame for all this. I mean, if they intern people without trial. . . .'

'But don't you think they had to do something?' Although Catherine would come up to Belfast to visit her friend, she was now too frightened to shop in the city centre. 'All through the summer the bombing was getting more and more dangerous and destructive—were they just to sit back and watch while the place was demolished?'

'That's beside the point,' Felicity turned up the flame of the gas fire and crouched closer to the heat. 'In the early days they had a sense of honour about the bombing, they only attacked property. And they did make some effort to avoid casualties— they played fair. But all that came to an end when the Army went into their houses and started rounding them up. Of course they feel bitter knowing that their friends are in concentration camps.'

'So it's all right to bomb property? What about the night-watchman who gets caught in the blast?'

Felicity got up and wandered round the room in search of cigarettes. 'I can see that it would be difficult for you—for someone from your background—to understand that for them this is also a class struggle. By taking action they are working for justice.'

'But what justice? Most of the Civil Rights demands are being met. So what else is there? A united Ireland run by the Provos? Even in the South that would hardly be popular!'

Felicity stood by the window, looking down into the street with its yellowing trees. 'I really don't know,' she said at last, 'I can't work it out in my own mind. In a way it's easy to see this as ethical violence—and yet. . . . But one thing I am certain about is that detention without trial is against all democratic principles and there'll be no peace in this country until the boys have been let out. They've always said that this society was rotten and now that it's seen to be repressive as well, it stands to reason that they'll continue to fight against it. Internment is proof of injustice!'

'Well, there's not much that either of us can do about it,' said Catherine, trying to avoid a quarrel. It seemed to her that a side-effect of the Troubles was an embittering of personal relationships. Nowadays she even quarrelled with John—for all that Felicity had told her she had no mind of her own and only

97

echoed the opinions of her husband. 'Can't we talk about something more cheerful ?'

Felicity came over to her and bent down, her large, grey eyes peering into Catherine's face: 'You're an awful softie, aren't you ? You can't bear an argument.' She lifted a strand of Catherine's auburn hair: 'It's time you learned to stand up for yourself!' Giving her a maternal pat, she began tidying the place, removing empty beer bottles and overflowing ashtrays. 'What a dump! I can't imagine you ever living in conditions like this.'

'Perhaps in some ways I think it's enviable ? It must be nice to have lots of interesting friends dropping in. Now that Patrick's at school. . . .' Her gaze drifted around the darkening room. There were many pictures on the walls, some by Felicity and her friends and a number of childish works which she had brought home from the school where she taught. 'Perhaps I should take up painting, or learn a musical instrument—though, I suppose, if I were to have another baby. . . .'

'D'you only think of your future in terms of babies and family ? Felicity paused before a chipped mirror and ran a comb through her short, curly hair. 'D'you really believe that's the only thing of importance in a woman's life ?'

'No, not for you—but I can't see what else. . . .'

There was an explosive noise and they both ducked instinctively, covering their heads with their arms. But it was only Aramanta banging the kitchen door. She now entered the room.

'You mustn't slam doors like that, lovey—it's bad for the nerves.' At night Felicity was sometimes kept awake by the sound of machine-gunfire. 'Go and put on the kettle, there's a darling! I'm sure Catherine could do with some tea ?'

The child's clothes were too small and her nose was running. She stared at Catherine in a way that made her feel uncomfortable, as she had been thinking of the contrast with her own healthy, well-cared for children.

'Do you have favourites,' Catherine asked Felicity as the girl left the room, 'Or are you a good impartial mother ?' Before Felicity could reply, she added: 'I have an attachment to Patrick that's almost neurotic—if anything happened to him I think I would feel that there was nothing much left for me to live for. . . . Although Edward is much the nicer person of the

98

two, Patrick's a spoilt little devil and can twist me any way he wants. And yet there's something about him. . . . Even if I have to get up to him in the night I really don't mind as it gives me a chance to touch him. I can't keep my hands off the child—it's like a love affair! Not that I've ever felt anything like that for John.'

'Perhaps it's what you need?'

'What?'

'An affair—I know a number of men who think you're rather dishy!'

Catherine blushed: 'I may be under-employed, but. . . .'

'D'you mean to tell me that in all the years you've been married you've never had a lover?' When there was no response, she bent forward, teasing: 'And looking like you!'

'Well, I haven't,' Catherine said flatly. An expression of obstinacy had come into her eyes.

With a faint, sly smile Felicity glanced at her: 'Perhaps you're one of those lucky people who find married sex quite adequate?'

'What? Saturday nights after he's had a few drinks at the golf club?' As soon as she had said this Catherine felt ashamed of her disloyalty. She did not add that she, herself, had little interest in this aspect of her marriage, and that the thrill she had imagined as a girl now seemed to her to belong to adolescent fiction.

'Kettle, Mummy!' shouted Aramanta from the kitchen and, rather reluctantly, Felicity got up and went out to make the tea.

While she was waiting Catherine picked up a newspaper which she found lying under her chair. As she skimmed through page after page of brutal incidents, she tried to remember what the contents had been in normal times. Today the worst account was of a torso that had been discovered with the dismembered limbs scattered over three suburban gardens. The dead man, it appeared, had been a member of the I.R.A. and was a victim of the bomb that he had planted unsuccessfully. A few months ago this story would have sickened her. Now, although Catherine's first feeling was relief for the innocent people who had been spared (the news had announced that a girl of eighteen had had her leg blown off at a village dance) her dominant sentiment was vindictive pleasure and she re-read the passage, almost with relish, wishing that more of them might succumb to the same fate.

Furtively, she laid the paper aside, knowing that John would have been disgusted to know what she was thinking. The boys who planted these bombs, he said, were very ignorant, often very young. Every death was a tragedy: the Troubles were for nothing!

Felicity came back with the tea and sat down at Catherine's feet in front of the gas fire. 'Where were we? We were talking about something interesting. . . .'

'I ought to be going soon,' the room had become very dark, 'John doesn't like it if I'm back late.'

'You mean he doesn't like it if he knows you've been to see me?'

'Oh, no!' Catherine lied. 'No, it's—well, the situation generally—he's a bit over-protective.' She decided to try one of Felicity's gauloises, but the strong tobacco made her cough. 'I hadn't told you he's joined the U.D.R. Rather a bore as he's often away in the evenings doing some sort of training. Seems to enjoy himself—playing at soldiers! He used to be in the T.A. before that was disbanded.'

'In the U.D.R., is he? Being a good citizen?'

'Oh, to be fair to him,' Catherine said defensively, 'I think he feels he must do something to help.'

'Yes, I suppose that's what he would feel—he's very conventional.' Over the rim of her teacup Felicity studied her friend's face as she stared into the fire. 'Tell me,' she hesitated, dabbed at her lips,' what about him—does he have affairs?'

'John!' Catherine backed away from the heat, feeling its glow on her cheeks.

'Not even if he goes away on business?'

'Oh, no! I can't say a worry about that is one of my problems.'

'All a matter of taste,' Felicity sounded peevish, 'but to me there's nothing more boring than the man who says proudly that he has never looked at another woman.'

'Poor old John,' Catherine began to laugh: 'That's exactly what he does say!'

'Perhaps it's poor old you?' Felicity suggested.

'Oh, I'm all right!' Catherine said with emphasis: 'I'm quite content—at least contented enough. It's just that it's a bit lonely and I miss having someone to talk to. Even when John's at home we often spend the evening stuck in front of the box.' She did not add that she was beginning to resent it that he refused to listen to her when she was trying to talk seriously.

'Why don't you come up here when he's out in the evenings? I've all sorts of people around—they bring their own booze, I'm afraid—but I daresay you could sneak something? Surely, John keeps a good cellar?'

'I'm tempted, but John wouldn't like it if I went out—he thinks it's too dangerous.'

'But he goes out himself.'

'Ah, that's different—I think he feels he's bullet-proof.' She glanced at her watch, finished her tea and got up preparing to leave. But when she was at the door she turned back impulsively: 'Whyever not? Better take a few risks than die of boredom at home!'

'There's my girl!' Felicity hugged her. 'You'll be quite an addition to my little circle. I've got a number of artists and some chaps from Queen's—I suppose you could describe them as the young intelligentsia of Belfast. But you're one of the beautiful people!' On the way downstairs she confided: 'Did you know that it's always been my ambition to have a salon?'

All but the essential exits had been bolted and there were guards on the few doors that remained open. As John walked round the workshop he thought of the damage that even a small bomb could do to the expensive machinery; if the whole building went up, not even Government compensation would cover the loss of orders and contacts while the place was being rebuilt. There had already been a blast nearby and one section of the factory was now artificially lit because the windows had been blown in and it was almost impossible nowadays to find a glazier to do repairs. 'Check your premises before leaving!' was the warning repeatedly given out after the news. Official posters had been stuck up on the walls as a reminder that a bomb could be as small as a cigarette packet.

The floor was thick with metal shavings and other debris, that crunched under his feet, and even the work-benches were permanently littered with dirty tea mugs, tins, rags, rubbish and an assortment of small bizarre objects whose usefulness would be known only to the worker on the bench. Although John had been talking to the foremen about the importance of each man clearing his own area at the end of the day, it was impossible to supervise the place really thoroughly. As he walked along he caught a glimpse through the machines of his brother, Peter, wearing a mechanic's overalls, and one of his uncles; the older man's face had become lined and haggard as he lay awake at nights worrying about the security arrangements.

'Good morning, Mr John!' a worker stopped his lathe to call out to him as he passed, and John paused for a moment, leaning against the bench. Harry Maguire had been apprenticed with them as a boy and his father had worked there before him. A few years earlier he had lost a couple of fingers in his lathe; although the workers were not well paid, it had always been the policy of the firm to be generous in cases of illness or accident. Nonetheless, when he watched him cheerfully smiling as he scratched his head with his mutilated hand, John wondered, for the first time, how it was possible that he seemed to bear his employers no grudge.

John bent down to peer at a newspaper folded back at the sports page, and the two men talked football. Then Harry touched his sleeve and jerked his head back in the direction of the office: 'Here comes the boss!' John looked up and saw his father walking towards him, frowning in concentration, his eyes glancing this way and that as he made his way between the men, all of whom seemed suddenly very absorbed in their work; even Harry had started up his lathe. When he caught his son's eye, Tom Mulholland beckoned to him, then turned back abruptly.

'There's a small point I want to discuss with you,' he said, once they had shut out the noise of the machines. John followed him into his office, a dingy room with bars over the windows in which there was a large desk, a swivel chair, a safe and rows of filing cabinets, the only decoration being photographs on the wall of the Royal family and his own father and some of the famous ships whose engines had been supplied by the firm.

'Sit down!' Tom removed a pile of papers from a chair in the corner of the room: 'I won't keep you too long.' He seated himself with his back to his son and stared at the correspondence on his desk for a moment before swivelling his chair round to say to him: 'As you know, Miss McNally is due to retire and we've been advertising for a new book-keeper. Now there have been a number of replies. . . .'

'You're wondering which to select?'

'Exactly! Well, for a start,' Tom made a jotting on a notepad, 'we'll eliminate the Catholics. But, that done, the question is. . . .'

'Steady on, Dad—I don't agree with this.'

Tom's eyebrows shot up; he was not accustomed to his authority being questioned. 'What's this? We've got to begin somewhere.'

'Yes, but we should first knock out the ones who are least qualified.'

'Now, look here, John we don't want to spend all day over this. As you know perfectly well there never has been a Catholic employed in this place—and now is hardly the moment to make a change.'

'Isn't it? I should have thought that this was a good moment. After all it's up to individual employers to make a break in their own traditions. You can't legislate against discrimination.'

There was a familiar rumbling noise. They listened in silence as the explosion faded.

'Hear that?'

John said nothing.

'If you employ a Catholic how can you have any guarantee that he doesn't have I.R.A. connections?'

John had got up and was looking out of the barred window to see if there was any smoke rising above the rooftops. 'Even so,' he said, 'surely, in the office. . . .'

'You might employ the most respectable-looking woman—she might even be the "good-living" type. But who's her cousin? And who's her nephew? All it needs is a little package hidden in the ladies lavatory. . . .'

John was still standing at the window, looking out; in his way he was as obstinate as his father. 'If we operate like this, then employers all over the country will be doing the same—only trusting their own, on whatever side they happen to be. The result of the terror is a vicious circle of suspicion and further resentment—and in the next generation things will be even worse than they were before. Even though there is a risk,' he turned to face his father, 'I think now is the time to make a gesture.'

The older man sighed, tapped his note-pad with his pencil. Then he glanced up shrewdly: 'Has Catherine been getting at you?'

John paused before saying: 'I'm capable of having my own thoughts on the subject.' He saw an angry gleam in his father's eye. 'And I've come to the conclusion that we were wrong.'

Wearily Tom pointed at the chair, indicating that he sit down again and listen reasonably: 'It's easy enough to say that we were wrong. But I grew up in the Twenties, you must remember. When I was a young man people were being lynched in the streets and drowned like rats in the harbour. The English complain that we have long memories but civil war is not a thing that's quickly forgotten. It wouldn't have been forgotten in England—they don't forget the War. If you've lived through trouble your opinions change. It may seem bigoted and narrow-minded but peace and an orderly working life where you can get something done are better than anarchy. And if the price of peace is to employ only one type, then. . . .' He shrugged: 'There you have it! And it goes both ways, of course—there are many Catholics that won't employ a Protestant.'

'But more Protestant employers.'

Tom frowned at his hands, which he opened and closed abstractedly, his thoughts elsewhere. He was wondering about his daughter-in-law, whose influence he mistrusted; the girl had always seemed to him somehow 'not quite'—he did not expect much from her. 'Well, where do you have utopia?' he said at last: 'Not here, not anywhere else. You just have to take the world as you find it.' His chin had sunk into the folds around his neck and he suddenly looked much older. 'The tragic bit about all this, son,' he laid his hand momentarily on John's knee, 'is that things had been getting much better. In the last ten years there's been an easing of the old grievances and even I'd begun to notice the change. I had thought,' he looked up at the ceiling, his eyes wandering a little, 'that by the time you'd reached my age how different it would all be—in your lifetime it might have been possible to take a more open line. The one thing I had never imagined was that I would live to see history repeat itself.'

'Well!' John was again on his feet, pacing up and down the congested room, cracking his knuckles. 'Which brings us back to the book-keeper. . . . What are you going to do?'

'I'll get Peter in,' his father exclaimed irascibly: 'He'll give me a hand in sorting this out!' And the two men stared at each other, their faces flushing with temper.

Tom said: 'If you bring a Catholic into a Protestant shop there is one other thing you have to take into account—the risk to their own safety. I saw you talking to Harry, there. Did you know that his neighbour had been found dumped on a waste lot? Ears off, nostrils slit—the man was hardly recognisable! And young George Magee on the next bench, his brother-in-law was in the police—that is, until he heard a knock at the door one night and peeped out of his bedroom window to see what it was all about. Shot where he stood, with his wife watching—he's not dead, just a vegetable. . . .' He muttered to himself, spitting into his handkerchief: 'And to think they were trying to disarm the police!'

'But I've had enough of this.' He handed John the list of applicants: 'You take that away and sort it out. Only one thing —no Catholics! If you bring one of them in here you don't have to use much imagination to work out what our boys might do to them if something were to happen that made their nerves give— and there's plenty happening, more's the pity, every day of the week. It's all very well for an educated man to have liberal sentiments, and even perhaps,' here he looked at his son with apprehension, 'to think himself above fear. But you must remember—if you have their interests at heart—that the ordinary people are afraid.'

'I'm sick of being cooped up in this house,' said Catherine. 'If you're going to be busy all weekend I shall take the children away to Fermanagh. You're out at the U.D.R. on Friday night, you'll sleep in all Saturday morning—and now you say you're going to golf in the afternoon. Which means, of course, that you'll spend the evening playing poker at the Club!' John was sitting with his back to her, watching an indifferent programme on television. He was very tired, having lain awake the night before wondering whether or not the firm should open up another factory across the water so that production could be kept going if they were bombed out in Belfast. He did not turn round to look at his wife as she paced the room working herself up for a scene. 'Well, what about it?' her voice was shrill: 'Why don't you answer?'

John reached across and adjusted the set, switching over to another channel. 'I'm sorry about the golf, but I can't get out of it. I'm playing with some business contacts Dad wants me to chat up—you don't like it if I bring them home.'

'Your father! What he says comes first? With you it's always business first!' She stood behind him, looking down on his sun-reddened neck and his broad inexpressive shoulders. 'If you'd rather, on the other hand, I could go and see Felicity in the evening—she's taken to giving soirées.'

'Soirées—really?' John covered his mouth to conceal his smile; he had recently annoyed Catherine by referring to her friend as the Queen of Bohemia.

'You just sit there. . . . What d'you expect me to do with myself if you're out all the time? You might as well be living in a hotel!'

'I suppose it was Felicity,' he now turned and glanced up at her, 'who gave you the hotel bit? You should watch her—people with broken marriages often enjoy stirring up trouble between their married friends.'

'Then can I go to Fermanagh—as the lesser of two evils? I take it you could just cook your own breakfast?'

'For Christ's sake, go—if that's what you want.' He poured himself a whisky. 'I don't run your life for you.' He had begun to drink more heavily—he must be careful not to let it become a habit. His eyes were again fixed on the television: 'When will you be back?'

Catherine hesitated, made nervous by his cold manner. Then she braced herself in defiance: it was time she became more independent, stood up for herself. Never before had she made a decision to go away without him. 'I had planned to stay for the weekend. . . .' He did not comment. 'You could come up, too, on Sunday—you could make it by lunch-time if you set out early.'

'I've no wish to come on Sunday—it's a long drive for one day—but I will if that's what you'd like.'

'Anything for peace, is that it?' said Catherine; although he did not want her to go, he had, nonetheless, managed to put himself in the right.

'Anything for peace.' He drained his glass and re-filled it, hoping the whisky would help him to sleep.

On the following day after breakfast he kissed her good-bye, perfunctorily, on the top of her head. She was annoyed that his last words were a reminder to take extra clothes for the children in case they fell into Desmond's pond. But later in the morning, she began to regret that they had parted on bad terms and rang him up at work; he was out visiting a customer and, when the telephonist put her through to his father, she felt embarrassed because she could not think of a message to leave.

Although it was early September, the woods around Castle Hardwicke were already yellowing and a damp, autumnal mist was rising from the ground. The house, set on a slope above Lough Erne, appeared less substantial behind the mist and the austere grandeur of the facade was softened. As she approached her family home through the familiar landscape, Catherine felt as though she were looking, not at a real building but at the ghost of something past; the reality was in her memories. The children, sleeping in the back of the car, wakened on the bumpy drive and started to cry. They, too, were growing older and it seemed to her that yet another period of her life was drawing to a close, being sealed off. She had left John behind on a restless impulse; now, at a distance from him, she felt anxious at the risks he might be taking as he trained in the fields late at night. The children whimpered. The melancholy stillness of the evening infected her, the countryside fading, vanishing, and she began to panic. But her fear was also for herself, for a cinematic sense of her life unfolding by stages and passing, while she, Catherine, had remained somehow on the outside, a viewer, as though she had never quite existed.

Her brother bounded down the steps to embrace her and she clung to him, enjoying his animal warmth, his buoyant laugh; he had been riding and his clothes smelled of horses and an elusive, indefinable smell of the land. Once they had entered the house and were inside the hall with its swords, flags and antlers, the children revived and rushed off to find their cousins. Sonia descended the stairs wearing evening dress, fastidiously elegant, although as she explained to Catherine there would be no one but the family.

'The hoi-poloi are coming tomorrow,' she said, 'to go shooting with Ambrose. Tonight we can be civilized.' She led the way into the drawing-room where Uncle Hugo was standing against the handsome mantel, looking quite spruce with a rose in his button-hole, although still wearing his hat. Stooping over Catherine, he greeted her with extreme courtesy:

'How very delightful it is to see you here, my dear! They've got nothing but foreigners around these days—the place has become like a transit camp! D'you know that one of those young Army chaps had the impertinence to land a helicopter on my lawn? And Desmond, there, he'll be bankrupted at the rate they put away his liquor.'

'Your brother-in-law, George is coming tomorrow,' said Desmond, 'with his whiny wife.'

Catherine grimaced: 'I thought I was getting away from all that.'

'Did you?' Desmond glanced at her. Then he said: 'Old George, he's not so bad—at least he gets around.' Recently George had taken a rod in Desmond's fishing syndicate. 'Seen his latest car? A Lamborghini! Fairly flashes the money about.'

'All the wrong people have got money these days,' said Hugo; 'Look at me, for instance, driving a Mini-Cooper!' He did not mention that the three Bentleys rusting in his stables had been abandoned on each occasion when they were in need of simple repairs.

'Desmond had some luck on the horses and we bought this.' Sonia led Catherine into the corner of the room to show her a painting, very large and darkened with varnish, of fantastic crags and whirlpools. 'It was sold to us as a Salvator Rosa, though I don't suppose it is—you know these Dublin dealers. Quite fun, though.'

Over dinner, seated far apart at the huge table whose surface reflected the family silver, Sonia talked about her horses and her impatience for the start of the hunting season. The view from the window was indistinct in the ebbing daylight, although a gleam was still visible on the lough. The room itself was dim, lit by candles that cast faint wavering lights on the high ceiling but obscured a damp patch and the cracks in one corner.

'I should like to hunt again,' said Catherine, remembering the sense of freedom, the danger. 'But I don't think I'd have the guts for it now—I've become very tame. Still it would be nice for the boys to have ponies, and we've got the space. . . . Something to keep me occupied at any rate.'

'I didn't know you were at such a loose end?' Casually, Desmond reached out for the wine.

'It's partly the Troubles,' Catherine avoided her brother's eyes. 'Rather a bore—one can't go anywhere because of the bombs.'

'So John's joined the U.D.R.?' said Hugo, 'Guy too. I expect you were wondering why he's not with us tonight?' He mumbled to himself, fearing for his grandson. 'Training part-time soldiers would make sense if the Army themselves were allowed to get on with the job—but as it is they've got their hands tied.'

'You're not joining, Desmond?' asked his sister.

'I don't see much point in getting a bullet through my skull for the sake of appearances. Uncle Hugo's right—if the Army were given the go-ahead to sort the buggers out it would be a different matter. As it is, civilians only add to the targets.'

'Bad show this bombing,' said Hugo. 'John's factory's still there, is it? Make quite a blaze, what!' He got up and laid his hand on Catherine's shoulder, gallantly offering to take her plate. 'Worrying for you, my dear—and for all of us. Of course, the extraordinary thing is that all this should be *allowed* to happen—but then what's intolerable for us is quite easily tolerated by politicians in Westminster who don't have to put up with it. What it boils down to is the political approach. The I.R.A.'s last round in the fifties never got off the ground because there was internment in the South as well as in the North. Those johnnies in the grocers' Republic were as determined as we not to stomach any nonsense and the whole thing fizzled out. Democracy doesn't work in Ireland—all they understand is force. Now if those windbags at Westminster. . . .'

'We've got one of them coming tomorrow,' Desmond

smiled, anticipating a row with his uncle: 'At least I'm not quite sure what he is—he's certainly not Army.'

'Why d'you have 'em in the house? It's these people with their woolly-mindedness who are responsible for the trouble in the Province. It could all have been dealt with,' Hugo crumpled up his napkin and flung it down on the table, 'but the blunt fact is that the British Government *condones* the violence in Northern Ireland.'

Lunch for the shooting party took place in Ambrose's kitchen because his wife, a recluse, did not appear, and refused to allow the sportsmen (who were clients not guests) to use her dining-room. Desmond had left the house before his wife and sister were awake and they followed much later, Sonia having had a few drinks before leaving, as one glass of beer was the ration for lunch. On entering the huge, grimy kitchen in which an unappetising stew was being consumed, she said loudly: 'Who are all these people?' and scanned the faces around the wooden table. 'I've never set eyes on half of them.' She waved at Davina who was chatting animatedly to a fair-haired man with un-usually pale blue eyes. 'Now who's he?' Sonia frowned: 'I ought to know his name—I believe he's staying with us. He's in the Diplomatic or something. . . .'

'What? Foreign Office in Northern Ireland!' Catherine was indignant.

'Best-looking man in the room!' Sonia pronounced, after a quick study of the other faces. 'But you can tell he's not an Army type by the way he uses his hands when he's talking—something almost effeminate. . . .'

At this the man looked up and the two late-comers by the door became the object of a rather calculating glance from his pale eyes, as though he, too, were in the habit of taking in everything that was going on. Catherine returned his stare and he looked away, offering a cigarette to Davina. He's conceited, she thought, he knows he's attractive. There was a delicacy in the gesture with which he opened his cigarette case and held it out in his tapering, over-sensitive fingers. She noticed, with a certain malice, that his wavy hair was greying at the temples.

'Why, it's little Catherine!' George Mulholland shouted

across to her. 'What are you up to, you naughty girl? Here all by yourself?' Again Catherine was conscious of the blue eyes upon her and felt, absurdly, that this fact, also, had been noted. 'What have you done with the old man?'

'He's coming tomorrow. I'm a golf widow.'

There was a movement along the benches round the table and the stranger edged closer to Davina to make room on his left. Davina looked peeved. But Catherine seated herself at the far end and it was Sonia who took the place, exclaiming:

'Tonight you will be my guest—perhaps you had better introduce yourself?'

'Martin Evans.' The civilized voice was too carefully modulated.

After lunch they were allowed into the drawing-room for coffee and the girls were offered liqueurs. The room was un-heated and the best pieces of furniture had been covered by dust sheets. Catherine stood by the window with George's wife, Liz, who was grumbling because she was pregnant and unable to ride: horses, she said, were the only thing that made life in Ireland worthwhile. While Liz complained about her nausea, Catherine's attention was distracted by fragments of other conversations, Ambrose who was planning to go shark-fishing, and an Army officer telling Desmond that the Troubles would be over by Christmas.

'I see you're an optimist! Then, if that's the case,' Desmond turned to Martin, 'what are *you* doing here?'

Martin smiled, but without showing his teeth. He has a concealing manner, Catherine thought. Although he held himself with a stiffness that was almost military, there was something nervous and volatile in his movements; when on the defensive, he kept his hands inside his pockets.

'Well, why are you here? What are you up to?'

'An official secret I'm afraid!'

'You're being very cryptic—are you trying to make a mystery of yourself?'

'In a sense I'm not really here at all,' Martin was still smiling: 'We're not supposed to make ourselves known to the public.'

'We?' Desmond was now glaring at him and he backed away slightly. To avoid the aggressive stare, he glanced around and caught Catherine's eye.

'Wouldn't you like to sit down somewhere? Are you sure you're all right?' Catherine whispered to Liz, turning her back on him. But, although the voice was discreetly lowered, she could not help over-hearing him ask:

'Who was that girl who came in with your wife? Is she a friend of hers?'

'They're sisters-in-law,' Desmond's amiability had returned: 'Which might or might not make them friends.'

'*Your* sister?'

'Want to meet her?'

Catherine had a sensation of *déjà vu*. She looked out, wondering whether the rain would keep off until tea-time. It was only when Desmond summoned her, calling imperiously across the room, that she remembered the party where a soldier had kissed her.

They were introduced. When Martin Evans bowed over her hand, she glanced down at his shoes, half-imagining that she had seen him clicking his heels. She was surprised to find that he was wearing a wedding ring and there was also a signet ring on his right hand. Although nothing amusing had been said, she felt that she might start laughing inappropriately, as if the too-gentle contact with his fingers were tickling her skin.

'You must think us very eccentric here,' she said, 'very peculiar?' He looked perplexed. She withdrew her hand and indicated the shrouded furniture: 'All those dust-sheets. . . .'

'Where's your wife, Evans?'

He coloured very faintly. Then he drew himself up and again his hands were in his pockets: 'Margaret? She's in England for the moment. She's refused to come over here until we're offered a house she can bear to live in—she's fed up with being moved from place to place.'

'Indeed!' Desmond looked interested: So you're here for some time?'

Martin evaded the question: 'She's got rather a lot on her plate at the moment, translating some correspondence on the Dreyfus case. She read languages at Oxford,' he glanced at Catherine: 'We met when we were undergraduates.'

'That must have been a fair while ago!' Desmond was becoming bored.

Catherine was embarrassed by her brother's rudeness. 'It

must be tedious for you being separated?'

'Yes and no. I don't like living in a hotel. But otherwise it's not too disagreeable to be on one's own for a bit. After all,' he gave her an avuncular smile, 'we have been married a long time.'

The coffee cups were being laid aside. 'Time to go,' Desmond touched his elbow and abruptly led him away. The party then drove off to a piece of wild ground where the men went on ahead across the bogs. It was a mild, clammy afternoon with low clouds, very midgy. Although Uncle Hugo was carrying a gun, he remained behind with the girls, most of whom were unsuitably dressed for tramping over the heather.

'What d'you think of Martin Evans?' Davina glanced up from under the rim of her hat.

'Sexy!' Sonia raised her binoculars to look after the disappearing figures. 'You can always tell with men of that type—it's those very light blue eyes.'

'He's a member of the new class—the meritocracy,' said Hugo: 'Done a bit of work on his vowels.'

'So much the better! Everyone knows,' Sonia's white face was impassive, 'that common men make excellent lovers—none of your English public school inhibitions!'

'You emancipated young women don't seem to mind what you say! Or perhaps it's just in front of an old buffer like me? I suppose you think I'm past it, what? Well, you're right,' Hugo chuckled to himself, 'I am.'

Liz complained about feeling sick and went back to the car. The others walked on, the girls with their long skirts hitched up, under a sky that was gradually darkening. Just before it began to rain the aromatic smell of the bogs became very intense.

'The thing I'd like to know,' Hugo craned back his head to look up at the dissolving clouds, 'is what a fellow like that is doing over here? The Army's one story, but these political wallahs. . . . There's something fishy going on—I'll lay you a bet on it! They don't trust us to manage the show by ourselves.' He put his hand under Catherine's elbow to help her over a marshy spot: 'He seemed to take rather a fancy to you, I noticed. Perhaps you can do a little espionage?'

'Lucky Catherine!' giggled Davina.

'Well, I'm damned!' Hugo tilted back his hat to peer through

113

the drizzle, 'He's chickening out! Well, on you go, my dear,' he gave Catherine a little push, 'see what you can make of him.'

Martin was returning towards them, accompanied by one of the labradors, the other men having disappeared over the hill, where muffled shots could be heard. 'Go on!' Hugo encouraged her, making the others hang back while she walked ahead to meet him.

'Are you giving up because of the rain?' she called out.

He waited until he had caught up with her before answering; 'No, I'm a rotten shot—but I'm perfectly happy just walking if it's in pleasant company.' He smiled, and it seemed to her that there was a certain professionalism in his charm. When she did not reply, he added: 'It was very kind of your brother to ask me along today. I find Irish—that is, Ulster people quite unusually hospitable.'

'Yes,' she said, 'they are.'

He watched her striding over the hummocks in her flowing dress and Wellington boots, a woollen shawl over the shoulders. 'I must say you do seem to have a sublime disregard for the climate.'

'I should have brought a mac,' she said, 'but it's only a shower. Look over there!' She pointed to an opening of brightness above the hill where the rain had already stopped. Her hair had come down and she picked out the pins, rather crossly, then shook it free.

'If you'll permit me,' she felt a light touch behind her ear, 'you missed one.'

She looked at the hand holding her pin. She hesitated before taking it and his finely-shaped fingers trembled a little. It was a caressing hand, she observed, then was surprised at herself, unaccustomed to thinking of men in intimate terms.

'Thank you,' she took the pin and threw it into the rushes. 'I've been told to spy on you. Uncle Hugo wants to know what your job is over here. You're in the Diplomatic, aren't you?'

'One of the functions of a diplomat,' he lowered his voice, 'is to be in the right place at the right time.'

'You certainly have a diplomat's knack for avoiding the question. D'you like it over here?'

'Yes. Does that surprise you?' She hitched her dress a little higher to jump over a pool and he caught sight of her bare

114

thigh. 'It surprises me, as a matter of fact. In the Foreign Service one is moved fairly rapidly from post to post. It's a point of policy, the idea being that one remains impartial, not too involved. And this is the first place I've ever had a feeling for. I'm not quite sure what it is—a sort of ambivalence. . . . Or perhaps it's just the landscape ? I can't get over the colours, the changing light effects. I suppose it's too corny and obvious to say that I find Ireland romantic ?' He smiled at her 'I could quite easily fall in love with your country.'

'You talk of it as if it were a foreign country. You'd better be careful. People over here don't like being treated as foreigners —at least not if they're Protestants. The first thing you have to find out when you meet someone new is which foot they dig with.'

'I'm sorry ?'

'Which religion.'

'Ah! Maybe that's what I mean by the ambivalence. There seem to be so many pitfalls—one can never quite tell who's friend and who's foe. Perhaps you could give some instruction on basic etiquette ?'

They had now reached the crest of the hill from which there was a wide view of the landscape with its small marshy fields and ragged trees and, here and there, a patch of green so intense it was almost garish.

'It seems to me,' he said, 'that the real problem is that Ireland needs to be less poor.' Catherine pulled her damp shawl closer around her shoulders. 'Would you agree ?'

'Oh! I hadn't realized you were asking my opinion. . . .' She looked over to the west where she could just see the islands on Lough Erne. 'I suppose so—certainly there's a lot of poverty. . . But, in a way, that's not the point. One of the virtues in Irish people—and perhaps that is what makes it difficult for the English to understand them—is that they're not very materialistic. For a start, family life is much more important here than in England. And then, of course, there's religion, which adds an extra dimension to the place and you'll never get the hang of it if you under-estimate this. The English are practical people, but for the Irish things of the spirit, in one form or another, have more influence over the way they behave than—well, common sense.'

Below them the shooting was intermittent and, now and then,

one of the frightened birds, fluttering in bewilderment in the middle air, would drop into the scrub.

'One has the impression here,' he said, 'that time has come to a stop—it doesn't seem to matter much when things get done or even if they're done at all. There's a seductiveness about it.' He watched her descending the hill with her head bowed, her auburn hair in a tangle over her eyes, like any peasant girl. 'One could lose oneself—forget. . . .'

'Forget what?' She looked up at him, shielding her eyes against a sudden gleam of watery sunlight.

'Oh, it might be difficult for you to understand. . . . I've reached a point in my life—I shall, alas, be forty in a few month's time—when, having spent years scratching my way up the ladder, I can now see exactly how far I'm going to get. With a bit of luck, that is.'

She had turned away from him, perplexed that he should confide in her. His personal manner was curiously intrusive and she asked herself: what does he want?

'For me all the mystery has departed—I would like a holiday from myself. I sometimes feel,' his hands were restless, as though he would like to touch her to ensure her attention, 'that I've spent far too much of my life looking after my own interests and not enough being a human being.'

The men were emerging from the bushes, patting their dogs. 'They've had enough,' Catherine said, and turned back up the hill to rejoin her friends.

In the evening the remnants of the shoot met again for dinner at Castle Hardwicke. It was late when they sat down to eat and extra places had to be laid as Sonia had forgotten how many people were invited. George and his wife and Martin were staying in the house and a distant cousin had turned up unexpectedly. Also Guy had brought along his latest girlfriend, a young married woman he had lured over from London while her husband was away on business; to Guy's annoyance she was placed between Desmond and Ambrose, who competed noisily for her attention and later succeeded in making her very drunk. The other end of the table was dominated by Uncle Hugo's reminiscences.

116

It was a long time after dinner was over and the candles were almost extinquished when they rose. Liz nagged her husband who refused to follow her up to bed, saying the evening had just begun. In the drawing-room Ambrose seated himself at the piano. He played a Schubert sonata, very softly, as if to himself. Martin came over and stood beside him, amazed that the brawny fellow he had seen mauling Guy's tipsy young woman should perform with such sensibility.

'D'you play?' Ambrose asked him, raising his bloodshot eyes.

'I'm afraid not—I'm not really musical at all. But I enjoy listening.'

'There are a number of good amateurs round here. Helps pass the time—we're rather cut off.'

'What about something more cheerful?' said Desmond. 'A tune we could dance to.' He had his eye on Guy's girlfriend who was standing by the window trying to cool her forehead against the glass.

So they started dancing and the lights were dimmed.

'Been waiting for this all evening,' George pulled Catherine out of her chair and put his arms round her: 'I've always thought it a pity we were related.' She felt his moustache on her cheek and tried to turn her face away, but he was holding her too firmly and she did not like to make a scene. As they circled in a dark corner she thought of her husband who was so like and so unlike his brother: where John was straight, the other was false, a snob, a hypocrite. She was repelled by the sweet smell of his after-shave lotion. He stood still for a moment and tried to peer into her eyes, murmuring: 'Hello!'

'You've had too much to drink!'

'Don't be like that. . . .' He tried to kiss her.

'Why chase me? I don't see the point! And with Liz sick upstairs. . . .'

'That's half the trouble,' he was slurring his words, 'supply's been cut off.'

She looked round and was embarrassed to see that Martin, who was sitting by the fire with Sonia, was watching.

'Get me a drink!'

'Squash?'

'No, tonight I want a drink—whisky, anything. . . .'

When George returned with the drinks he was apologetic. 'No hard feelings ? You're not going to lodge a complaint with Big Brother ?'

Catherine was amused: 'Don't tell me you're afraid of him ?'

But, instead of replying, he patted her cheek: 'A sweet little girl, that's what you are!' They sat down on the other side of the fire and George compensated by recounting to her the indiscreet details of his pre-marital affairs. He would talk of a new car, she thought, with the same mechanical relish. Opposite her Sonia had fallen asleep and Martin was moodily drinking.

She got up, feeling rather unsteady as she did not normally drink after dinner, and leaned against the mantel-shelf. At once the two men were standing on either side of her, talking across her back. She did not quite observe how Martin managed to elbow George out so that he was left alone with her, both propped against the marble staring down into the dying fire. Ambrose had stopped playing and people were now dancing to gramophone records.

'Shall we ?' Martin suggested.

She had meant to say she was tired, find some excuse, but instead she allowed him to lead her away into another part of the room. Unlike George, he was very circumspect. They danced in silence, not quite looking at one another. If he'd only cuddle me, she thought, I wouldn't have to talk to him. To break the tension she asked tritely:

'Do you like your job ?'

'Yes, on the whole. One meets interesting people and I enjoy the travel—the variety.' As he said this he pressed her hand very lightly and she sensed another meaning under the commonplace remark. He's rather cold, she decided, but highly-strung; she could not take her eyes off his face. 'The disadvantage of the Foreign Service is that one's social life tends to be superficial. As a result one depends much more than is usual on one's marriage partner.'

Marriage partner! she echoed to herself, trying to guess at what was lacking. 'But aren't you happily married ?' He looked down at her with his lips sternly compressed and she realised that she had gone too far.

He said: 'Let's sit.'

They returned to the fire and sat on the floor, warming their

118

backs. The room was growing cold. Ambrose was again at the piano and the others were leaning against it, singing Irish songs.

'But tell me about you—that's much more interesting.' It now seemed quite natural that he should hold her hand, caressing the inside of her wrist.

'There's nothing interesting to tell. I've got two children. . . . I'm not like you who's been all over the world.'

'Then tell me what you think about.'

She laughed: 'An Irishman would never be curious to know what a woman thinks about. The female function in this society is not to be a companion.'

'What is it then?'

'Oh, the usual, mother, house-keeper—and the rest.'

'So you're lonely?'

'I didn't say I was lonely,' she withdrew her hand.

'And proud?' She said nothing. 'It's your upbringing—you were bred proud.'

She turned away, thinking: it's my connection with this house that intrigues him, there's something wrong with his voice—he's a mushroom!

'I hope you won't be angry with me,' absently he stroked the material of her dress, 'if I say that—to me at least—you seem the image of the romantic Irish beauty? When you were walking through the rain. . . .'

'We think of ourselves as English—my name is Catherine not Kathleen!'

'So you won't allow me,' his voice was teasing, 'to find you mysterious?'

A little later, when she went up to bed, Catherine paused outside the children's room to listen for their breathing. She was surprised to hear Patrick wide awake, singing:

'Furry jackie, furry jackie dormay-voo?'

The sound of the child's rather tuneless but sweet little voice was somehow painful to her in its innocence.

Martin was wakened early by children playing below his bedroom window.

'Patrick, it's you must be the bomber—you're the one with the Fenian name!'

He got up and looked out. They were playing with guns, but they did not look like toys, reminding him of the antique pistols in the hall. He opened the window and called to them, but they ran into the woods, chasing Patrick with bloodthirsty cries.

His room was in the front of the house looking down over the croquet lawn and pond, and below to a stretch of grassland that had once been lawn and was now rough, which descended to the lough between an avenue of trees. It was a mild morning, very quiet, apart from a few birds. The grass was pale with dew and the trees only showed their autumnal colours in their upper branches where the ground mist had begun to dissolve.

While Martin was dressing, he noticed, with a heightened interest, the old-fashioned detail of his surroundings: a ewer on a wash-stand, the enormous bath, a tarnished set of silver brushes. In the corridors the smell of the moist countryside seemed to have infiltrated the house. Downstairs there was no one around and he wandered from room to room ending in the kitchen where there was a woman at the stove. He called out: 'Good-morning!' rather too heartily, and she mumbled about breakfast. She worked on the farm and was wearing a cloth cap to protect her hair from the cows. When she saw him still standing there, looking at the blackened cooking pots and a half plucked pigeon on a ledge, she spoke to him again, but it was only after a while that he understood he was to wait in the dining-room.

It had been partially cleared, although there were crumbs on the table and empty bottles under the side-board. An unusual assortment of silver objects adorned the centre of the table, but in the daylight he observed that none of them had been polished for some time. A magnificent breakfast was wheeled in on a trolley. He asked the countrywoman for the morning paper and she regarded him with suspicion:

'We don't have none of that here, sir.'

When he had finished there was still no sign of the other members of the household, so he went out—he enjoyed walking —and followed the drive down to the shores of the lough. It was here that he had an encounter that he was later to turn into a party anecdote. A boy of around twelve years old, wearing shorts and a pair of Army boots that were too big for him, was fishing from a jetty. Trying to start a conversation, Martin asked what he hoped to do when he had left school. The question was of no importance, he was told, because the world was to come to an end within fifteen months' time: though most, but not all Catholics would be saved, every Protestant would be damned.

Although he had intended exploring the countryside, Martin now turned back to the house, walking rather fast. The boy's matter of fact conviction had disturbed him, and he found it oppressive that there were no clear outlines in the landscape, the banks of the lough and the islands merging with their reflections and the trees blurring in a fuzz against the sky. On the front steps he saw Catherine, wearing velvet trousers and an embroidered jacket, her hair in bunches, like a school-girl. He began to wonder if dressing-up was an entertainment in this part of the world, but before he reached her she had retreated into the house and he found her with her brother in the hall. They were talking about the missing pistols.

'Not loaded, are they?' said Catherine.

'I doubt it. Still,' Desmond's vivid blue eyes were creased with laughter, 'you never know.'

'The children have been thieving,' she informed Martin, 'they're such a pest!'

'Ah, Martin! Good-morning to you!' Desmond looked him over, rather languidly, his eyebrows raised: 'I expect you'd like to see round? Catherine, here, she'll give you a guided tour.'

'You mean round this house?' Martin glanced at Catherine.

'The house, the grounds—wherever you like!'

Although Desmond's smile, as he rocked from one foot to the other, could not have been more genial, Martin felt ill at ease, imagining himself lured into a trap with Catherine as the bait. All around, from the blackened portraits, the eyes of men who resembled Desmond, but were dressed in costumes of other periods, seemed to be watching him.

'That's my great-grandfather,' Desmond pointed. 'He soldiered for the Empire for a while—brought back plenty of loot! And the chap on the right, Hughie Hardwicke, he was in the Inniskillings—killed at Sevastopol. There's his regimental flag.' There were a number of flags hanging from the ceiling, mostly frayed and discoloured. 'Now Rory Hardwicke was one of the lucky ones—became a bishop and died in his bed. He fancied himself as a botanist and brought out a book on the local flora—we've got it somewhere. . . .' Desmond led on into another room and paused before a collection of plant studies. 'This is some of his work.'

'No, it was his wife,' Catherine interrupted, 'who did the illustrations.'

'Are you sure?' They began to argue. 'Anyway,' said Desmond, 'sketching seems to run in the family—we've had several sketchers. These, for instance, were done by my great-aunt, Clarissa. She was a traveller and spent her time disappearing into the desert.'

Martin, peering at the 'sketches', was surprised by their competence. 'I do a bit of this myself.'

'Oh, do you?' Catherine turned to him, but he could not tell whether he had succeeded in arousing her interest or if she was merely being polite.

The tour of the house continued. Martin had hoped that Desmond would leave them, but he became absorbed by his family's history and the anecdotes that attached to each room, to the individual pieces of furniture, the fabric of a chair brought back from China after the Boxer Rebellion, an unusual clock that had been a present from a Russian princess. From time to time brother and sister quarrelled over the merits of their ancestors:

'Now that grim-looking old bird,' Desmond glowered at the portrait dominating the stairs, 'was a Miss Stoker—you know, the Stokers of Stokerstown. You can tell she's got religious mania. . . .'

'But she didn't squander the money,' Catherine objected, 'if it hadn't been for her the front of the house would never have been completed.'

'All the same, I can't stand the sight of her—she depresses me every time I come up the stairs.'

'We won't go through all the bedrooms,' said Catherine, 'but I'll just show you this one as the bed is rather fun.' The room was badly lit and there were damp stains on the walls; the hangings on the four-poster bed, which had originally been made out of sumptuous material, were now in poor condition. 'This is the room where I was born.'

'Really?' Martin laid his hand on the silk coverlet, unable to think of an appropriate response. He was moved by a sense of pathos. 'You,' he echoed, 'born here?'

Watching him, Desmond chuckled to himself; then he backed away, rather stealthily, to the door and was gone.

'Where's he off to?'

'I wouldn't know—Desmond's like that.'

'What was he laughing about?'

Catherine shivered: 'It's cold in here.' She was annoyed with herself that she should feel so nervous at being abandoned in the musty bedroom with this stranger. If I don't move, she thought, he'll feel I'm waiting for him to kiss me. 'Let's go out into the garden. I'm sure you're bored seeing round all this? We're like care-takers in a museum!'

He tried to keep up with her as she ran down the stairs and out through a side entrance. 'I hope I haven't seemed bored?' She walked ahead of him and he noticed the whiteness of her skin where her hair parted. 'Quite the contrary, a place like this is very evocative, nostalgic. . . .' For a moment he indulged a fantasy of having passed his own childhood in such surroundings. He drew abreast of her: 'I suppose it's the sort of background I would have liked to have had myself.'

'This is the vegetable garden, all rather over-grown, I'm afraid. We get a good crop from that fig tree, but it attracts wasps.'

'I've embarrassed you?'

He received a blank look from the violet-blue eyes: 'No, not really. . . .'

'You must be aware that I'm a fraud?' He was amused to see that she was in fact embarrassed. 'Surely, to you it must be obvious that I've spent years trying to train myself to speak with a respectable accent, and I don't even have the glamour of having come up from the working class! My father died when I was six and my mother kept a small drapery shop, selling buttons and feminine bits and pieces, underwear, that sort of thing.'

'Well, does it matter?'

'I find it shaming that I am ashamed of it.'

Then why does he tell me all this? she asked herself. In exposing his Achilles heel, he was forcing her to treat him with understanding and with sympathy. The man's spurious, she thought, sensing a concealed motive beneath his apparent frankness. She glanced at her watch, wondering whether John would make it in time for lunch and, so that she could look out for his car on the drive, she led Martin round to the front of the house.

'The landscape here seems to be turned inside out,' said Martin, noting that the water in the pond was green and the trees surrounding it were bluish, as though far away in the distance.

'Perhaps this is him!' Catherine had seen the glint of a car passing along the shores of the lough. Martin looked puzzled. 'John,' she explained, 'my husband.'

'Oh! I hadn't realised. . . .'

'He's coming for lunch.'

Martin had moved away and was bending over a rose. She watched him inhaling its scent with a savouring voluptuousness.

John reacted with surprise when she flung her arms round his neck. He was tired after the long drive.

'Where are the children?'

'Oh, playing somewhere. . . . They've had a super time!'

'You seem all breathless!' He looked at her clothes: 'Where did you get this kit?'

'Don't you like it? I've worn it before. . . ' She drew back before her husband's disapproval. She thought it odd that she should not have noticed the sandy whiskers growing in his ears before.

'John, my dear fellow!' Desmond greeted him with a friendliness that was excessive, linking his brother-in-law's arm as he led him into the drawing-room to join the other guests.

After lunch John's good humour revived when they played croquet and the locals banded together to cheat against the English. Then, in the fading light, they went for a walk round the grounds and spent some time looking at a greenhouse where Desmond was thinking of growing orchids. On the way back to the house he murmured to his sister:

'How are you getting on with Evans?'

'What d'you mean?'

'I was wondering if he was going to become a friend of yours?'

She blinked at him: 'Oh, don't be so stupid!'

'Watch it!' he pinched her arm: 'Don't forget he's a bird of passage.'

Catherine had tried to avoid Martin, but, after tea, when people were preparing to leave, he came up to say good-bye to her, lingering while he shook her hand: 'We'll meet again, I hope?'

'Why don't you take him home?' said Desmond. 'After all, you've got two cars between you.' Martin had come up with George.

'Yes, that was badly managed!' John resented the waste of petrol. Without much enthusiasm he said: 'You can come with me if you like—at least it will be some company.'

Catherine was irritated when Martin in thanking him, added an admiring comment on his new car.

'Evans is over here on some political dodge,' said Desmond. 'I suspect he's trying to find out if we're fit to govern ourselves.'

'Now that,' Martin gestured vaguely, 'is open to inter-pretation.' Sensing hostility he tried to change the subject.

Desmond turned to his brother-in-law: 'Why don't you give him a game of golf sometime?'

John muttered, not committing himself. He distrusted Martin's evasiveness and the ringed and elegant fingers repelled him.

He complained when Catherine became flustered as she collected the children's clothes; he had still not forgiven her for leaving him on his own for the weekend.

On the way home he questioned Martin about his former postings and they talked of countries that were far away. After a while, John forgot his initial antipathy; any companion-ship, he felt, was preferable to being left with his own thoughts, which turned nowadays, insistently, on one topic.

'I don't suppose you've seen today's paper? Or heard the news?'

Martin shook his head. It seemed to him he had been away for much longer than the two days and his sense of perspective had become confused.

'They were up to no good in Newry last night. Have you ever been there? It's a pretty little town on the Border.' John gripped the wheel, reminding himself not to drive too fast and it was some time before he came out with the story: a Protestant warehouse had been set alight and the Catholic crowd watching the blaze had refused to allow the firemen to rescue a man who had been trapped behind a grille. In the morning two other charred bodies had been discovered—not, as the crowd had hoped, the Protestant employees, but members of the I.R.A. who had set the place on fire. 'Still, who they were is irrelevant,' said John: 'The horrific bit is the brutalisation of ordinary men and women—one must assume that they enjoyed the spectacle of a man screaming as he burned to death before their eyes.'

Martin then capped this with horror stories from the Yemen.

'That's not the point,' John snapped at him: 'Only a short while ago this was a civilised country. To get the measure of how much Northern Ireland has been degraded by the Troubles you have to set it against the pleasantness of the people—their love of children, their homeliness—a few years ago there was less crime in Belfast than in any other city in the U.K.'

In the Fifties, he went on to tell him, the I.R.A. had been active on the Border, murdering policemen. But the affair had come to an abrupt close one Sunday afternoon when a young constable, off-duty and unarmed, had walked across the mountains to visit his girlfriend on the southern side. On the way home he had been ambushed by an I.R.A. gang and over forty bullet holes had been found in the corpse. 'The interesting thing here,' John said, 'is that not only people in the North but also in the Republic were so revolted by this one atrocity that the I.R.A. were forced to give up for lack of popular support.'

By the time they reached home it was very late and, reluctant to drive on into Belfast, John suggested to Martin that he should stay the night. When Catherine got back she was annoyed to find the two men drinking whisky and went straight upstairs with the children.

'Did we have to have him here?' she asked when John had followed her up to bed.

'Well, it was your brother that lumbered me with him!'

'You shouldn't allow him to bully you.' With sudden venom she added: 'Desmond's a bastard!' As she watched her husband undressing she was wondering what it would be like to be with another man. She could hear Martin opening the window of the spare room. 'Did you find out what he's doing in Ulster?'

'Not really. He's a diplomat!' John pronounced the word with contempt. 'I gather he's involved in some sort of liaison between Westminster and Stormont—but I somehow feel that it's not quite as innocent as it sounds. It's not encouraging to think that a man like that might have some influence.'

'What did you think of him?' Catherine's face was half-hidden under the sheets.

'A light-weight.' When John got into bed he pulled his wife towards him and rather roughly made love to her.

In the morning Martin rose early and walked round the garden. Through the kitchen window he caught sight of Catherine tying a bib on Edward as she lifted him into his high chair. Without make-up she looked very young and he felt both touched by the domestic scene and a little guilty that he should be spying on her. When he tried to recall an image of his wife at the same stage he was disturbed to find that he could only remember her in photographs. Catherine started when he came in by the back door, opening it very quietly.

'I'm sorry, I must have scared you? You're deathly white.'

The colour flooded back into her face and she could feel herself trembling with the shock of seeing a man's silhouette at the door. 'You did give me a fright. One never knows these days. . . .'

'It's a beautiful place you've got here.'

'Yes.' She busied herself with the children.

'Can I do anything to help? I'm quite house-trained.'

'If you go into the dining-room I expect John will be down in a moment.'

'Will you be joining us?'

'Perhaps.'

But she remained with the children, feeling suddenly too shy to make conversation over breakfast. She heard letters being pushed through the front door and went out to pick them up. Among them was an evangelical pamphlet with a photograph of a furnace on the front page and in flaming letters written across it: 'Is this your tomorrow?' When Martin came to say good-bye she handed it to him:

'Perhaps you should take it away with you. It might be

helpful for you to remember that there are people in this country who still believe in that sort of thing.'

'Oh, don't pay too much attention to Catherine,' John was in a hurry to get off: 'She's full of notions.'

Martin telephoned to thank Catherine for having put him up, but when he tried to prolong the conversation she cut him off. He was, therefore, surprised to receive a call from John later in the week inviting him to play golf. He was finding it hard to pass the time at weekends and accepted readily, hoping that he would also be asked back for supper.

It was the first time that he had been to Newcastle and, although it was a grey afternoon, he was impressed by the view of the Mourne Mountains and the unspoiled beaches that stretched for miles on either side of the golf course. John introduced him to the other members of the foursome, a local businessman and a surgeon from Belfast. Almost at once he was asked his reason, since he was not in the Army, for being in the Province. His diffidence before the blunt question appeared to arouse their suspicion. Eyeing him with hostility, the surgeon remarked that it was part of his job to treat casualties from the explosions.

'You people in England don't seem to realise,' he said, 'what is actually happening in this country.' Martin recoiled, as he went into detail, saying that it was sometimes necessary for a medical team to sift out intestines in order to determine the exact number of the dead. 'Against a background of that sort of thing there comes a point when any means would be justified if the violence could be brought to an end. But it's your Government,' he looked at Martin accusingly, 'who are preventing this by putting the brakes on the Army.'

'You're not suggesting,' Martin was scandalized, 'a military solution?' He turned to John, who avoided his eyes, not liking to commit himself openly on the side of force. Martin informed them that the British Government felt no solution could be reached until the country was represented more democratically. 'With one party running the place for fifty years it's hardly surprising that things aren't what they ought to be. Of course, I can understand,' he smiled, having taken the trouble to find out that his companions were Protestant, 'that no one likes to give up a position of such influence.'

'But how are you going to impose "democracy",' John paused while one of his friends drove off—'when the only people with an active interest in politics are Protestant? Most Catholics, in spite of being such a large minority, opt out. Are you going to force them to stand for Parliament?' The Unionists, he explained, were not one party but two—moderates and hard-liners—the rivalry between them being fought out not in Stormont but in the constituencies when candidates were nominated. 'At the moment,' he said, 'we are fortunate in having a moderate Prime Minister who can keep the die-hards under control.'

Martin listened, murmured. He did not mention that he knew it was an aim of British policy to split the Unionists in order to break their power.

'However bad things may seem to you now,' John insisted, 'they would be very much worse if it was the hard-liners who called the tune. And it wouldn't do to set the Prod rabble in motion again. It's too soon for any of us to have forgotten the damage they did in August sixty-nine.'

'Oh, come!' Martin thought him preposterous: 'That sort of thing's been going on in Ireland for the last five hundred years—anyone who was shocked at what happened in sixty-nine just hasn't read their history books!'

The players separated to look for their balls. When they joined up again Martin sensed that, although treated with politeness, he was being subtly cold-shouldered, the Ulstermen talking among themselves about people he had never met, with all reference to the Troubles carefully avoided. Had it not been for the exercise in the salty air and the remarkable scenery, he would have found the afternoon very dull.

The game over, they went to the bar and the surgeon bought a round of drinks. Martin fidgetted with his glass, waiting to see what would happen when John was ready to leave. He wondered how Catherine amused herself when her husband was out. But, to his dismay, John bought another round and ordered sandwiches for himself, saying that he was going to stay on for a game of poker. For want of anything better to do Martin joined the game. He had no interest in cards and the only thing that kept him alert was the look of satisfaction among his companions when one of them took money off him. The conversation was fragmentary; he could not understand their sense of humour, the interminable jokes—there was a great deal of laughter when someone said that people came up from Waterford for a weekend's shooting in Belfast. It had become obvious that John was not going to invite him home. Glancing at him as he sat back from the table frowning over his hand, Martin asked himself how it had come about that a creature like Catherine, who seemed not quite to belong to ordinary reality, could be married to this prosaic fellow. To combat his ennui he began plotting ways of meeting her again. He thought he had seen her being kissed by her brother-in-law; certainly she had shown no sign of disapproval while listening to his ribald tales. . . .

John looked at his watch, sighed, 'I must be leaving you.' He gathered his cards into a neat pile: 'I'll be getting the rolling pin!' He turned to Martin, interrupting his fantasies about his wife. 'What about you—d'you want to stay on?' Catherine was not amused by his golfing friends and John hesitated before asking: 'Perhaps you'd care to drop in for a drink on your way home?'

'That sounds like a good idea.' Anxious not to reveal his enthusiasm, Martin languidly drew back his chair, taking his time before following him out.

When they arrived there was only one light on in the drawing-room where Catherine, in her dressing-gown, was curled up by the fire reading. Martin had been talkative in the car, but he halted in mid-sentence when he saw her and hung back in the shadows while John bent down to kiss his wife, murmuring: 'I hadn't meant to be so late,' then, apologetically: 'I'm afraid I've brought a visitor.' Catherine's book fell to the ground and she bent over to retrieve it, avoiding Martin's eyes as he came forward. 'Well, how are you, pet?' John picked it up for her. To Martin he said: 'Have you ever heard the Irish expression "ashy-pet"? The pet of the house was given the place closest to the ashes. . . .' Suddenly sentimental, he caressed her forehead, pushing her hair back out of her eyes. 'It's an Elizabethan word. There are a number of others that are still used over here— "thole" for example.'

'Thole?'

'It means to put up with—to endure.' John poured out a couple of drinks, without offering one to his wife. His mood of tenderness had passed and it was with controlled anger that he said to his English guest: 'The people of Northern Ireland have a great deal to thole.'

He seated himself on the edge of Catherine's chair and put his arm round her, while Martin remained standing, uncertain where to sit, his gaze flitting from object to object, as he did not want Catherine's husband to see him looking at her. Then, with a movement that was curiously stealthy, he reached across and removed the book from her hands.

'What do you read while you sit by the ashes?'

'Yeats' dream plays.'

'Yeats!' He looked up, into her eyes, and she adjusted her dressing-gown over her knees, embarrassed that he should be staring at her when she was so obviously dressed for bed. 'How appropriate!' He took the book away and sat down on the opposite side of the fire.

'The great patriot!' said John. 'I wonder what he would think if he was alive now? After all, he wasn't so keen on the "cause" after the Civil War. Didyou know the fighting went on in the South for fifteen years after independence?'

Martin smiled, incredulous.

'It's true. What was that,' turning to Catherine, 'you read me Yeats said—"the best lack all conviction and the worst are full of passionate intensity"?' Abstractedly he caressed his wife's hair. 'This remains true today, unfortunately, in particular the lack of conviction. . . . At Stormont we have a Government whose aim is to put an end to the violence, but it's frustrated at every turn, partly by,' he forced a friendly smile, 'you people from across the water and partly through lack of support from the moderates in our own country. They've become ashamed of the Unionist record, which was in any case not nearly as bad as it was made out to be—and certainly there was nothing that begins to justify all this bloodshed. . . . But it's no longer fashionable to appear to take a firm line—and be labelled reactionary. You've met Catherine's Uncle Hugo?' Martin nodded, his light eyes expressionless, and John asked himself why he should take the trouble to put his point of view to this stranger who was all too ready to deliver abuse on the iniquities of Protestant misrule. But Martin was on his best behaviour.

'It's a sad day,' John continued, 'when one has to re-examine one's liberal principles. While in normal times it's civilised to restrict the power of the Army and the police, in Ulster that works against the interests of the community as a whole. The British are so squeamish about facing reality over here that they miss the point altogether. Most other countries, if faced with an emergency like this, would have felt justified in having some form of martial law.'

'A very heated view, if I may say,' Martin's voice was measured, reasonable. 'Though perhaps'—he glanced at Catherine (he could never quite make out what these people were thinking) but she was gazing into the fire and was no help to him—'perhaps you're pulling my leg? I can hardly believe you could not be in sympathy with our opinion that persuasion is better than force? You see, we,' he paused for emphasis, 'we believe that one of the keys to the problem lies in a *rapprochement* with the South. If they could be persuaded, for instance, to be a little more co-operative on the question of extradition. . . .'

'And the supply of money and weapons, bazookas, rocket-launchers. . . . All that fancy equipment is smuggled through from the South!' Catherine, backing up her husband, spoke with exaggerated vehemence: 'Not to mention providing training grounds for the gunmen and interviews in Dublin for the World Press. An I.R.A. bomber killed "in action" in the North is taken over the Border to be given a hero's funeral.'

'That's right!' For no good reason Martin appeared euphoric.

'One doesn't have to be an Orange Protestant,' said John 'to prefer living in the North. This is a free society with no censorship. The country's more go-ahead and much less corrupt. Besides, we have the English system of social services so the poor are better cared for—it's the very poor who would suffer most from the change-over.' John had rolled up Catherine's sleeve and Martin's attention was distracted while he watched him stroking her arm. 'The political domination of the Catholic Church is not acceptable to people here—among other things it has consistently opposed humane reforms. Still, these objections would have applied before the Troubles. . . . D'you really imagine that any talking could now be done with the Republic when they openly support the atrocities? In Ulster there is a conviction that the British Government would like to offload the Province by handing it over to the South.'

'Oh, no chance of that!' Martin fluttered his hands and John glared at him. 'I do think they can see it would hardly be practicable.'

John lowered his voice almost to a whisper: 'Do you suppose that a united Ireland would be a good thing if it was achieved as the result of mounds of severed limbs?'

Catherine cried out: 'You're hurting me!'

'Oh, darling!' He had forgotten the guest and was bending over her, lifting her arm to see the place where his fingers had dug into her flesh: 'I didn't mean to hurt you—I hadn't known I was doing it. . . .' He was so distressed at the pain he had caused her that Martin felt a cad watching him when he slid his hand inside her collar and massaged her neck, compulsively murmuring: 'I'm sorry—sorry. . . .' Catherine's head had drooped forward and there was such an odd expression in her eyes that Martin wondered for her stability. He opened the Yeats and pretended to read it.

'Perhaps it's best not to talk about these things—it makes for bad blood. It's not easy for you to understand,' John picked up Martin's glass, 'what it's like to belong to a country being smashed up before your eyes and to feel that one ought to be doing something about it. And yet what? One is powerless. . . . Whereas to you,' again John felt himself becoming rigid with anger, 'the casualties are just statistics!' He turned to Catherine: 'D'you want a drink, darling?' She shook her head. In an attempt to be more sociable he said: 'She's a good girl, is Catherine. Doesn't smoke, hardly drinks.'

'Is she?' Martin caught her eye behind her husband's back.

John topped up the drinks and stood in front of the fire, his face lit up with artificial joviality. 'Oh, Catherine,' he raised his glass, half-emptying it, then leaned against the mantel-piece, 'I never told you about the Catholic priest and the Baptist?' With a look of apprehension Catherine tucked her feet under her, shrinking into the chair. 'Well, you see they've had a car crash and when they get out to inspect the damage the Baptist waves his fist saying, "If it wasn't for my cloth, sir, it's strong

133

language I'd be using!" And then the priest,' John was chuckling to himself, ' "Man," he says, "if it wasn't a Friday I'd chew the balls off you!" '

Martin laughed politely and Catherine flushed: the risqué story had made her over-conscious of his presence. In the dim light she saw, not that his hair was greying, but his conventional good looks (the bone structure well-defined, rather narrow) and his blue eyes, too watchful of her slightest movement.

She said: 'Perhaps one has to be Irish to be amused by jokes about clergymen?'

'Which puts me in mind. . . .' As John emptied his glass she realised that he was becoming drunk and she tried to quieten him before he made a fool of himself. 'There's the one about the clergymen who go to Heaven and are given different cars according to their merits. Now,' he scratched his head, 'I can't quite remember how it went. I know the Pope was given a bicycle. . . .'

'No, you've got it wrong. It was the Pope who got the Rolls Royce and Paisley who got the bicycle.'

'One of those stories,' John explained, 'that can be twisted in both directions. Catherine, you see, she tries to make out that she digs with the other foot.'

'Just because my father turned Catholic!' she flared up at him. To Martin she said: 'You've no idea the fuss that was made when I told my mother-in-law I might take the children to Midnight Mass!'

'You only said it for effect.'

'Not necessarily. Why shouldn't I take them? You said yourself it's a free country.' They began to quarrel and Martin interrupted:

'So you have Catholic friends?' He stretched out his hands to the fire, adding casually: 'Perhaps you might introduce me to some of them?'

John sobered up at once, thinking: he's making use of us. He treats the people in this country like exhibits in a zoo!

The husband and wife were both gazing at him in astonishment and Martin became aware, for some reason that he could not understand, that he had committed a *faux pas*. He was appealing to Catherine, in an attempt to win back her favour, when he said:

'Whatever its problems I do think Northern Ireland is a most beautiful country.' John sat down and remained morosely silent while Martin described˙the car journeys he had made throughout the Province and over the Border into Donegal. He spoke with admiration of the varied scenery, the friendliness of the people, the wildness of the Donegal coastline where many of the villages were falling into ruin. He had been making notes, he told Catherine, drawing his chair a little closer to her, of the legends and memories that seemed to attach to each neighbour-hood; in one place he had been informed—for a fact—that there were warriors under the hill, sleeping in their armour until the day came when they could fight the true fight for Ireland. While he was talking he kept his eyes on Catherine's face, her chin resting on her hand, the firelight illuminating her profile. He noticed that she had the translucent skin of red-haired people and that the fine veins in the temples were very blue.

John dozed off and dreamed uneasily, but was wakened by a log cracking in the hearth. He sat up in alarm, thinking he had heard a shot. He said: 'The Irish myths have a certain charm, but you don't want to take all that too seriously. It's one of the blights on this country that fantasy and fact are inter-mingled. . . . Even the fact of death, if one dies for Ireland, that is.' He had forgotten his animosity to the man who, while furtively studying his wife, was applauding the poetry of the landscape: 'If you don't watch out, you'll get lost in the Celtic twilight.'

'It does exist!' Catherine assured him so solemnly that Martin was tempted to give her a pat on the cheek like a little girl. John frowned at him and he instinctively edged back into his chair, suspecting that her husband could read his thoughts.

'You said you'd been over the Border?'

'Only into Donegal.'

'In a car with an English number plate?' Martin nodded. John rose to his feet, pointedly pushing back his cuff to look at his watch: 'Well, I wouldn't do that, if I were you!'

'But. . . .?' Martin smiled uncertainly at Catherine. All three were now standing. John was making his way to the door. As Martin followed, he said:

'You look conspicuously English.'

'Oh, do I?' Martin glanced down at himself, straightened his coat.

'No, really!' On an impulse Catherine clutched at his sleeve: 'You shouldn't go in that car—and certainly not on your own. It would be best if you didn't go there at all.'

Her intensity amused him. The hand laid artlessly on his arm he covered with his own: 'Perhaps one day you could show me the country?'

At the door John clapped him on the shoulder, not from friendliness but content to be rid of him, as if pushing him out. When he had gone, he said to Catherine:

'You like Martin, don't you?' Without listening to her reply he turned back into the house, muttering: 'I don't know why I have a fellow like that around the place. The Army are straight enough, but the others. . . . There seem to be quite a number of them about these days—I met a new one in the Ulster Club.' He raked out the fire, stabbing the smouldering logs: 'These English, they make me boke!'

Catherine recoiled at the coarse expression, and thought him uncivilized.

Although John had taken a dislike to him, he was disarmed when he received a letter from Martin, thanking him for the game of golf and the pleasant company, with even a suggestion of an apology for his tactlessness when talking about Ulster affairs. So, in the weeks that followed, John took him out again a few times, bringing him home afterwards and returning early because Catherine complained when she was left on her own. On one occasion Martin invited them to dinner in a little restaurant a few miles from Belfast, as it was no longer safe to eat in the city because of the bombs. The evening was rather strained. Martin fussed over the wine list and seemed unusually dispirited. He had been offered a house that contained nothing his wife could seriously complain about. When she came over, he said, he would be able to return their hospitality in more comfortable surroundings. While talking he kept his eyes on Catherine and she felt that there was some innuendo under his words, some catch. Earlier he had given them a drink at his hotel and they had driven to the restaurant in one car. At the end of the evening, when they got home, Catherine discovered that he had left his gloves on the back seat. She held

136

them against her cheek, sniffing at the leather, while John went on ahead into the house.

Martin had often told her where he worked and how he could be contacted, but, when she rang him about his gloves, it was the first time she had telephoned him and she was surprised to find that she had spent most of the morning trying to work up the courage to dial his number. They had fallen into the habit of speaking over the phone as Martin would call her on any flimsy excuse, and when it rang she would run to answer, hoping to hear his voice. At that time it seemed to her that something had gone wrong with the telephone system—or perhaps it was merely that the fragments of conversation she overheard so frequently were abnormal and gruesome. One morning, when it was announced on the news that a Catholic had been murdered for his eccentric support of Rangers football team, she had lifted the receiver to call her mother-in-law; but, instead of the dialling tone, she heard a girl's voice say very quietly: 'He was warned not to wear that scarf. . . .'

Catherine became conscious of how much time she had to waste during the day. Her home was run efficiently, Patrick was at school and Edward so well-behaved that he would play beside her for long periods while she stretched out with a book or listened to gramophone records. She took a dislike to her clothes and, in spite of the bombing, often went into Belfast, searching the streets for new boutiques. When she drove through the city she would see smoke in the distance or would pass through an area where floating ash was blowing about. Every week familiar landmarks would disappear. There was an unreality about the way in which the buildings were extinguished, as if they had been made of paper and a giant had squashed them in with his thumb. Once she passed a shop selling bridal gowns where yards of lacy material were still fluttering from the shattered windows. Sometimes the ruins looked disgusting, like carcases showing their innards, or very garish, a pub decorated with the Irish love of bright colours, the flattened edge of what had been an orange room, a purple room, a room papered in turquoise and emerald stripes. The bare, useless walls would be scribbled on with slogans and insults or hung with religious posters: 'Get right with God!' or, 'Thy sin shall find thee out!'

137

When she dropped in to see Felicity, she told her about John's new friend, whose visits helped to enliven the monotonous days.

'He's called Martin Evans, is he? I've heard people talking about him. . . .' She looked at Catherine out of the corner of her eye: 'And he's John's friend?' She teased her. For the first time it seemed to her that she had a slippery way of laughing—nothing Catherine could say would shake the conviction in Felicity's mind that Martin would become her lover. 'Why, you're half in love with him already!'

'But I've never been in love!' Catherine protested before she had time to think what she was saying. To herself she added: this is what I have missed.

When she arrived home, with a new record, new shoes, two new blouses, she felt annoyed at her slip of the tongue and thought how disloyal it was—and how untrue. She had been in love with her husband. She still loved him—in a quiet way, perhaps—but there was no question which of the two men she preferred. She was then annoyed with herself for having compared them and thought how disorganized she was, with so much leisure: she must do something useful—she would make clothes for the children. She even went out and bought some dress-making patterns; but, when she spread them open to look at them, they were mostly for girls' clothes. If only she had a little girl, she thought, and the longing, the unexpressed excitement that had begun to stir in her found an outlet in fantasies about an unborn daughter, the image becoming so vivid that she could actually see the child at different stages, a toddler in a diaphanous dress playing on the lawn, or an older girl who would be her companion. She lost interest in her sons, even Patrick irritating her with his love of gadgets and war games. One frosty morning, watching her little girl in imagination (around three years old at the time) she looked up suddenly and in exactly the position where she had so clearly seen her child, saw Martin walking towards her, quite naturally, crossing the lawn and smiling at the glistening day.

'I've come for my gloves,' he said. He had left his car at the bottom of the drive because he wanted to walk through the garden. After a vague greeting, she led him into the house.

'Well, there they are!' The gloves were on the hall table. He picked them up and she offered him some coffee. When she went to the kitchen she found Ellen and her daily whispering to one another, their eyes bright with curiosity about the man who had come to the house at an unusual time of day. It was a comment on the society, Catherine thought, that a visitor for coffee in the morning should appear improper. After all, she told herself, it's not as if I was having an affair with him!

They drank their coffee, but Martin seemed in no hurry to go, so they walked round the garden. She showed him the trees they had planted and laughed at her mother-in-law who would descend on them with buckets of horse-manure because they did not feed their plants properly. Martin compared the shrubs with those in his own garden in Essex. 'I rather like gardening,' he said, smiling at her with a tenderness inappropriate to the subject; she thought it curious that she felt moved by this trivial remark. In the frosty sunshine every blade of grass was distinct, every twig on the bare trees.

Martin told her that for the first time in their married lives they had bought a home of their own and he described the house in detail; his wife, naturally, was reluctant to leave it to come to Ireland. His twin boys were at boarding school, which meant that Margaret, who in her day had been a brilliant student, now had a chance to return to other interests. While he was talking about his wife, it seemed to Catherine that there was a complicity between them, as if the open reference to his marriage lent a cover of respectability to what might have been a different conversation.

Margaret had bought the house; she was the one who had the money. 'But it doesn't come between us,' he said. She glanced at him, wondering if he was trying to be funny, but he went on to tell her, unsmiling, that he was indebted to his wife who had worked on his accent and taught him how to behave. Catherine looked away: this information was too personal, shaming. As at Castle Hardwicke she felt that he was trying to win her sympathy. When he said: 'I married above myself,' she turned on him in exasperation, about to ask why his wife had chosen him. But on looking into his eyes with their equivocal expression (even when he was trying to be sincere there seemed to be an underlying cynicism) she realised that the answer was obvious: his wife had married him for sex!

'The only thing I don't like about your island,' (it amused him to think of the island in terms of fairy-tale, the sleeping princess hedged by thorns) 'is that rock on the causeway. It gives one rather a turn to be driving along, thinking how idyllic it is, to be faced with this ominous message: "Prepare to meet thy God!" It does make one feel,' they had gone down to the shore and he watched her picking her way over the stones, 'as if one were somehow in danger.'

Although there was no reason to feel ashamed, Catherine was uneasy when, two days later, she was introduced to Martin's wife. For a start he had not mentioned that Margaret would be coming over and he, himself, seemed equally taken aback that they should meet at a cocktail party given by one of the Stormont Cabinet Ministers. The party was large and formal, the men greatly outnumbering the women because so many of the English had been invited: Army officers, a journalist, a few Foreign Office officials that no one had seen before and who were as elusive as Martin when questioned about their jobs.

'Here are John and Catherine Mulholland, darling—the people I was telling you about who have been so kind to me.'

When Margaret turned to them there seemed to be no alteration in the fixed cheerful smile with which she had been surveying the room, a highlight glinting on her narrow-arched teeth. Catherine's first impression was of disappointment; she had expected someone more glamorous than this middle-aged woman wearing a dull but obviously genuine diamond brooch pinned to the shoulder of her dateless little dress. She was tall and slim, if somewhat angular, and her greying hair had been cut short, it seemed, for practical reasons. Although she appeared to have left every kind of nonsense behind her, there was still something youthful in her manner, almost adolescent, which showed itself in the vivacity with which she discussed subjects that interested her. Her character, Catherine was later to tell Felicity, must have been formed when she was a school prefect.

After the introduction Martin sidled away, leaving the women alone as John, too, had drifted off, bored by Margaret's chatter about house prices in the south of England. Looking at her,

140

Catherine was surprised that, married to a man like Martin, she could afford to let herself become dowdy: then realised that this was a sign that she was confident of his loyalty and, perhaps, of his dependence on her. The party depressed Catherine. As she watched, out of the corner of her eye, Martin suavely conversing with the other guests, she thought: this is a man for whom career comes first.

Margaret talked about her house in Essex, bitterly complaining that Martin had been posted to Belfast—of all places! She quizzed Catherine on the price of groceries in Northern Ireland and looked shocked when Catherine told her she ordered her food by phone and did not know how much it cost. She then asked if one was obliged to wear a hat to functions at Government House, adding, with a girlish toss of her greying curls, that she couldn't be bothered with hats! Catherine was surprised when they were joined by Carol Mulholland that Margaret should seem so much at ease with her suburban sister-in-law. Having expected to be intimidated by her intelligence, Catherine found instead that her attention wilted under the trite exchanges and, while Margaret enthusiastically accepted Carol's invitation to a coffee morning, she edged backwards to eavesdrop a conversation between John and an Army officer, who was telling him that he had seen a couple of men roaring with laughter as they watched the explosion they had caused and the people rushing into the street as the building burst. One of the Army's worst problems, he said, were the women and children, who would stand in front of the gunmen so that they could fire at the troops at close range. One of his men had been taking aim at a sniper when a toddler had appeared and jumped up and down on the pavement, jeering at him: 'You can't shoot now!' Catherine had seen women rioting on television; the sound of a mob shrieking with high-pitched voices was somehow more disturbing than rioting men. She looked round at the polite gathering and tried to imagine the female guests hurtling through the streets, wearing curlers and banging dustbin lids, using language that would scandalize even the most hardened soldiers.

Margaret was talking about her children. 'Babies,' she insisted to Carol, whose only child was a year old, 'are just a nuisance—but the reward comes later.' Itemizing the idio-

141

syncrasies of her teenage twins, she paused, her face becoming suffused with gratification, as she exclaimed: 'Gosh, they're fun!' The Christmas holidays were the problem: 'I'm not allowing my children to come to a place where one can actually hear the bombs going off. Martin can jolly well see to it that he gets some leave so that he spends Christmas at home!'

When the party was at an end Catherine maliciously observed that Margaret looked respectable rather than smart in her good fur coat. She asked John: 'What did you think of her?'

'Who?'

Catherine could feel herself blushing: 'Margaret Evans.'

'Nothing particularly—she's one of those people one has difficulty in remembering. But I did notice,' he turned to his wife, expecting her to share his amusement at the expense of their new friend, 'that he seems to have a knack when it comes to getting himself introduced to the right people—rather too smooth an operator, if you ask me!'

As they drove up and away from Belfast they looked back at a curve in the road and saw a huge fire near the docks (at first it seemed as if a large area of the city, itself, was ablaze), the flames reflecting in an immense glow on the water, while even the surrounding hills were reddened. 'There's that big timber-yard away,' said John, who knew the owner. 'I wonder just how many million pounds worth of damage. . . .' He stopped the car and got out, shivering in the wind as he gazed down at the astonishing spectacle. His sense of doom was aggravated by the knowledge that the fire was now so widespread that there could be no checking it until it had burnt itself out. Trying to make light of this, he said to Catherine: 'How's that for a vision of damnation?'

'Lovey!' Felicity kissed her effusively as Catherine entered the studio, which this afternoon was full of people. 'What luck that you should have come today—I've got a surprise for you!' The surprise was Martin. He was sitting cross-legged on the floor amid a group of people discussing internment to whom he was listening with an expression of concern. 'I met him at one of those Arts Council gatherings and we had quite a talk. . . . I would say,' she squeezed Catherine's arm, 'that he was as interested in you as you are in him.' Catherine glanced appre-hensively across the room, but the angry voices made such a din that it was not possible he could have overheard. 'He's very intelligent,' continued Felicity; 'And he seems to have got the hang of things over here. His sympathies are in the right place! He was telling me about his job. . . .'

'Really? He's never told us about it! What exactly does he do?'

'Well, there are going to be some changes,' Felicity frowned knowingly, 'important changes. The days of Protestant in-justice are numbered!'

'What d'you mean?' said Catherine. 'Tell me more!' But her friend refused to be drawn. As she looked round the room, Catherine was suddenly aware that she had become a misfit among these people, most of them with Catholic names, Rory, Siobhean, Mikhail, who were arguing, intractably, on the side of the terrorists on the grounds that any violence was per-missible so long as there was detention without trial. Amid all this talk the carnage seemed somehow irrelevant. It was when she thought of the victims that she realised how much her personal views had become formed along different lines and she remembered John, regretting the hardening of his own feelings, who had told her that a civil war divides a community at every level, brother from brother, friend from friend. Martin caught sight of her and at once, with a litheness that she found repel-lent, he rose to his feet. He had abused her husband's confi-dence; she had been tricked by his seductive manner—he had come to their house to spy on them!

'Well, I don't think I need introduce you?' Felicity slyly smiled. She left them to attend to her guests who were con-suming beer and cakes. Martin took her place at Catherine's side:

'We seem fated to meet!'

Catherine was abrupt: 'Where's Margaret?'

'She's gone back to England—she'll only be over at weekends for the time being.' He put his arm round her, touching her delicately so that she could hardly feel the pressure: 'Where would you like to sit? Not that there's much room except on the floor.'

She leaned against him, whispering: 'I see you've managed your Catholic entrée!' then freed herself.

143

'Felicity did mention,' he smiled, but she looked past him, 'that I might meet people here who would be of interest to me. . . .' He took her hand and led her over to the window where there was less of a crowd. 'You seem out of sorts. Have I annoyed you in some way?'

Instead of expressing her real grievance, Catherine replied petulantly: 'You hardly talked to me at the cocktail party.'

'Oh, is that all?' He looked relieved. 'For me it was more or less an offiicial function—I was on parade, as it were.' Catherine's eyes remained shadowed, sullen. With an intuition that unnerved her, he said: 'You're wondering why I don't tell you more about my job? I'm a sort of observer—we're here to sound out possibilities.'

'Possibilities of what?'

'Well,' he gestured, 'that remains to be seen, doesn't it?' He then confided to her that he was a socialist. For Martin this was an admission, as he was secretive about his real opinions, and he made a point of emphasizing: 'I don't normally tell people which way I vote. We're supposed to be above politics.'

He's trying to absolve himself, Catherine thought, glancing at the wedding ring on his mobile hand. She had been mistaken about him: there could be no risk with a man who had chosen a wife like Margaret!

Martin described the evening when he had met Felicity at an exhibition of architectural designs. These had interested him: he had once thought of becoming an architect and since he was a boy he had enjoyed drawing buildings. She softened towards him when he lamented the destruction of Belfast. After a while he began to complain of the noise and said it was time he must go. Perhaps she might give him a lift as his car had broken down? When they left together Felicity winked at Catherine behind his back and, once they were in the car, she explained to him that Ulster society was so strict that someone would be bound to observe her in the company of a man who was not her husband. Accustomed to being driven by John, she felt nervous with Martin in the passenger seat and was concentrating so hard on not making mistakes that she failed to notice when they entered a street that had been emptied. There were soldiers watching from the doorways, then making a run for it to the next door. When Martin remarked that it might be best if she

144

turned off into a side street, she was more agitated by her own stupidity than by the fear of a sniper's bullet.

'You'll come in for a drink?' Martin suggested when they arrived at his hotel. He patted her knee, thinking that she had been frightened: 'Might soothe the nerves.' Although it had been gaudily modernized there was a dingy atmosphere in the hotel lounge where the tape for the piped music seemed to have been worn thin and cigarette smoke competed with the smell of frying food. 'Pretty awful in here!' he said, sensing her thoughts. 'Perhaps,' he hesitated, 'maybe we should go up to my room?' She looked up at him, then quickly away. 'No?' He watched her fidgetting. 'No, better not.' He asked her what she would like and went up to the bar.

When he sat down beside her she told him that she visited Felicity because she had not enough to occupy herself. 'Oh, you mustn't think I'm Women's Lib!' she glanced at him anxiously: 'But I do sometimes resent it that I spend so much of my time servicing other people—you know, picking up toe-nails from the carpet! It's degrading to find that one has no existence in one's own right.' He listened sympathetically: poor Margaret, he said, had felt frustrated when the children were small— things would be better when they were old enough to go to boarding school. 'But then I'll miss them!' Martin laughed. He curled a strand of her hair round his finger, twisting it to see the sheen glisten in the light.

'You must often have been told you have beautiful hair?'

'Not so often.' She had become very tense, her hands primly folded. 'John, of course, but not other people.'

Martin was annoyed that her husband had been brought into it. Playing for time, he re-arranged the objects on the table, their glasses, a saucer with lemon slices, a dirty ash-tray.

'What are you doing?' she snapped at him in her nervousness.

'Oh, nothing really!' His hands were now under the table. 'A mechanical habit. I suppose it's rather irritating?' He could see that she was looking for her bag: in a moment she would be gone. 'It had occurred to me, if you're really such a lady of leisure'—he waited, her back was still turned to him—'that perhaps you might take me sight-seeing if I could get an afternoon off?' He was not prepared for her direct reply:

'Yes, if you like.' She thought for a moment: 'We might go to

145

Downpatrick. That's where St. Patrick is supposed to have been buried. Or Inch Abbey is very pretty—you might like to draw the ruins. . . .'

He got out his diary: 'Next Tuesday? I'll pick you up and take you out to lunch. And then we can go exploring.'

'No, no! I'll meet you somewhere!' Catherine rose to her feet and pulled on her coat, tugging at the sleeve, astonished at her own impulsiveness and trying to hide from herself the knowledge that she had taken the first wrong step.

In the hotel courtyard, as she was about to unlock her car, Martin bent down and kissed her on the cheek: 'I think I now know you well enough?'

Catherine glanced around furtively. 'You shouldn't do that—not here. There are too many people. After all, coming out from a hotel, they'll think you're my. . . .'

Martin stood beside her, rigid. Then he burst out laughing: 'Unfortunately not!' He stooped, kissed her on the other cheek, indulgently, as if he were saying good-bye to a young relative. 'They might think you were my niece.'

On Tuesday it rained. She rang Martin, but he told her that this was the only day when he would be able to leave his work— he had taken some trouble, he added, to manipulate his absence. They could go out to lunch and perhaps it might clear up later in the afternoon. 'Or I could give you lunch here?' he suggested. Catherine took so long to reply that he thought they had been cut off and he began calling anxiously: 'Hullo? You still there?'

For Catherine the empty morning seemed to linger without end as she tried on her new clothes, keeping her eye on the door in case Ellen, who would at once become suspicious on seeing the untidy bedroom, should walk in unexpectedly. It was still raining when she set off, the landscape uniformly grey and limited in visibility, the hilltops obscured. She could not see the far side of Belfast Lough as she drove towards Martin's house, which was in the same residential suburb as the houses of her in-laws, John's parents and his brother, Peter. It was the fault of the community, she told herself, if the worst was assumed when you merely went out to lunch, and, on seeing Brenda

McTaggart driving past, she waved in defiance. But, when she entered the rusticated gateway into the garden with its dripping rhododendrons and secluding privet hedge, she felt suddenly so depressed that, if she had not seen him watching for her from a window, she might have turned back and gone home.

He opened the door and waited while she climbed the steps, his face appearing so warm that she wondered if he had been drinking. He then closed the door, shutting out the wet day, and led her through to the drawing-room; but he did not kiss her and she felt stupid because she had hovered in front of him expectantly. She found the room depressing with its patterned fabrics and darkened woodwork, a picture window looking out on the misted view, too many china ornaments.

'Not our taste,' he handed her a drink. 'We took it over wholesale. But I expect Margaret will find some way of cheering it up.'

They exchanged banalities about the climate, Martin making rather too much of his regret that their trip was called off. The lunch that he had prepared for her was surprisingly delicious; there were even napkins and flowers on the table. He would not allow her to help and, while he was attending to her, she was momentarily overcome by a sense of the absurd; she watched the deftness with which he uncorked a bottle of wine, and thought that, given a different twist to his fortunes, he would have made a good waiter.

As lunch drew to a close there were repeated silences and Catherine felt herself blushing every time she looked up and found his eyes on her. When they went back into the drawing-room and he seated himself on the sofa, she chose a chair at a distance from him. 'Why don't you sit down beside me?' Obediently she got up. 'You look nervous!' Again she blushed, knowing perfectly well that, in agreeing to come to the house, she must play his game. She kept saying to herself: I'm still free to leave, I must go—now I really will go! And all the time, while she was fidgetting indecisively, she was conscious of him watching her with an expression of mockery.

'I haven't any etchings to show you—but perhaps you would like to see my drawings?' He went into another room and returned with a folder containing pencil sketches, each page covered by tissue paper, that had been produced over a number

147

of years in different parts of the world. Although his subjects were romantic—mosques, ruins, a lonely tower—the execution was dryly meticulous and their lack of any panache or style reminded Catherine of the humble illustrations of Irish scenes that were produced annually by one of John's foremen for the works calendar. She felt, too, that the drawings revealed the intimate nature of the man and she was dismayed both by the painstaking attention to form and what seemed to her to be an aridity of feeling. Now I really can go, she thought, as, politely murmuring, she returned the drawings to their folder; now—this very minute—I will get up from my chair and. . . . Martin was watching so anxiously for her approval that she felt embarrassed by her lack of enthusiasm, almost sorry for him. He looked quite crushed when she stood up, trying to remember where she had left her coat.

'Here it is.' He held it out for her. But, instead of waiting till she had her arms in the sleeves, he let it fall to the ground and kissed her, taking her so much by surprise that she thought she would faint. 'You must be aware,' he whispered, the tone accusing, 'of the effect you have on me!' He was shivering but his skin felt very hot. He led her over to the sofa; while he caressed her, she lay passive, thinking of the contrast between her husband's clumsy affection and Martin's expertise. He slipped his hand between her thighs: 'Is this all right?' She was put out that he should ask and remained silent. 'I don't want to force anything,' he insisted. And she thought: he's a diplomat in all things! He's covering himself so that whatever happens there'll be no question of the blame being pinned on him. . . . He had become quite pale.

She touched his cheek: 'That's all right.'

'Well then!' He got up, suddenly matter of fact, and led her into a room with a single bed that belonged to one of his children who were at boarding school. 'I'm sorry it's so cold in here,' he switched on the electric fire. 'I'd have heated the place before but—' she was kicking off her shoes, like a bad-tempered child, 'although I hoped this would happen, I felt superstitious about it. . . . Besides, I daresay you might have thought that too calculating?' She had moved away from him and was hurriedly unfastening her clothes, an obstinate expression on her face, as though having stumbled into this predicament, she was determined to go through with it, if only out of bravado.

'Why don't you let me undress you?' He began by taking the pins out of her hair.

He's making a ritual of it, she felt, he's too practised: 'How many women have you had?'

Put out by this blunt question, Martin left her alone and started unbuttoning his own shirt. The narrow morality of his upbringing had been modified into a more sophisticated desire to be thought of and to think of himself as a 'good chap'. Basically circumspect about his marriage, he had a set of personal, if devious, rules about infidelity: if he was separated from his wife, in particular if it was through her choice that he was left to fend for himself, he then felt justified in exploiting his freedom.

He said: 'What about you?'

Out of pique, Catherine was equally non-committal. She had climbed into bed with the sheets pulled up to her ears. Watching her, Martin thought: this is not going to work—this is not how I had meant it to be. He sat on the edge of the bed and drew back the covers, but, as he gazed at her, she avoided his eyes. He knew that he must say something, reassure her, but every phrase that came to his lips seemed tastelessly conventional: he had not before realized that she might only have slept with her husband.

When he got in beside her, he said: 'I've wanted you since I first met you—I even dream about you!' Although he had so often elaborated her seduction in his mind, from the moment he touched her he became so excited that afterwards, when he was telling her, repeatedly, that she was beautiful—he even used the word 'love'—he felt he had merely been enjoying himself at her expense. 'Go to sleep!' he closed her eyelids, unnerved by her vacant staring.

They lay there till the light faded and the windows had steamed with moisture. It was Martin who became anxious about the time. He got up and made some coffee. When she had dressed, Catherine looked at herself in the mirror, thinking: now I am an adultress! But the word had no meaning. She was wondering why she had bothered, as it seemed to her that the difference between Martin and her husband was less physical than social—with Martin she was not sure how she was supposed to behave.

She went into the drawing-room and waited till he brought in the coffee. Although she felt cheated, (she had sinned for nothing!) when he appeared in the doorway, his normally tidy hair tousled and frowning in concentration in case he spilled the cups, she felt as if her well-being depended on whether he sat beside her, where she could touch him, or in another chair.

She said: 'I suppose this is what's called chemistry?'

He stiffened, handed her the cup and sat in the chair.

'My parents-in-law live round the corner from here. . . . if they only knew!' When he saw her eyes shining at her own wickedness, Martin thought: this is a schoolgirl. What have I let myself in for?

On the way out he asked protectively: 'You sure you'll be all right on the way home?' He kissed her good-bye, trying to remain detached, but, when his lips touched her skin and he felt her clinging to him, he began to tremble. 'Well, thank you for coming,' gently he pushed her away. 'Perhaps we'll have a look at the country some other time?' He paused and she could hear his breathing: 'There will be another time?'

As she looked into the ugly hall mirror at their two reflections, she thought: either this will be very embarrassing or I will fall in love with him. She hurried out into the rain and did not look back.

When she got home, having driven too fast over the slippery roads, all was as usual, Ellen with a towel over her arm and the children shrieking in the bath. She looked in the fridge, trying to remember what she had planned for John's supper. But, once she had laid out the food and had started to prepare it, she was overcome by the banal repetitiveness of her domestic routine—nothing had changed, no one had noticed, she would spend the evening sitting with her husband as if the day had been as uneventful as any other. . . . She went upstairs and continued trying on the new dresses that she had left scattered all over the bedroom. When John entered, she was still in front of the mirror, staring at herself.

'Oh, that's where you are! I looked in the kitchen and found that the cooker was on—and the door of the fridge wide open. . . .' He frowned at the clothes on their bed. 'What's all this?' She had clipped on a pair of earrings and was turning her head to see their effect. Through her open zip he glimpsed the white skin of her back. 'I must say, Catherine, you really are the most awful slut!' He slid his hand inside her dress and she shuddered.

'Why shouldn't I sort out my things?' She had turned on him with such viciousness that he drew back in astonishment. 'You're always scolding me—you treat me as if I were about five years old!' In different places around the room there were photographs of their wedding, their parents, their children in infancy with silky heads and trusting smiles: she resented it that she should feel reproached by so many eyes. 'In some ways it's all your fault!'

He raised his eyebrows, perplexed: 'What's my fault?' But she turned away sulkily and began tidying the room.

Martin sent her a pot of gardenias with a note attached: 'Am I forgiven?' The note displeased her—she mistrusted its humble tone—and she promptly threw it on the fire. She thought it odd to have sent a pot plant instead of flowers and the gesture, itself, made her ill at ease: she had a premonition that one day he would retire behind such a gesture. She spent a long time staring at the plant, wondering what to do with it and how to explain it to John: it would die in the garden and Ellen would notice if she threw it out. In the end she said merely:

'Martin sent this.'

'Did he?' John bent down over the white, clammy flowers, whose insidious perfume was filling the room. 'I wonder where he got those? One doesn't often see gardenias nowadays.'

'I expect it was for all the meals.' The word 'meal', she thought, was disgusting. 'There was a note, but I don't know what I've done with it. . . .'

'Well, that was nice of him.' John looked cheerful and she felt frustrated by his pleasantness; she was surprised at the ease with which she had lied to him.

Martin telephoned but she found excuses not to speak to him; once, when she was standing close to the phone and could be overheard, she told Ellen to say that she was out. The girl eyed her curiously, but she had become careless of appearances as if trying to prove to herself that there was nothing to be ashamed of, nothing to it—it was a mistake, she had decided, that would be better forgotten. There's a moment of choice, she was telling herself, there's still time: at this point she could put a stop to it, say no! But because she lacked the courage to talk to him, she knew that she was really waiting for something quite different to happen, that she would drift and there would be no choice, and the price must be paid. For she was convinced that in the end it would turn out badly—that punishment must follow.

The dreary weather continued and she shut herself in at home, spending hours in the kitchen or in her sewing-room, making clothes. But, though her hands were occupied, her domestic affairs required little thought and she had too much time to indulge her fantasies when she re-lived the afternoon that she had spent with Martin, remembering each nuance of conversation and going over the detail of his profile, which she had peeped at when she was supposed to have been asleep; he had looked vulnerable with his eyes closed, his handsome features become gaunt and drawn, rather ordinary; she had been most moved by a sense of his limitations. It was a lonely face, she thought—they had lain together in solitude—and the guilt that she had at first felt towards her husband became merged with a fear that she had disappointed her lover. As the days passed she began to think about him so constantly that she was not really surprised one morning to see him looking in at her through the streaming window when she was wearing her spectacles bent over her sewing-machine.

She went to the front door and called to him: 'Why didn't you ring the bell? You're soaking!'

'I might have been told you were out.' It seemed to him that she was not at all excited by his unexpected appearance. 'After all, you're out whenever I telephone.' She led him back to her sewing room at the far end of the house. As he watched her walking ahead in her tight jeans, he thought angrily that she had allowed him to become obsessed with her and was now teasing him.

'You look ill,' she said, as she closed the door behind him. He leaned against it, staring at her. 'Why don't you take your coat off?' He removed his coat and crossed to the other side of the room, fearing that, if he touched her, he would lose his self-control. He had intended to be gentle, to appeal to her—on his knees if that was the way she wanted it—but the sight of her studying her sewing pattern, humming to herself, so enraged him that it was only with an effort that he broke the silence:

'I left work this morning to come and see you!'

'Oh?' She appeared not to appreciate his recklessness and again he felt thwarted.

'You're a bitch—you just sit there! It's years since I've been so excited by a woman. . . .' He watched her pressing her knees together, shrinking from him and sensed that he was repeating his mistake. He had played it wrong, he had realised, he should have taken more trouble to make love to her verbally, to appear to commit himself: it was her naivety that he had underestimated. With the single-mindedness with which he had won scholarships as a boy and then later had pursued his professional career, he was determined to find some way of dominating her affections. However, in planning his approach, he had twisted his own motives, not liking to see himself as too calculating, and he had thought with remorse, even gallantry, that he had been far too abrupt and had abused her feelings. Trying to calm himself, he sat down. 'Catherine, please listen. . . .' He fondled her hand. She did not draw away from him, but her fingers were very cold. 'Look I'm sorry if I took advantage of you. . . .'

'It's not that—I didn't have to sleep with you.'

'Well—no. But perhaps you have regrets. . . . Do you?'

'I don't know.' Her eyes seemed out of focus.

He hesitated before suggesting: 'We don't have to continue with it—you mustn't think that I'm only interested in. . . . If you prefer we could forget that it happened and go back to being friends?' He dropped her hand, nervous lest he be betrayed by his anxiety that she might agree. 'You do still like me, don't you?'

'Oh, yes,' she softened, 'yes, of course I like you.' When she smiled at him he felt ashamed that he should have prepared the scene in advance.

'But you think I'm playing with you?'

'I don't know what to think.'

'I should have talked to you more openly.' He pulled her towards him and sat her on his knee. 'You asked about other

153

women. . . . At the time I didn't like to tell you that I've quite often amused myself. Margaret and I have been separated fairly frequently—usually because of things to do with the children. But it was never more than a game, light entertainment —never what one might call a love affair.' She looked miserable. 'Is that,' he touched her cheek, turning her face towards him, 'why you want to push me away?' She lowered her eyes and he watched her fingers nervously clenching. She'll only do it, he thought, if she believes she's in love and I'm equally involved. 'Maybe you're right. When one is happily married it's a mistake to play around unless it means a bit more than. . . .'

'I see you have a double standard! It's all right for you to, as you put it, amuse yourself, but a woman who does the same thing is degraded unless it's a grand passion—and she suffers!'

He looked at her warily: 'That's not quite what I said.'

'What about your wife? Does she "amuse" herself?'

'Margaret? Oh, no, she's not the type!'

'And I suppose you respect her for it?'

He evaded the question. 'My marriage has been a good thing for me. It works as a partnership—we're a good team. But it's never been at any time,' he paused, appearing to search for the word, 'poetic.' He caressed her face, touching her lips with his fingertips. 'When people say that if one has been married for some time one's feelings deepen, I'm afraid the sad fact is that they often deepen into boredom.'

'It is sad,' she agreed, then felt disloyal.

'But this still doesn't explain why you should have affected me in this extraordinary way. . . . It's different for you—you're young, you've got all sorts of things ahead of you. But I've reached a point where there's a kind of futility. It's as if I'd dried out. I've felt that here, in this country, and,' he lowered his voice, 'with you. When I'm with you I sometimes feel that I've missed out on the things that are really important.' She looked away and he was touched to see that his words had made an impression on her. He was speaking the truth when he said: 'I suppose what I would really like is for something to happen that would lure me beyond myself.'

'Isn't that what one always wants?'

'But one is seldom,' he looked into her eyes, 'lucky enough to find.' He kissed her and felt for her breasts under her thick

154

jersey. When he touched her nipples, she thought: If I go on with this he'll spoil me for everything else. Clinging to him she whispered: 'Why d'you excite me if we're just to be good friends?'

He let her go and stood up, turning away from her to straighten himself. He smoothed his hair, trying to sound casual: 'I'm too late to get back before lunch, so why don't you let me take you out somewhere?'

She looked at her dirty jeans: 'I'd better change?'

'Why?' He laid his hands on her shoulders: 'Do you believe me if I tell you I think you're marvellous?' He tried to think of a better word, then of the other things he had planned to say; but the phrases sounded empty, a verbal trick. He shook her: 'You must believe me!'

They went out and she told Ellen she would be gone for an hour or two, closing the door quickly before she could be questioned. In the car he said:

'It's rather out of the way, but you wouldn't mind if I went home first? I'd like to change my wet shoes.' When she smiled, he slowed down and laid his hand on her thigh: 'You really don't mind?'

They did not go out to lunch, nor did Martin return to work. She was making him lose his sense of proportion, he told her; he had not even rung up to say he would not be back. On the return home he kept stopping by the roadside, but she no longer cared if she was seen. It was only when they were back on the island that she became cautious, asking to be let off at the gate.

'I don't want to cause trouble,' he looked at her anxiously, disturbed by her radiance.

'What does it matter?'

They arranged to meet again and she watched his car driving back over the causeway and the headlights travelling along the far shore to vanish inland. The rain had cleared and a brilliant evening was reflected on the water. There was a smell of frost, but she did not notice how cold it had become as she walked through the wintry garden, listening to the wind in the trees, a solitary bird, a dog barking far away in the distance. What does anything matter? she asked herself, thinking that she had found what she had been waiting for all her life.

155

There was a brief period of extreme happiness, an age of innocence in the affair itself, unspoiled by deceit or mistrust or practical difficulties. Margaret had decided not to settle in Ireland until their children were back at school after the Christmas holidays, so that even at the weekends Martin was still free to play golf and John, unsuspecting, would invite him back to stay. Martin was embarrassed the first time he heard John's voice on the phone, but he managed to persuade himself that it would sound suspicious if he were to refuse. Catherine was amazed at the simplicity of her double life. Instead of guilt she felt a heightened affection for her husband; the eveningt when Martin came to the house as a friend and the two men talked politics were a relief from the intensity of their private meetings.

She told Ellen she could stay at home with her parents on the nights when John went out to the U.D.R. and Martin would enter the house so stealthily that she wondered where he had acquired his animal caution. 'Which room?' he had asked her on the first visit and she had realised that, while he seemed to have no qualms about accepting her husband's hospitality, he would still have disapproved of her if she had not taken him to the spare room. She told him that John spent one evening a week at a club, fearing that he would think badly of her if he knew the real reason for his absence; even at this stage she felt that he was looking out for her faults so that, when the time came, he would be able to abandon her with an unworried conscience. It was a bit of luck, Martin observed, it was not a Tuesday when John went out, as that was the night his boss borrowed his car to visit a lady friend. This surprised Catherine: the community was very strict. 'Not now it isn't,' he laughed at her: 'You're not original in your wickedness!' She did not like it when he suggested that the Province had become an adventure ground for the many strangers, separated from their wives, who were temporarily stationed there.

In the mornings Martin sometimes rang up saying he could get away for lunch and she would leave whatever she was doing to drive off to meet him; it added to the excitement if she had to cross Belfast where the bombing had become so intense that the

156

shops in the city centre, lit up with their Christmas decorations, were deserted. By now all the windows of John's factory had been blown out and his men had resigned themselves to working by artificial light. John was obsessed by the damage; he told Catherine that the sound of broken glass being swept off the roads had begun to get on his nerves almost as much as the bombs themselves. He had seen people walking along with blood on their faces; it was not unusual to find a crowd on the pavements looking up at the building from which they had been evacuated because of a bomb scare. On one day in Belfast alone there were explosions in a co-operative store, a café, an antique shop, an insurance office, a furniture shop, a television office, a clothing factory, a hotel and a railway station. In the empty streets teams of cameramen photographed the destruction of the city.

On the days when they did not see each other, there were long telephone conversations; it became a game with Martin to keep talking when other people entered his office. But there would be eerie interruptions. Once, when Catherine lifted the receiver she heard a voice saying: 'That's the British Home Stores gone up, Brigit—quite a big one! Now put me on to D.J. . . .' Catherine stopped breathing, irrationally afraid of letting Them know she had overheard. Two hours later she heard on the news that the British Home Stores had been bombed. Another day she heard a woman whisper: 'He was caught in that blast, but his wife hasn't been told yet. . . . Oh, yes, he's bad!' This time Catherine laid down the receiver and ran from the room, tormented by the contrast between her own private exaltation and the woman who was soon to be told that her husband had been crippled.

At night when Martin came to see her she would be unable to say good-bye to him, clinging like a child till he would say, rather irritably, as he unlocked her arms from around his neck: 'Catherine, I really must go!' The morbidity she had experienced after Patrick's birth returned in a fear of ambush as he drove home in the dark. But for herself she had become careless of the surrounding danger and, where her friends were doing their Christmas shopping in the villages outside Belfast, she made a point of going into the city and, when she heard an explosion, she thought: If it happens at least I will have lived— I will have been complete! If she were to die tomorrow, she would not have to pay the price when the affair came to an end and Martin's term was over.

'I hadn't understood what the fuss was about,' she was to confide in Felicity: 'I never knew it could be like this!'

'That's what's usually said—don't think you're the only person in the world it's ever happened to.' Although she had encouraged her, Felicity was nettled to see Catherine so transformed, thinking it unfair that her friend seemed to have had the best in all ways. 'One over-rates the beloved. Conventional women like you blow up the whole thing into a noble passion in order to justify it.' But, when she saw Catherine's languorous expression, she felt pleased that the wife of John Mulholland should be cheating him; he belonged to that part of Ulster society by whom she had felt rejected. 'Don't take what I say too literally. I can see what you fell for—Martin has a vibration. I wouldn't have said no to him myself!'

Catherine glanced at her in suspicion, wanting to know if Martin still came to visit her. But Felicity merely smiled, amused to see her jealous. Although she knew no cause, Catherine now found herself eroded by jealousy. Women that he had never seen, a girl in a shop, would suggest themselves as potential rivals and she would look in to their faces wondering what they might be able to offer him that she lacked—whatever she had seemed not enough: her demands on his affection were insatiable.

John took her up to Castle Hardwicke for the weekend and her brother remarked on her glowing appearance. 'How's that friend of yours?' he asked: 'What's-his-name, the fellow that's had the elecution lessons?' Catherine felt apprehensive that he should so easily have guessed; she observed, too, as if it were a foretaste of the world's condemnation, that Desmond and Felicity, who had tried to lure her towards the affair, were sneering at her now that it had happened. Not that she cared! When Martin touched her, it seemed that she could feel his soul through the skin. She awoke and saw snow on the ground and the children crying out in excitement. Although it melted after a few hours, the vision remained as she had perceived it through her heightened responsiveness, glistening, paradisial.

John came up behind her when she was dressing and held her in front of the mirror: 'Look at yourself—you get prettier every day!' But she could not face his reflected smile nor her

158

own treacherous eyes. 'Go on—look at yourself!' he insisted: 'Why should you feel ashamed of being so delicious?'

In the mornings Patrick went to school with extra sweaters in case he caught cold during bomb drill. John held Catherine's hand while they watched the school's Nativity play where Patrick, with the other fair-haired boys in his class, was dressed as an angel. Towards the end of the play the angels came to the front of the stage to sing in their thin voices encouraged by the lady at the piano: 'If you're happy and you know it clap your hands!' When this was over, there was a hush before the audience remembered to applaud: in certain districts the current version of the song was: ' "If you'd kill a British soldier clap your hands!" ' It was being said that in a school in the Falls, casualties among soldiers and police were charted on the blackboard. A man John had met in the U.D.R., who worked in a Catholic shop, had told him that Army deaths were greeted with cheering and patriotic songs.

Driving home through Belfast they saw painted on the walls: 'Informers beware! Informers will be shot!' They were shot through the knee-caps as a warning, and maimed for life; the corpses of more serious offenders were often burnt or mutilated, sometimes with 'I.R.A.' branded on their backs. A pregnant woman was tied to a lamp-post and beaten with hurley sticks; but, while immense publicity was given to a girl who was tarred and feathered, there was little emphasis on the humdrum cruelties inflicted by the I.R.A. on their own people, like the man who was 'punished' by having his legs repeatedly run over by a car. When bombs went off by accident the victims were Catholic boys who had been flattered or intimidated into 'doing a job for Ireland', as the terrorists were reluctant to waste skilled men by planting the explosives themselves.

It was incongruous, said John, as he wired up the Christmas tree, to be celebrating in such an atmosphere; he was thinking of the children in the back streets, a generation numbed by savagery. But he complimented Catherine on the decorations: she had out-done herself, he had never seen the house look so festive! Insisting that they all needed cheering up, he opened a bottle of champagne when Martin came to say good-bye to them before going home to England. Martin was surprisingly inarticulate, almost wistful and, to cover his awkwardness, he made overtures to Patrick. This was the first time that Catherine had felt hostile to him and thought it in bad taste that he should insinuate himself with her child. As she watched Martin playing with him, tickling him, throwing him up in the air, she wondered what he would be like as a father—then as a step-father. It was an unpleasant surprise to her to realise that, although she felt she could not live without him now, this alternative was not what she would choose.

During the few days when Martin was away, Catherine listened for the postman, tearing open the pile of cards then casting them aside in disappointment when she did not find his letter. However, although she did not hear from him, their parting had been so tender that she could persuade herself that in spirit he was still with her and she could feel his caresses, could even remember the smell of his skin. She talked to him interminably in her imagination, re-phrasing her ideas in a form that might meet with his approval. On Christmas day when a large party of John's relations came to lunch her mother-in-law congratulated her on her efficiency and the hard work that had gone into preparing the food; even Tom Mulholland praised the turkey. An incongruous influence of her liaison was that, while she went around the house, her eyes glazed with erotic dreaming, in her practical life she was renewing her effort to live up to the bourgeois ideal of the married woman whose role is to serve her family with devotion.

Martin rang from the airport as he got off his plane and she spent an hour with him before he went back to work. She was surprised that he should be so passionate after spending a few nights with his wife. 'This can't go on much longer,' he told her, 'it's not going to be so easy for me to get away from the job.' He hinted that there were soon to be important changes and tried to explain to her that he was anxious to do well in Ireland where his position was unusual. But she looked so crestfallen that, to make amends, he took time off on the last day of the year and, instead of staying in his house with the curtains drawn, they went on the outing they had first planned to the ruined abbey near the coast.

The abbey had been built in a green hollow at the mouth of an estuary. As they walked along the deserted path at the water's edge there was no sound other than the birds in the rushes or seagulls whose wings dazzled against the blue sky. Martin was enchanted with the ruins. They talked about Celtic culture, the land of scholars and saints. Twisting his hand inside her sleeve so that he could feel the delicate skin on the underside of her arm, he spoke of his sympathy for the vision of a united Ireland: he had been infected by the myth-makers. She must let down her hair, he insisted. Did she object if he thought of her as his colleen? The countryside moved him to lyricism, the gentle colours, the peacefulness, the illusion that time and the modern world were of no consequence. He told Catherine that she was making him lose his sense of reality. They laughed about the I.R.A.'s aim for a Gaelic-speaking Ireland divided into pastoral units of farms and villages where life would be centred on the family. But was this so absurd, he asked, when the consumer society, the forces of progress were merely polluting and devouring the world? He said he would like to find a cottage, somewhere in the lonely west, where they could spend a few days together instead of having to snatch their moments. Would that be possible? he gripped her arm so tightly that she caught her breath. She could not bring herself to admit that it would never be possible. There was a place he had in mind that he had seen when driving through Donegal, and he went on to describe it. They sat down under a broken arch.

'I feel I could stay here,' he buried his face in her hair, 'I could settle in your country.'

She listened, feeling his lips on her neck, and searched for another meaning under his words. The fact was that in the autumn he would go. But there was still time, more than half a year. . . . If we were to die now, she wanted to ask him, would you choose to spend your last hour with me?

'Oh, no, not here!' he had unbuttoned her coat: 'We'll be seen—even when you think you're alone there's always someone lurking in the hedgerows. . . .'

'Don't look then!' He pulled her hair over her eyes and made ove to her, straddled on the broken stones, while the crying gulls circled above the silhouette of the ruins. The risk, even the sense of sacrilege added to his delirium. 'I never knew I had it in me to feel what I feel for you—I don't think you quite appreciate what this means to me. . . .'

You will go, she thought, and I will be left.

'At a time in my life when I found myself descending gracelessly into middle age. . . .' He saw tears in her eyes. 'Don't be sad. One should feel gratitude for the extra things that happen—regard it as a bonus. After all,' very gently he caressed her cheek, 'who would have expected us to meet, two strangers, and that it should be like this?'

They drove up into the Mourne mountains where snow glistened between the rocks and the farm dogs were so fierce that they attacked the car, scraping their teeth against the windows.

'Before I met you, he said, 'my life had gone grey. But with you I can see the colours. . . .' He slowed down so that he could look at her. 'I want you to remember—whatever happens—' moved by the despair in her eyes, he kissed her hand: 'even after we have parted I will never forget. . . .'

'Later!' she covered his lips with her hand: 'You can say all that later.'

'This has been one of the best days of my life,' he told her as he opened the car door to let her out at the garden gate. He did not at once drive away and when she reached the house and looked back, he was still standing in the shadows gazing after her.

Although they would normally have expected to go out, for the first time in their married life John and Catherine spent New Year's Eve watching television at home. As usual Northern Ireland featured on the news. John stared gloomily at the screen, wishing he could feel optimistic that the situation might improve; as he got up to pour himself a whisky he decided to make it his resolution to lay off the drink. Where John was depressed about his country, Catherine thought only of Martin: will he go at the beginning or at the end of the autumn? This will be my most marvellous year and also the most miserable. . . .

The next morning they went to see John's parents. It is a tradition that the ships in Belfast harbour welcome in the New Year by blowing their sirens, an event which can take some time while the crews compete with one another. This year, Tom told his son, midnight had come and had passed without a sound. There must have been an agreement; not a single ship had broken the silence. It was the worst New Year, he said, that he had ever experienced.

1972

'The Protestant back-lash is an empty phrase!' Tom Mulholland looked at the newspaper close up, then, as if not quite
believing what he had read, he held it away from him at arm's
length peering at it over his spectacles. His eye travelled down
the page: on the hills above Belfast a man's head had been seen
emerging from the snow as it melted, the corpse being dug up
with great care in case it was booby-trapped. . . . Rustling it in
disgust, he turned over, but even the inner pages were so
monotonously packed with horrific incidents that he wondered
how they had managed for news in the old days. A small
paragraph told of a corpse that had had to be identified by the
dead man's dentist as the eyes had been removed and the face
was unrecognisably mangled. He let the paper fall. 'The one
thing that really is remarkable,' he removed his glasses, rubbing
the bridge of his nose, 'is the restraint of the Protestant population—so far.' He bent down, superstitiously touching the
wooden leg of his chair. He had heard that Protestants were
saying to the soldiers: 'Give me your rifle and I'll do your job
for you!' ' "Back-lash" ', he muttered. Then he glared at his
son: 'How can they under-estimate the force of Protestant
feeling? Just because the Protestants are on the whole fairly
law-abiding it doesn't mean. . . . Why, one only has to remember
the way they sacked the Falls in sixty-nine. In the Province
there are one and a half million people and by this time there
can hardly be a single adult who doesn't know at least one

person who has been murdered or injured.'

John lifted the poker and prodded the fire. 'Why doesn't Mother use proper coal instead of all this slag?' Although he now visited his father quite often, his parents' house depressed him; the welcoming blaze which Catherine would have ready for him when he came home was a symptom, he felt, of a more generous nature.

'I suppose you'd like a drink to warm yourself up?' his father said grudgingly.

'I'll wait till I get back. I've got to drive.'

'Which route d'you take?' The tone had become anxious.

'Oh, don't worry about me, Dad. I'm old enough to look after myself.'

'People are talking,' said Tom. 'Your Mother has heard them in the shops, whispering over the counter—"It'd take three weeks to wipe Them out. . . ." They've had enough. It's the Abercorn that's done it.' The two men stared into the smoking fire, thinking of the explosion where nearly a hundred and forty people had been injured, including a girl who had lost both legs, an arm and an eye. A few weeks earlier a crowd had been deliberately lured by a false alarm into Donegall Street—when the bomb went off amid the panicking throng there had been six deaths and over one hundred and fifty injuries. A young constable had fainted before the dismembered bodies, the mass screaming. It was only by being almost jocular about it that the older policemen had been able to do the job of collecting into plastic bags the arms, legs and hands that had been strewn about, some from the dead, some from bodies that were still alive. 'They do say,' although John was wearing his coat, he shivered, 'that the reason the atrocities have become so bad is that the Army has got them beaten and they're desperate.'

'How can you be so naive!' Tom thumped the arm of his chair. 'Your trouble is that you've got too many friends among the English. English people are themselves too fundamentally decent to believe that anyone could do such things on purpose. If it happens they feel there must be some mistake or there's a special reason behind it that makes it in a way excusable. When the fact is that the I.R.A. just don't care what suffering they cause—they've as little human feeling as the creatures that staffed the concentration camps during the War.'

166

John avoided his father's eyes. Catherine, too, had heard things: in a bakery, with its genteel sugary smell, a woman had murmured of an acquaintance that had been kidnapped, her face prudishly inflamed: 'They cut off his privates.' It was said that there had been an attempt to quieten publicity in the case of the policeman who had been strapped to a tree with his limbs splayed out. The rumour was that he had been very slowly shot up both legs, then both arms; when he was dying a Union Jack had been plunged in his stomach, which was later sent, stained with his blood, as a momento to his girlfriend.

John said. 'What's to be done?'

'That's up to your English friends,' his father was looking at him as if he was a traitor. 'It's up to them to decide, un-fortunately, what's to be done—or not done. There seems to be no doubt that even at this stage the Army could still deal with the terrorists. But they've got their hands tied behind their backs. All one hears is talk of a "political" solution. As poor old Faulkner keeps pointing out, politics are irrelevant against a background of violence. Today in Northern Ireland anyone at all can commit a murder and get away with it. It's absurd to think that the I.R.A. can be *persuaded* to give up.'

'Stormont still has some power,' John said doubtfully, and he thought of Martin whom he had not seen for some time. With revulsion he suddenly realised that the man he had entertained so frequently was Catholic-biased. Two years ago he would have argued with his father on the side of the Civil Rights Movement: it had been a shock to him to find he had not even noticed that the society he lived in was so unfair to some of its members. However, although he still liked to think of himself as a moderate, he had been dismayed to find how much his own feelings had hardened, the discovery coming to him by accident when, on entering a village shop, he had heard a Mass being played over the radio and he had listened to the Southern voices, thinking: the enemy! He said: 'To begin with the English Press had it that the Catholics were goodies and the Prods baddies, but now, since the bombings, they're all bad—it never seems to have occurred to anyone that there might have been some justification for Protestant fear of the I.R.A.' He glanced around the room, irritated by his mother's plants whose fronds trailed over the furniture. 'I suppose it's bad

167

luck, too, on the Catholic community most of whom have no more liking for trouble than the rest of us, that they should be banded together with the terrorists.'

Tom grunted. He had always accused his son of taking too soft a line; he was as squeamish as people from across the water when it came to facing the reality. He regretted now having sent the boy to an English school. 'Would it be Catherine that invites the English to your house?' His brother, Arthur, had seen her with one of them, drinking in a hotel.

John flushed, resenting it that whenever he disagreed with his father the blame should be laid on his wife. 'She doesn't run me, if that's what you're asking?' He was about to add something more abusive in her defence, when his father stopped him, laying his hand on his knee:

'Let's have that drink. I could do with one myself.' He got up, rather stiffly, from his chair: 'I know you're very fond of her—and it's none of my business.' But, as he poured out the drinks, he noticed that his hands were shaking—he was becoming an old man. He felt apprehensive for the well-being of his favourite son. 'We can talk ourselves blue in the face for all the difference it'll make. There'll come a day when everyone gets tired of the upheaval and it'll fade away as inconsequentially as it started.'

'I think you're wrong.' John tried to ignore the spilled drink that his father's trembling hand held out to him. 'I don't think it has much to do with the local population—it's a disaster that has come upon them like a plague or a war. The real issue is between the I.R.A. and the British Establishment—but it's the ordinary people of Ulster who suffer and not the British who see no real urgency to end the trouble. In Britain the disturbances here are taken for granted. Maudling,' he spat the name, 'actually spelled it out when he said that what Westminster wanted to achieve was "an acceptable level of violence in Northern Ireland". No one seems to remember that a few years ago this was a country with practically no crime.' He picked up his father's newspaper and looked at a photograph of a policeman who had been shot while rescuing victims of a blast and had received brain injuries which meant he would spend the rest of his life in a mental home. The face looked honest, dutiful, simple. 'A situation like this inspires the average man to heroism—but what's the point of it when even their sacrifice brings no improvement? I hear there's talk,'—it was Martin who had mentioned it—'of easing security. The presence of an Army, which is not allowed to be effective, merely provides a curtain behind which the violence can continue indefinitely. Any member of the security forces who is murdered trying to protect the place in effect dies for nothing.'

Tom's drink tasted bitter and he put it aside. He did not look his son straight in the eye when he suggested: 'The same would apply to you in the U.D.R.—I'd like to see you out of that.' John said nothing. 'Oh, I know you feel you must do your duty. . . .'

'I can't get out of it, I'm committed. No one likes to be seen as a coward.'

'But there are plenty of fellows who join because they need the money,' Tom was trying to be persuasive, his voice gentle, 'and they like a bit of excitement. But for you, it's a waste of your intelligence. . . .'

'You think I'd be more useful in politics?'

'Politics!' Tom gripped the arms of his chair: 'D'you want to have your house blown up?'

It was a long time before John answered: 'This must have been what happened in Germany before the War. I've always wondered how it was possible that the German people permitted a regime like Hitler's—but now one can see how it could have come about. In this country the civilized man didn't dirty his hands with politics and now that it's risky he holds back even more. But let it go till things become intolerable it's then too late and too dangerous and no one but a fool would stick their neck out.'

'Fine talk!' to cover his anxiety his father appeared to be sneering at him: 'That's not a parallel, it's not the same thing at all!'

But John was thinking that the reason why he would find it difficult to enter politics was that in his mind there was a split between practice and principle: in principle all his instincts were revolted by the idea of a military solution; in practice he could see no end to the Troubles without the ruthless use of force.

'Here, I must tell you!' The older man's face was creased with contrived cheerfulness: 'Brenda's old man, Henry McTaggart, he goes around with a gun in his pocket—even takes it to church.' When he laughed the veins stood out on his temples: 'But then he always was a pessimist. At least I'm not as bad as that!'

John smiled, but he did not think it particularly funny.

'Would you have believed this possible?' John held up the newspaper for Catherine to see the headline: the introduction of Direct Rule was a shock for which no one in the Province had been prepared. They watched on television the demonstrations in Belfast. When the announcement had been broadcast the shipyard workers downed tools almost to a man; they marched in their thousands round the City Hall where they listened to speeches from hard-line politicians, then in total silence they returned to their work. There was something ominous both in the spontaneity and in the extreme orderliness of this protest. Shortly afterwards there was a meeting at Stormont attended by a crowd of over a hundred thousand, waving Union Jacks but again very orderly. Then a two-day general strike. Although it is a remarkable achievement to bring a country to a standstill, the English Press managed to ignore its significance because they chose not to see the force of resentment felt by the majority in Ulster that their Prime Minister had been humiliated and his Government sacked. 'The lesson people will draw from this,' said Faulkner, appealing for restraint in his final address, 'is that violence can and does pay.'

Protestant strikers expected their employers to back them up by giving them their wages for the days when they had been off work and Tom Mulholland called in his directors to decide on the manner in which this demand should be rejected. 'If they want to lose two days' money that's up to them. We're running a business. We're not interested in politics.' He publicly attacked his eldest son: 'It's time you saw sense and buried your head in the sand. Politics no longer exist in this country!' Exasperated to find himself being stared at, John got up and went out. Direct Rule, he realised, would mean the end of any attempt to govern the country from within as the 'bigoted' Protestants, who tended to be the only people with a practical interest in politics, were giving up, discouraged, after too many years of bad publicity. On the way home he heard a man outside the City Hall calling through a loud-speaker for the population to be mobilized. Disregarding the rain, which streamed down his collar, he shouted: 'Whitelaw has come here to sell us out to the South. . . . We've no alternative: Eire must be overrun, Dublin must be bombed!' John's father had told him not to forget the fear of the ordinary Protestant for the Catholic employer; his gardener, Nathaniel, had thought of emigrating when he had heard that Stormont had been suspended. Overhead the usual helicopters were hovering above the city; John had come to hate the sight of these buzzing machines.

The days were dark and it was very cold during the general strike when there was no electricity. There were unpleasant stories of intimidation, with bands of youths roaming the country, bullying little shopkeepers into closing their doors. While the I.R.A. were returning from hiding across the Border, hooligans from Protestant districts, though not yet organized, were beginning to give trouble to the Army. A 'low profile' was announced on security and internees were released. Shooting incidents became more frequent and after two or three weeks of the new regime there were bombs exploding on an average of one an hour at some point in the Province. Although the violence had got very much worse, Northern Ireland was less in the news and it was suspected that a degree of censorship was being employed in order to lull the British public into thinking that Direct Rule was working. Meanwhile, the new Secretary of State, adulated by the Press as 'the Supremo', made appearances on television to explain his policy: 'Softly, softly,' was the phrase. Not at all the pin-striped, bowler-hatted Englishmen, but a gemütlich figure, who seemed blinded by vanity at the idea of his own charm. 'Just let them see me!' he would say: 'Let them see what sort of chap I am—and then it will be all right.' He was filmed walking through the streets, making himself known to the people; like a king he granted a pardon to the husband of a woman who plucked at his sleeve. Regularly on the news, after the usual list of fires, bombings, shootings and mutilations, would come an announcement that at the personal request of Mr Whitelaw numbers of detainees

171

were to be set free. As these men returned to their activities casualties among the security forces increased. There were sensational murders of Catholics who had joined the police or the U.D.R., one man being shot in front of his wife and five children; the gunmen, in passing, also wounded his ten year old daughter. After such events there would be photographs in the papers of the bereaved—a look in the eyes as if they would never smile again.

A new slogan now appeared on the walls: 'Whitewash out!' Special privileges were given to 'political' prisoners so that a man who had murdered a policeman enjoyed an easier time in jail than a common burglar; this much-publicized gesture merely inflamed the loyalists without appeasing the opposition. While the new administration seemed prepared only to listen to the views of the minority and Stormont politicians were in disgrace, a hearing was, nonetheless, given to the leaders of the Protestant rabble who were getting ready to practice violence in competition with the I.R.A. The line here, too, was conciliatory and they were not prevented from setting up an organisation, training in the fields and marching through the streets, wearing stocking masks and dark glasses.

'We live under a dictatorship,' said John 'but without the advantages of firm rule.' Coming home late one night he had been stopped and searched by a gang of Protestant roughs; they were mostly boys, some only about twelve years old. The police had watched from one side of the road, the Army from the other. When he protested the constables had looked away in embarrassment; it was the soldiers who allowed John to understand that it was Government orders that these boys were to be allowed the freedom of the streets. Catherine woke up when he got into bed. He told her what had happened and she sat up and stared at him with an extraordinary expression in her eyes. She flung her arms round his neck, shuddering with suppressed hysteria, because, while he was out and in danger, Martin had been to the house.

She had become very temperamental; on some evenings when he came home he would be astonished by her gaiety, but there were other days when she appeared so closed in on herself that she seemed not to hear when he spoke to her. Where she had once been vague and easy-going she now talked politics with intensity, her voice shrilly rising if he disagreed with her. He was sometimes surprised that she should appear so well-informed. 'Where did you hear that?' he would say. But she would shrug it off: 'Where does one hear anything—the radio, the telly, things people say. . . .'

She lay on the floor, reading from a newspaper, 'Listen to this: "The constable's widow, whose only brother was machine-gunned to death a few months ago, collapsed, sobbing, in the street as the cortege left the church. . . ." ' The lines on John's forehead deepened, but he made no comment. 'Why is it allowed? Why isn't something done about it?' She jumped up and was clawing at him: 'Why doesn't someone put a *stop* to all this?'

'Oh, Catherine, please!' He could feel her nails through his clothes. 'Why attack me? What can I do about it?' In self-defence he caught hold of her wrists. 'If everyone took each dreadful incident to heart we'd all go out of our minds. One's got to keep going. There's nothing for it but to hope that something will eventually be done and that one day things may improve.'

'Nothing is being done—nothing will be done!' she picked up a fashion journal and threw herself on a sofa, scowling at advertisements for summer dresses.

John lifted the discarded newspaper and began to read, but the contents sickened him. He let it fall, thinking that in contrast to Catherine's emotionalism, his own feelings seemed to have deadened; there was too much to be angry about, too much to grieve over. He glanced across at the woman who lay sullenly sprawled out. She might have been a stranger. It startled him to discover that he had had a physical misconception of her: the fey girl, towards whom he had once felt so protective, he had thought of her as slender, fragile, but, when he looked at the curve of her hip, he realised that she was much more robust; in middle age she might become heavy. He went over and sat down beside her, but she did not raise her eyes from the magazine, merely shifting her legs to give him more room. He leaned against her, disturbed by her brooding sensuality.

'Catherine,' he touched her hand and she let the magazine flutter to the ground, 'what's happening to us?' The look of fear in her eyes was quickly glazed over and she lay torpid,

173

waiting for whatever it was he had to say. 'You've changed.'

'We've all changed. Everyone I meet seems altered in some way by what's going on—usually for the worse.'

She's at it again, he thought, exaggerating! He put his hands round her face, meaning to be tender, but instead he was sadistically excited by the malleable softness of her cheeks. She was gasping for breath as though suffocating and when he kissed her she yielded with a moaning voluptuousness that he found alien. As if there was nothing left but sensation they lay there, reckless of intruders, with the doors unlocked and the curtains undrawn.

'There are days,' she whispered, 'when I wish that I had never been born.'

He closed his eyes against the sour light of the spring evening. Normally he would have replied: you're too extreme. Instead he began talking to her about the things he usually only discussed with his father. 'I'm becoming unbalanced about it myself. With every death it's as if I felt somehow personally ashamed.'

'Ashamed?' she echoed, thinking of the things that could not be undone, the passion she could not control: while John despaired for the victims, she lived from moment to moment waiting for the telephone. 'I do love you best, you know,' she avoided looking into his eyes, 'I mean better than the children— better than Patrick.'

From then on when he came home John would enter the house quietly or, pretending to walk round the garden, he would peep in through the windows, trying to catch sight of her before she knew he was there, so that he could guess at her mood. It was as if she had changed from being his wife into a difficult and unreliable mistress.

When Direct Rule was announced Catherine's one thought was: will I see more of him or less? Although Martin had hinted that something was about to happen (he had annoyed her by his air of secret knowledge) he had been too discreet to give away the details. Catherine had been astonished that the change-over had been so abrupt and so careless of Protestant feeling. 'They may not be very eloquent when it comes to

174

putting their own case,' she told him, 'but they're a proud people—it was tactlessly managed.' But Martin assured her that the Government at Stormont had done nothing but harm; it was time they went—and good riddance to them! He spoke enthusiastically about his new chief, a 'lovable' character to whom all his staff were devoted. It was irritating that he should be criticized by the deposed Prime Minister who insisted that conciliation could not work against a background of anarchy. 'I'm going to write my own slogan on the walls,' Martin said: 'B.U.F.—belt up Faulkner!' He was elated by a sense of power at finding himself part of the team running the country whose democratic rights had been waived.

When he telephoned he talked so much about his job that she began to wonder if he was losing interest in her. Once she became so exasperated she told him that it was the British Government that was responsible for the continuing and worsening of the violence. 'It's their fault,' she shouted into the receiver, 'not the fault of the Ulster people most of whom want peace at any price.' He hung up abruptly and she wept because they had quarrelled.

Normally she fell in with all his plans. Since the beginning of the year, when Margaret had come to settle in Ireland, it had become much more difficult to meet. On the nights John was out he would not find excuses to come to see her if Margaret was at home. 'It's a game,' he said, 'life is a game—one must observe the rules.' Although he seemed untroubled by practising a major deceit against his wife, his rule was that he would not tell her a direct lie. When he discovered that John was in the U.D.R. and not at a club as she had first told him, he scolded Catherine, telling her that she was unfeeling and disloyal. 'But it's the only night he ever does go out,' she protested, 'if you don't come then it won't ever be possible.' He looked cornered and she thought: although he complains about them, he's as devious as the Irish. 'All right I'll come,' he had said coldly, 'but that's your decision, your problem.' Occasionally Margaret went away for a few days to see to their property in Essex and they would meet at his house. When this happened he took great trouble over her and she wondered if it was another of his rules that even in love he must play the hospitable host.

But, on the whole, they were limited to outings during the lunch hours, sometimes in restaurants, where Catherine, entering first, would look around to see if there was anyone she knew; then on other days, when there was less time, they went straight up to the hills. They would leave one car by the roadside and drive on together, but there was a risk that the abandoned car would be stolen by terrorists and Martin always looked in the boot in case explosives had been planted in them. Though the countryside seemed so quiet, it was surprisingly difficult to find an empty lane where they would be unobserved. After these hurried encounters Catherine would return home, wondering what to do with the rest of the day. She tried to take an interest in the garden and would attack the weeds that had shot up during the spring rains; but whatever she could do in the home she still remained mentally unoccupied with too many hours in which to brood. She thought of Martin back at work, exhilarated by his snatched adventure: his job in Ireland, he said, was the most exciting of his career. Whereas on her side she was beginning to feel that the tedium and loneliness of domestic life in themselves constituted grounds for divorce. This thought frightened her; she had not considered divorce as one consequence of the affair. The more likely end was simply that when Martin left she would remain in this place where he had visited her and where she had thought about him so obsessively that every tree, every shadow would be a taunting reminder of his absence—and she would be trapped.

There was a brutality, too, about the speed with which they met, made love, parted, with hardly a moment to discuss more than which route they should take and where to park. Everywhere the vegetation was coated with lemonish fronds vibrating in the changeable light as if the whole landscape had become effervescent. 'You're fantastic,' he told her, 'I haven't felt so lit up for years!' So that is all I mean to you, she thought; she could not have put into words what he meant to her.

Once, when she was at a private view with Felicity she caught sight of him at the far end of the gallery wearing his spectacles and holding hands with Margaret as he led her through the crowd. They looked like elderly undergraduates. Margaret was glancing around with her fixed, cheerful smile and Catherine realised that the woman was completely self-satisfied—she had no conflict between what she wanted to do and how she felt she ought to behave. She left the gallery and went home early when it was still light. As she drove through Belfast, where there were gilded gleamings on the wet roads, she became aware that among the people she saw walking the streets that evening it was probable that at least one would have died unnecessarily by the following week. Thereafter, when she was lying in bed missing Martin, she would sometimes suffer a physical nightmare, thinking that, if she was to live through the flesh, she should be grateful that at least her arms and legs were still attached to her.

She was afraid of John, of a man's face in the window. Like Martin, he, too, would approach quietly, spending a long time in the garden after she had heard him garage his car. (Isolated houses had been burned down, particularly those belonging to men who worked for the security forces.) In the old days he had run up the steps, calling to her as he opened the front door, exuberantly pleased to be home. Now he would creep up on her, a dark look in his kindly brown eyes and she would wonder if she had been seen—and exposed. She would slip away from him to make him a drink; she made an effort to see that his dinner was ready when he came home so that there would be no time to wait, or she would bring in the children in their dressing gowns. But after dinner he would complain that he was tired and wanted to go to bed early and she did not dare refuse him in case he guessed from her coldness. The evenings were getting longer and she drew the curtains so that he could not see into her eyes. Even when they were first married he had not been so demanding, but at that time, she remembered nostalgically, it had all been so much simpler and more affectionate. Now, although she had to force herself to lie down with him, his first touch would inflame her as if she had become the victim of her own awakened appetite. Later, when he was asleep, she would be imprisoned in the strong arms she had once found so comforting, and, trying not to wake him, she would ease herself out of his embrace to get up and wander about distractedly. While she was with John she felt that in her body she was lamenting Martin's absence, but the mixture of fear and distress merely added to her excitement and then she would feel degraded by her treacherous response.

In the dark hours it seemed to her that she was being used by Martin: he might think of it as the thrill of a lifetime, perhaps—but still only a thrill. Was it worth it? she often asked. It was with him that she had had her white moments, but the price she paid was the long periods of misery when he was not beside her. If only she could have taken a worldly and rational view, regarding the affair as an enjoyable sideline. . . . But had she been 'amusing' herself, Martin would not have been so interested in her. Men like to make women unhappy, she realised: it flattered him to think that she pined when he was not with her. Once when she had arrived late, she had found him waiting for her in a hotel lounge, bespectacled and reading a newspaper, in the pose that he presented to the world, and she thought: what am I doing with this pompous old man? But the image had vanished when he hurriedly took off his glasses and looked up at her with his exciteable pale eyes. Once when they had been lunching in a restaurant a policeman had rushed in to the phone to report that he had been shot at, and she had stared at the man who had had the luck to survive, thinking that love leads to selfishness: the sufferings of people all around her were nothing more than a back-cloth to her private pain when he said something she found hurtful—or merely inadequate. She tried to make herself despise him for his wariness about expressing his feelings: he was emotionally parsimonious, he should not have allowed her to see his coward's eye glancing at the eventual exit. She should give it up, get her own back, recover her self-respect. But there was no longer any choice. . . . Before returning to bed she would look first at her sleeping husband, over whose features there seemed to be an uneasy shadow although his eyes were closed, then at the photographs of her children. But even Patrick had become repellent to her with his endless war games and his clever little drawings of tanks and gunfire and bombs falling out of aeroplanes. In one of the cupboards John's revolver was hidden on a top shelf out of reach of the children. He left it at home during the day and had taught her how to use it and which window to shoot from if a sinister stranger were to come to the house.

In the liverish spring evening, greenness seeped into the room.

They kept away from the windows and talked in whispers.

'Do you love me?' she asked him.

He was edgy: 'Better not use the word "love". It means too much and too little. . . .' He was avoiding her through sophistry. He looked at the greenish glow on her drooping hand, thinking that in Ireland all is decline, a melting and merging, the romantic allure a deception. 'One's got to keep a sense of proportion.' He braced himself, holding out his glass to be re-filled. 'I say, that's rather a strong one!' He held up the dazzling glass in which the sunset was reflected, the purple sea.

'All right. I don't love you and you don't love me. *On s'amuse.*' He appeared injured. 'One plays the game,' she said, 'your game.'

He drew himself up, sipping; he might have been at an Embassy cocktail party. Glancing away from her with extreme irritability, he changed the subject, turned his eyes towards the sea, asked about John's boat.

'I suppose that's something else you'd like to cash in on?'

A professional smile: 'Why not? I'd enjoy that—if he cares to ask me.' The smile was replaced by severity: 'I like your husband.'

'Is that a reproach? You can stand here, in his home, waiting to. . . .'

He watched the movement of her breasts as she struggled to suppress her anger and concentrated on trying to see her nipples under her thin blouse.

She pushed his hand away. 'Your wife has been in this country for several months and it's part of your job that she must entertain for you. And yet, although there was a time when you practically lived with us, we have never once been invited to your house!'

He flushed; he did not like to see himself as a sponger. 'The only entertaining we do is rather dreary and official—you wouldn't enjoy it.'

'That's not the point!' Felicity had been befriended by Margaret who had told her that they had no intention of wasting their time by becoming involved with the Protestant establishment. 'Dreary or not, you would have asked us if you had thought we might be useful to you.'

'Now, steady on!' He made sure he had finished his drink

before reaching out to grip her shoulders: 'That's bloody well unfair! You're being unreasonable!'

Because your wife doesn't want us, she thought, and I refuse to sympathise with the problem. Because you don't want to risk upsetting your menage as mine has been upset. In a moment he would kiss her and, once she could feel him she would be lost. If only I could stand up to him, she realised with momentary self-knowledge; if I insisted on it he would treat me better, if I could be angry I would no longer have that awful feeling—there would be no need to weep. But, instead of objecting to his hypocrisy, she turned away; 'I've got a head-ache!' she said. Her annoyance had been overtaken by distress at antagonising him.

He sat down beside her and they talked about sailing.

'Yes, I daresay John probably would take you out in his boat.'

'To hell with the boat!' He looked at her accusingly: 'You do make me feel the most dreadful cad!'

They wrangled for a while, but in the end he managed to persuade her to get into bed with him, which was what he had come for.

While he made love to her she determined: whatever happens I refuse to cry. To stop herself crying she kept her eyes on the window, which opened to the back on the green hump of the island, patched with tiny fields, a landscape a child might have drawn with geese, pigs, a goat and a donkey all mixed up, like animals from a toy farm, in one paddock; then she concentrated on objects in the room which she remembered buying with John during the first year of their married life.

He sighed and rolled over. She looked Pre-Raphaelite, he thought, with her auburn hair spread out all over the pillow, which was no whiter than her face. There were greyish hollows under her eyes. What had he done, he wondered, that she should look so ill? He could think of nothing to say. Morbidly drawn to her, he rested his head against her breast and lay for a long time, listening to her heart beats. When he raised himself to glance at his watch, she was lying as before, quite expressionless, but with her eyes closed.

'I don't want to go—but I must. Darling,' he whispered, 'please look at me. . . .'

A few days later when John came home he found Catherine in such a benevolent mood that she actually kissed him at the door.

'Surprise, surprise!' she said, 'an invitation from our new rulers!'

Although it was two months before the Twelfth, the bands were already out on the streets and everywhere there were crowds on the pavements, waiting, staring at the passing cars, little boys holding Union Jacks and waving at the soldiers; there appeared to be more jeeps, camouflaged lorries and armoured trucks than civilian traffic.

'All those people, they give me the creeps,' said Catherine. 'It feels like the end of the world.'

John had heard the spectacular explosion earlier in the afternoon in which, it was said, ten million pounds worth of damage had been done. As they drove through Belfast on their way to Martin's house they saw, from a long way off, the smoke from the bombed building ballooning upwards, then dispersing high above the roof-tops, puff after puff; the smoke was so active it seemed odd that it should make no noise. On the motorway leading out of the city they passed an abandoned car whose windows blazed with golden light. At this point the traffic was very fast, each driver accelerating till the suspect vehicle was well out of range. It was a watery evening, melancholic and luminous where the sky seemed not empty but transparent as if it were a window on to something beyond.

The party was mostly composed of English people, Martin's colleagues, some journalists, a few soldiers. John was taken aback to find that among the Ulstermen there were only one or two Protestants. Felicity waved to Catherine across the room, but she was too busy helping Margaret to exchange more than a few words with her friend. A nickname could be heard repeatedly; it seemed that everyone was on intimate terms with the Supremo. As a man-to-man gesture Martin made a point of introducing John to the most important official in the room. When he handed Catherine a drink he touched her fingers, but did not talk to her and she felt miserable with jealousy as she watched him flirting with his boss's wife. Although he would tell her that he was trying to allay Margaret's suspicions, she also observed that in doing so he was achieving something useful on his own account. As she watched the woman warm to him, she heard someone say:

'My remedy would be take off the children under four, float the whole island out into the Atlantic—and sink it!'

Meanwhile, John was being told: 'What we think we will see in Ulster is not just a solution but a good solution. Once we have split up the Unionists and broken their power. . . .'

John interrupted: 'You'll only break the moderate Unionists. When they've gone you'll be left with the hard-liners.'

'You think so? Well, if they're going to be silly about it, then it's themselves they'll have to answer to. As we see it. . . .'

These people are over-educated, thought John, to them the problem is theoretical. He restrained himself from saying that in Northern Ireland English politicians could make as many mistakes as they liked because it was the opinion of the British public that the Irish were ungovernable and if things went wrong it was they who were to blame and not the new administrators.

'Of course the position is very complex,' John's companion gave a fluttery little laugh, 'I'm afraid we do rather feel that we've been obliged to take up again the white man's burden.'

'Oh, I see. Natives?'

Discreetly, while he was opening an elegant cigarette case, the man eyed him: 'I think I can assure you that everyone involved is desperately sincere in their concern for the situation.'

'You talk of a "solution"?' John was thinking of the illusory comfort of certain words. 'The ironic fact is that if, because they are exhausted, the people of Ulster accept whatever package is imposed on them, then British policy will appear statesmanlike.'

'The joke, my dear fellow,' the Englishman regarded him coldly before turning away, 'is that people think we have a policy!'

The party had divided into little cliques with some antagonism between the military and the diplomats. An Army friend of John's complained to him that the soldiers were being used as target practice for the snipers while the politicians marked time. 'Look at them,' he glanced round the room, 'they're all preparing to write their memoirs.'

'The thing that amazes me,' said John, 'is that there's so little sympathy for the people who have been killed and injured. One gets the impression that if there's suffering in Ireland the English merely think this is what they deserve.'

'There's no point in making such a fuss about it—you've got to see it in perspective.' They had been joined by a P.R. man. 'After all, when you think of the actual number of deaths there have been in Ulster it is nothing compared to catastrophes in other places. Why, in Britain alone seven thousand people are killed on the roads every year. . . .'

With an effort John controlled himself and asked calmly: 'So it doesn't matter?'

'Not if you look at it from this angle—no, it doesn't. . . . You see, the really interesting bit is the television coverage. When things blew up in Northern Ireland it was the first time that people all over the world could see it happening in their own living-rooms.'

'So the news has become entertainment?' said John. 'I suppose the time will come when TV companies pay people to start wars in order to keep the masses happy at home.'

'It's begun already,' came the cheerful reply: 'Only the other day a couple of Frenchmen were fined for shelling out fivers to a crowd that had rioted in front of their cameras.'

John moved away and looked for Catherine. He found her fiercely arguing with a glamorous young woman attached to the Foreign office. The girl was saying:

'Northern Ireland is like a family and in that family there's a naughty little brother—the I.R.A. Now it's up to the other members of the family to be kind to him and teach him how to behave.'

Catherine's face was scarlet. 'What about the men the I.R.A castrate alive?'

The girl also flushed: 'It doesn't help when people get stupid and emotional.'

'You're not talking politics, are you?' John tried to draw Catherine aside.

Martin appeared. He laid his hand on the girl's shoulder. 'Poor old Anne's just back from the Middle East—she's used to dealing with Arabs. Doesn't understand when people over here don't react in quite the same way.'

At a sign from his wife Martin stopped pouring drinks and the party came to an end precisely at the hour indicated on the invitation. He stood at the door with his arm round Margaret's waist and gave John a friendly smile, but seemed not to notice when Catherine passed in front of him.

In the car John complained: 'Dismal party—I could be breathalyzed and no problem.' For a while neither spoke, then he asked: 'Did you meet anyone interesting?'

'I don't know what's coming over me—if you hadn't turned up I'd have slapped that girl's face!' She glanced at him but he was concentrating on the road. 'You heard what she said, didn't you?'

'I heard.'

'Well, can't you see. . . .'

'Yes, but you bang your head against the wall if you start quarrelling with the English. However wrong they may be, they still have a knack of retaining the advantage. It's easy enough to appear reasonable when you have no personal stake involved.' He patted her knee, condescendingly: 'Do me a favour, will you? Lay off the Troubles!'

'Why?'

'There's no use getting excited. You've got to have facts, statistics, dates. . . .'

'To hell with statistics! Why can't they see it's a simple human reaction that if your brother is murdered you're not going to be sweet and reasonable about it? They make a mistake if they ignore the feelings of ordinary men and women.'

John sighed and she burst into tears. He said irritably: 'The worst thing about arguing with women is that when they run out of steam they start to cry.'

Catherine had doubled up on the seat and was weeping hysterically: 'That's not why I'm crying.'

John drove on, bored, alienated: 'Then what is the matter?'

'Too much to drink.'

'You were lucky!'

He saw her putting her hand over her mouth. As soon as he had stopped the car she got out and vomited by the roadside. She thought of Martin linked with his wife; she felt he had snubbed her in public. The head-lights illumined a rock on which had been painted the word: 'Eternity!' She stared at the irregular letters wondering if in hell there could be punishment more extreme.

'You've got it on your coat.' John rolled down the window to air the car as she climbed back inside. On the way home he appeared so sombre that she was convinced he had found out. She was astonished when he helped her gently over the gravel saying, 'I know how you feel. It's not easy to keep calm when one is talking to people who seem to have no understanding at all of what's going on. It's a pity they've got total power.' He mopped up her soiled coat.

'Oh, don't do that—it's too revolting!' When he smiled at her and she looked into his trusting eyes, she again began to cry. She wished Martin had never come to Ireland.

Martin surreptitiously re-filled his glass while his wife counted the empty bottles.

'These Irish,' she said, 'they fairly drink!'

As he crossed the room to give her a hand he bumped against a table. He must keep sober, he reminded himself, or she would notice. She was standing with her back to him, calculating the cost of the party.

'Did we really have to have all those people? Your Unionist friends, for instance, I didn't think they added much. The wife was most frightfully rude to poor Anne.'

'Was she?' He watched her tipping out the ash-trays, flinging open the windows. 'I must say,' he could hear himself slurring his words, 'I thought Anne looked rather dishy tonight.'

'I thought you thought so,' the tone was arch, 'I was keeping my eye on you.'

Martin gulped his drink wondering just how much she had observed. He had to force himself to eat the supper she laid before him. It seemed that the hours would drag on interminably while he listened to her bright chatter. When they went up to bed she sat in front of the dressing-table laughing at her grey hairs.

'There we are—got you!' She plucked one out. 'I suppose another seven will now grow in its place?'

He climbed into bed and lay with his back to her, thinking of Catherine. The room swam. He had spent the evening in

185

tension lest Margaret should suspect, but, instead of relief that she should be sitting there chuckling to herself, he was offended by her obtuseness. She got in beside him and he felt her arms round his neck, then her hands running down his body.

'Oh, no!' He saw her smile fading and a look of astonishment. 'I couldn't,' he curled up his knees, apologizing, 'I seem to have had one too many.'

'That's unlike you!' She dug her fingers into his shoulder and he winced before shaking her off. 'I must say it's a bit hard when you're forever complaining that I don't take enough interest.' Crossly, she rumpled the bedclothes, put on her reading glasses and picked up her book.

He slid away from her, repelled by the way she licked her finger as she turned the page. How would it end, he asked himself, as he tried to stop the characterless wall-paper wriggling before his eyes, if he let things go so far that he could never face her again?

Martin looked up but he could not see the larks singing overhead in the warm, white haze where even the glare of the sun was bland. There was an azure bloom over the landscape whose other colours had paled, the effect at midday being of a brilliant twilight. He peered into the hedgerows and commented on the number of wild flowers, the flitting butterflies.

'That's because we're so backward,' Catherine told him, 'the farmers around here don't use so many chemicals.' When they got near the village the hedges were stuck with rubbish and a sodden mattress blocked the lane. 'You'll be annoyed,' she said, 'if I tell you this is a Catholic village?'

'Is it?' He looked away from the rusting bed springs. 'It seems just Irish to me.'

'Well, yes, it is all a bit like that, but it does vary—it's a question of degree. . . .' She picked her way over the rushes at the verge, looking up at him anxiously lest he lecture her for being prejudiced. He shared with his colleagues a facile condemnation of Protestant attitudes, but was touchy about the slightest criticism of the other side. It was absurd, she realised, that she should fear his disapproval when he knew so little of the country and his interest in it would fade once he had moved to a new posting. He had the twin English vices of hypocrisy and moral arrogance, his image of himself being of more concern to him than the real effects of his behaviour. Trained to be impartial and above emotion, his understanding was limited by a set of principles to which he would adhere irrespective of their relevance to a situation. He conforms to type, she thought, he's rather ordinary; but, as she gazed at the sunshine on his fair, greying hair, she knew that it made no difference to the craving so acute that even to be with him was painful—even when she was in his arms the ache would remain. I'm neurotic, she told herself, I want more of him that there is to have.

They climbed a gate and crossed the fields through flowering gorse bushes that were full of bees attracted by the curious scent. He looked down at the prickly ground: 'Well, this won't do!' He laughed and entangled their arms, twisting his hand round her wrist. 'There seems to be gorse everywhere,' he complained, 'it's very pretty, but. . . .' Eventually they found a protected hollow where the grass was dry. All around they could hear the tiny noises of the countryside, rustling, humming, scratching, sighing; there were grasshoppers hidden in the bushes.

'I can't bear to think that one day I will have to live without you—I don't know how I'll get over it.' She looked away, thinking: he's here now—this moment should be enough. Her head drooped and she murmured: 'You give me *douceur de vivre*.'

Her lips were slightly parted. He looked at the movement of ribs, as if with each breath she was making an effort to contain herself—and he thought of the contrast with his passionless wife.

'D'you think we should do anything about it?'

She raised her eyes, incredulous: 'You mean. . . . ?'

'Well?' He lifted her hand and turned her wedding ring. But, as he spoke, he knew he would never have the energy—and nor would she. I'm too weak, her eyes were saying to him: you must decide! In offering her the choice he was intensifying her distress.

'You're always wanting me to tell you that I love you? I do, Catherine.' He stroked her face compulsively, exploring each feature. 'Don't you understand that my life is over-burdened by my feelings for you?' The hollow where they were sitting

187

was filled with a yellow light that in Ireland is nostalgic even in the present, a softness, melting, caressing, vanishing. . . . The landscape was in dissolution.

He had told her what she wanted to hear. But nothing would come of it, they would neither of them have the courage to face the other people involved. He would go and there would be no comfort, no consolation. 'Perhaps,' she said, 'one might manage better if one was a Catholic. . . .' The power of the Catholic Church lay in its understanding of human feebleness, its probing of the dark places cleaned bare by Protestant reason.

'You are a funny girl,' he pushed back her sleeve and touched the downy hairs on her arm: 'What an extraordinary thing to say!' But he was relieved that she had changed the subject. He sounded more cheerful when he asked: 'Well, shall we stay here or do you think we can find a better place?'

They stayed until the moving sun had cast a shadow over the grass, which became damp at once.

When Catherine got home she found that John had returned early. He was in their bedroom, sitting in his shirt-sleeves with his head buried in his hands. This time! she thought. She did not dare approach him. He dropped his hands and she saw, before he blinked away from the light, that his eyes were bloodshot.

'It's Danny McQuade,' he said. 'I don't suppose the name would mean much to you? He's been with us since he left school. Both legs blown off.' He got up and stood in front of the mirror, tidying his ruffled hair. 'Nothing out of the ordinary—a tragedy is happening to someone every day of the week.'

A month later, when John parked in the narrow street, people appeared in doorways to stare at his car and he saw faces behind the curtains of upstairs windows. The houses with their decorative victorian brick-work appeared quite cheerful from the outside, although he knew that the interiors would be cramped and the plumbing inadequate. They were without gardens and there were no parks in the area; the many children playing in the road, skipping and chanting, stopped their games for a moment to watch in silence while he knocked at the door.

It was opened by a thin young woman with her hair in

188

rollers, who laid her hand over her mouth and gazed up at him anxiously through her spectacles. Then she fled, calling: 'Mammy!' Mrs McQuade shuffled to the door. She was a small, stout woman with dark hollows under her eyes.

'I'm John Mulholland,' he held out his hand. 'I was wondering how Danny is? I heard he had come out of hospital.'

'Mister John!' Her face glowed with mingled pleasure and dismay and she patted her hair, glanced down at her slippers. She wiped her fingers on her overall before shaking his hand. 'Come in, come in!' He followed her inside and a crowd gathered in the street around his car. 'You must excuse me— if I'd known that you'd be coming. . . .' She fumbled with the buttons of her overall, puffing slightly in her haste to remove it. 'I'm afraid you'll just have to take us as we are,' she apologised, leading him into a tiny room that was full of women and children. There was an overpowering smell of frying food and he glanced at the window, wondering if it was ever opened. 'This is Mister John,' she announced importantly, 'from Mulhollands!' The adults rose to their feet, pushing the children off their laps. She offered him the best chair: 'Won't you sit down?'

'No, no! I'm all right.' There were not enough seats to go round. They were looking up at him with the traditional respect of Irishwomen for their menfolk. He felt too tall for the room and ducked instinctively to avoid the lights. A very old woman edged away and scuttled through another door.

'You mustn't mind Mother,' said Mrs McQuade, 'She's a bit backward—she wouldn't feel it was her place to be passing the time of day with you.'

He shook hands with the daughters, the girl who had timidly opened the door to him and her married sister, a heavy young matron, who might have been quite pretty a few years earlier.

'Mary!' her mother scolded the girl, 'take them rollers out of your hair—you're not fit to be seen!' She pulled up the chair and he felt obliged to sit. 'Dad's out at a meeting. He'll be sorry to have missed you.'

A meeting? thought John, hoping that the man was not a member of a suspect organization. Perhaps it was something to do with whichever church he belonged to? They were obviously a 'good-living' family; it seemed to him ironic that the text over

189

he mantel-piece should read: 'Become acquainted with Him and be at peace!'

'And Sandra,' Mrs McQuade was plumping up the cushions, shooing the children from the room, 'go you into the kitchen and make Mister John a wee cup of tea. And tell Mary to give a hand tidying up upstairs. Danny has the room covered in newspapers,' she explained to John, 'And there's the cigarettes he smokes, dear help him!'

When the tea was brought in, it was so heavily sugared that he could hardly swallow it. The two women sat opposite, Mrs McQuade touching her hair and bending down, surreptitiously, to smooth the creases in her stockings.

'How is he?'

His mother took out her handkerchief and dabbed at her eyes: 'My poor boy. . . .'

'He's doing his best,' Sandra answered for her, 'it's not an easy thing to bear.'

'No,' he said, 'it's not.' He tried to imagine himself in the same position—and failed because each individual believes he has a charmed life and that catastrophe comes to other people. He sipped his tea slowly in case he was offered a second cup.

Mrs McQuade was making an effort to control herself. She sat up very straight, twisting her handkerchief on her lap: 'It was very kind of you to take the trouble to call—Mulhollands always was good to their own.'

John glanced round the dingy room, thinking of the mean wages his father paid the workers. 'It was no trouble. I only wish. . . .' He faltered, at a loss for a phrase that would be in any way adequate.

'It happened in the evening,' she said, 'when he went out to the pub to buy some cigarettes. But don't think he drinks.' she added hurriedly: 'He took the Pledge when he was eighteen and hasn't touched a drop since.'

'You should have seen the place the next morning,' said Sandra, 'all that broken glass—and the blood. . . .'

Mother and daughter then competed to describe the deafening explosion, the sirens, the screams of the injured, the neighbours rushing in to tell them the bad news. Each stuck to her own story and they became quite quarrelsome, contradicting one another.

'No, you've got it wrong, Sandra, it was uduer the counter that they left the bomb—in a paper bag. You'll be getting poor Mister John all muddled up!'

Mister John! he echoed to himself, suddenly disgusted by his paternalist role. The mother's face was shining, her eyes luminous with gratitude; it was as if Danny's accident had almost been worth it for the honour of his presence. He thought of the old grandmother who had felt herself too far beneath him to shake his hand.

'May the Lord forgive them!' Mrs McQuade raised her eyes to the text: 'I lie awake at night praying for an answer—I just can't understand why it should have happened to him. You see, Danny, he was always such a good boy. . . .' She paused to blow her nose, then looked up at John, questioningly, through her tears: 'But perhaps it was done for a purpose? Perhaps the Good Lord has singled us out?'

John found himself unable to reply. Her acceptance of the disaster struck him as both pathetic and repulsive—she was not even bitter about it. He thought of the many funerals he had seen on television with weeping mourners trailing in front of the cameras; in addition to bomb casualties the corpses were being discovered each morning of people that had been assassinated after dark. Though it was popularly feared that the Britsh Government might give in to the I.R.A., there was no official disapproval of the enraged Protestants now rallying in the streets. But while violence was fanned rather than appeased by the new policy, no protection was given to the very poor whose tragedies left them bewildered.

John laid down his cup. 'I'll go up and see him now if that's all right?'

The mother preceded him to make sure that the room was in order, and was sharp with the younger girl for not having seen to it that the ashtrays were emptied. The room was hazy with cigarette smoke and he noticed that the hand held out to him was nicotine-stained to the knuckle. He pulled up a chair by the edge of the bed.

'How are you, Danny?'

'Oh, not so bad, not so bad.' He turned awkwardly to fumble under the pillow for his cigarettes. 'D'you smoke?' John shook his head. He tried to return Danny's smile when he added: 'It's about the one thing left—that and the telly. . . . I was watching a grand race this afternoon!' He was thinner and more lined than when John had last seen him and his skin was in poor condition. John wondered if it was his mother who had brushed his hair so neatly; a man in his late thirties, he was one of those Irish bachelors who never quite make up their minds to leave home and get married. Thick lace curtains across the window meant that nothing was visible outside the room where there was only space enough for the bed, a cupboard, the television set. Danny asked after his work-mates, some of whom had visited him in hospital. 'People have been very kind—very kind,' he looked pointedly at John, who turned away in embarrassment. He tried not to stare at the flat centre of the bed where his legs should have been.

John asked him about his treatment in hospital and if he was still in any pain. 'I was nearly in the papers,' Danny told him. 'Some journalists came round who were doing an article on the Troubles. The nurses thought it'd be me they'd pick—but in the end it was a little boy.' He looked disappointed. 'It was an arm he'd lost and his right foot. . . . I suppose,' suddenly there were tears in his eyes, 'with a kiddie it's even worse.'

Better news value, thought John, remembering the relish with which the Sunday papers portray anguish and misfortune —better entertainment!

He explained that in addition to government compensation Danny could expect to receive something from the firm. They talked about artificial limbs and employment for the disabled. 'But in the meantime,' said John, 'is there anything I can do for you? Anything you need?'

'Now that's civil of you,' Danny twisted towards him, knocking his cigarettes on the floor. When John picked them up he whispered conspiratorially: 'If you could get me some of these? Ma rations me!'

John lifted the packet, glanced at the brand name. 'Well— yes,' he was taken aback by the request, 'are you sure that's all?' When he got up to go he saw the real misery in the man's eyes.

'It's nice to have a visitor—the days drag.' Danny clutched at his sleeve: 'Why did it have to be like this?' He was looking up as if expecting John to say something that might help. 'What did I do?'

John's face contorted; he did not at first understand that he looked on this as some sort of judgement. 'You've done nothing, Danny! You can't surely think of this as your fault?' John tried not to sound too abrupt as he pulled away from him. He could hardly bear to look at the man, so pitifully humble, who would have to find some way of enduring the rest of his legless life. Why don't you hate the people who did it to you? he wanted to say. He said: 'Don't worry, Danny, I'll get you your cigarettes.' He left the room and descended the narrow staircase to where the women were waiting, listening for the sound of his footsteps.

He thought with loathing of the I.R.A.; then it seemed to him that the blame lay almost as much with the politicians who felt no urgency about putting an effective end to it all. In the beginning it could have been dealt with by the police with a little assistance. Now the thousands of troops stationed in the Province merely provided an illusion that something was being done. The Army was so restricted that it could do little more than contain the violence. But, while the policy-makers discussed other things, casualties continued day after day, week after week, and could go on indefinitely—among the poorest and most helpless members of the community.

In the street children scattered in alarm at the sight of the tall, angry stranger advancing towards them who did not seem to notice that they had been climbing over his car.

'Good gracious, it's John!' his mother opened the door to him, 'this is an odd time of night to be dropping in.' She peered at him more closely: 'Is something wrong?'

He moved past her and looked around inside: 'Where's Dad?'

'I expect he's gone up to bed. I thought I heard him pottering about some time ago. . . .' Alicia followed him into the sitting-room, her face suddenly brightening. 'Now that you're here, you could do something for me—I've got some cuttings I'd meant to give to Catherine.' She opened the curtains and looked out: 'Let me see, I think it's still just light enough . . . Hang on while I get my secateurs.'

'That's not what I'm here for!' He caught her by the arm, then let go at once, appalled that he should have used even this mild force against his mother. 'It's Dad I came to see. Your wretched cuttings can wait!'

She stared at him, astonished. 'Very well, then.' She stumped out of the room and stood at the bottom of the stairs with her hands cupped over her mouth, calling: 'Thomas! You've got a visitor. . . .'

The old man came down in his dressing-gown. 'Why John!' He looked both pleased and wary: 'What brings you here at this hour?'

'There's something I want to talk to you about.' John glanced at his mother, who was still in the room, frowning at her plants.

Tom switched on one bar of the electric fire. 'Won't you sit down?' John was standing by the window with the curtain parted, looking out at the late glimmering view of Belfast Lough where the lights of a ship were moving slowly towards the open sea. Catherine never closed the curtains until after dark.

'I suppose you're trying to get rid of me?' said Alicia and her husband gestured. 'All right, all right—I know when I'm not wanted.' John did not turn round until she had closed the door behind her.

'I've been driving through the city looking at the bomb damage.' It was like a ghost town, he thought; apart from Army vehicles the streets had been empty.

Tom poured him a drink, but made no comment. A short while ago he would have scolded him for his recklessness.

'Earlier on I'd been to see Danny McQuade.'

'Ah, did you now? That's a good lad!' His father smiled approvingly. 'How is he?' John shrugged. 'It's fortunate he's not married.'

'I suppose so: He'll be alone in his old age. . . .' They discussed Danny for a while, then the Troubles in general. 'I can't help feeling,' said John, 'that if it was people like us it was happening to things would be rather different.'

'What d'you mean?' Tom glanced up at him under his eyebrows.

'There'd be more fuss about it.'

'And would that make any difference?'

'Yes, I imagine it would. If all the people with any position in the country—and in this I include the rich Catholics—were

194

to put pressure on the British Government to bring the violence to an end, they would have to listen.'

'And who's going to get them to do that? When Westminster disposed of Faulkner they got rid of the one man who had any hope of uniting the greater part of the population.'

'While I was driving around looking at the wreckage I kept thinking of that phrase the newspapers use, the "silent majority"—they're supposed to be sickened by the whole business, and yet, where are they? Everyone we know is astounded at the way things are being mismanaged—negotiating with the I.R.A. as if they were respectable politicians! That's something the average Protestant won't forget or forgive. . . .' He knotted his hands together, cracking the knuckles. 'But when I think of my friends there's hardly a man among them who would publicly raise his voice in protest. They're like us —they put extra guards on their factories and hope it won't happen to them. And for the rest they fold their hands waiting for it to blow over.'

'Which it will,' his father tried to soothe him, 'in time it will blow over.'

'But they won't be the ones to suffer. It's the Danny Mc-Quades, men and women who are so socially insignificant that their sufferings pass almost unnoticed. There's no labour movement here, they've got no one to stand up for them. The only way they can express their grievances is by counter-violence—on the streets. Whether we like this or not it is a patriarchial society that we live in and it's the duty of people like ourselves to protect the under-privileged.'

'You're getting into deep water,' his father smiled uneasily. 'Here, let me top you up!' He took John's glass and re-filled it, then sat down again, not looking into his son's eyes as he said: 'It's early days yet. I think most people feel that Direct Rule should be given a chance.'

'But it's been bungled already! Can't you see that it doesn't matter how many people get killed in Ulster provided the British image is kept clean? So long as they appear to be benevolent—so long as they talk about conciliation. . . . They actually go around congratulating themselves on their good intentions! It's too late to ask whether British policy will succeed or fail in Northern Ireland. It has already failed—and the extent of that failure will be the number of the dead.'

Tom sighed: 'I'm not disagreeing with you. . . .'

'They say that "desperate situations require desperate remedies". Although the idea of martial law is against all one's civilized instincts, by now it's quite obvious that the only solution is in some sense military. It's no use waiting and hoping that it will stop—because it won't. It's got to *be stopped*! And the trouble is that no liberal person—no one in a position of power has the guts to say this. The price that is paid for bashfulness in high places is the monotonous slaughter of simple little people who, unless they leave the country, can do nothing whatsoever to defend themselves.'

The older man pulled his chair closer to the fire and switched on another bar. 'Look, John, it's not pleasant to see someone whose had his life smashed. It was nice of you to visit Danny, but. . . .' He paused, thinking of the difference between the generations; unlike his son, he had grown up during a period of civil disturbance and he had fought in the War. 'It's a hard world—for the unlucky—but there's no point in becoming emotionally excited over the one tragic case. The thing's happened and can't be mended. And, while practically everyone in this country would like to see an end to the terror, there's not much that we can do about it—the decisions are out of our control.'

'You don't seem to have listened to what I've been saying. That's exactly the attitude I've been complaining about. We all make noises in private, but no one actually does anything.'

'And what would you propose to do?' His father had had enough of the conversation, the tone was sneering: 'Write letters to the newspapers? You can hardly enter politics as we no longer have any political representation!' When John did not reply, he became quite jocular: 'Going to train up your own army? Do a bit of gun-running?'

John reddened. 'I had thought I might speak to various members of the business community—one by one if necessary— to try and persuade them to put their money and influence. . . . You're quite right when you say that politics are at an end here —the democratic outlet is closed. But money still talks, money is power.'

Tom leaned back in his chair, finger-tips touching eyebrows

incredulously raised, as if he were listening to a child. 'And how would you use that power? Provided you had it, of course!'

'I would use it to try and bring about a change—and by this I mean a determined and, if needs be, ruthless campaign to stamp out terrorism, not a wavering policy of repression one day and appeasement the next. It's not good enough for the authorities to say they won't give in to the "men of violence"—there must be a resolution to *defeat* them. If the present administration won't listen to this point of view, then one uses the money for publicity. One of the most striking aspects of the Troubles is the importance of the media. And yet I have never once seen a television film directed against the I.R.A. or criticizing the Republic for its encouragement and support of violence in the North. Although there are documentaries about conditions in the bad areas, this is presented as being somehow endemic to Irish life, unfortunate perhaps, but just one of those things. The fact is that the intolerable state of anarchy is not normal and could have been—could still be—avoided. If enough people were prepared to give their backing to getting this across they could make such a nuisance of themselves that I think it would be bound to have some effect.'

'You'd get nowhere! If the I.R.A. were burning down the houses of the rich and there was no government compensation when a factory was blown up so that they felt it in their own pockets—then yes, you might make some headway. But as it is,' Tom opened his hands, 'you'll turn yourself into a laughing-stock! Who's going to act in the public interest these days when it means risking a bullet through the skull?'

'It would only work,' ignoring him, John continued, 'if it were joined by members of the Catholic community—Catholic businessmen, Catholic lawyers and professional people—there are plenty of them. . . .'

'You're talking about some sort of coalition?'

'And why not? This is a disaster that hits the country as a whole, not just one element. The worst damage has been in the Catholic part of Derry. . . .'

'My dear boy, it was one thing to have a coalition during the War when there was unity against a common foe. But don't forget that the aim of the opposition parties at Stormont was to destroy the State—to many people on the Protestant side what you're suggesting would seem like a coalition with the enemy.'

'Is this your view?' He looked at him challengingly, but his father had sunk down in his chair, his face sagging and tired. 'The only hope for this country is for both sides to co-operate in bringing the violence to an end. It's a shocking thing that after years of upheaval so few are prepared to cross the barrier to shake hands and forget. If this is to happen, then someone will have to make the first move.'

'You?' Tom mocked him, then he mumbled to himself: 'dreams, theories. . . .'

'The initiative must come from the Protestants—they are the doers in this community. When the average Catholic hits trouble he bows his head and retreats to his own patch, instead of trying to find out what can be done.'

Tom stared gloomily into the empty grate, which was full of plants as the fire would not be re-lit until the autumn. 'How much of all this is just talk?' He glanced at his son, whose eyes seemed not to be focused on the objects that were ahead of him. 'Where d'you go from here?'

'I'm not sure. I've not worked it out.'

'So you're really. . . . ?' In alarm his father leaned forward and laid his hand on his knee. 'Tell me, John, have you discussed this with Catherine?'

'No—not yet.'

'But you will?'

'I don't know.'

'Well, you should!'

John turned to him, his eyes cold.

'If you're going to get involved in some sort of agitation it's only right that you should talk it over with your wife. You must consider her—you must think of your little boys. . . .' The wife, Tom thought, was probably not much help. But he persisted: 'D'you want to find a package on your front doorstep?'

John remained obdurately silent.

'What can you hope to achieve? You know perfectly well that if you meddle in this sort of thing, you put not only your own life in danger, but your family, your home. . . . Why sacrifice yourself for a principle?' He watched his son getting up from his chair.

'I'll have to go now. I shouldn't have kept you up so late.

198

His father reached out and caught at his sleeve, a light of desperation in his watery eyes. Gripping his arm, he tried to summon up the eloquence of old-fashioned authority: 'John I *beseech* you. . . .'

John spent several hours driving around the quiet countryside. He was disturbed not so much by his father's fears for his safety as his cynicism about the effectiveness of any action taken by an individual. He thought of the hard-line politicians, who had no qualms about making themselves heard, but who were too extreme and too ill-educated to have any credibility outside their own following. Meanwhile, the people with real influence had become spectators. His father was right: he would make a fool of himself. He would be alone.

There was not a sound from within the house, only a faint sea breeze rustling the garden. It irritated him that there should be so many bolts to unlock where once the doors had been left open, and he swore as he fumbled with his keys. It was stuffy in the bedroom and he pulled back the curtains and noisily opened the windows, complaining to himself about his wife's personal habits. Moonlight flooded the room. She was lying on her back, half out of the bed-clothes, as though her dreams had been restless. At the sound of the windows being opened her eyelids fluttered, but she did not wake. She was moaning in her sleep. The sound angered him. What had she got to moan about? He stood over her, casting a shadow across her pale face. She looked like a crazy woman with her hair spread out all over the pillow and her lips twitching. He felt a need to humanize her:

'Catherine!'

She sat and stared at him, terrified. Her night-dress had fallen off her shoulder and he could see her breast, silvery-white against the dull whiteness of the cloth.

'Oh, it's you!' she said crossly. 'Whatever time is it?' Her first thought was that if she had known he was going to be so late she could have telephoned Martin.

John was about to tell her where he had been, but she turned over and huddled under the blankets, and he felt his isolation return. Undressing, he said: 'You could have been a little more welcoming—for all you know I might have been shot on the way home!' But then he was ashamed when he saw the fear in her eyes. He climbed in beside her and pulled her towards him.

'Oh, no!' she complained, 'I'm too tired!' He put his hands round her head to stop her turning her face away while he kissed her; then she was fighting him off. 'What's this? Are you trying to rape me?' She had forgotten how strong he was.

'You're my wife, aren't you?' As she struggled, he understood for the first time in his life why lust was regarded as a sin. She might have been a stranger, any shabby old whore from the back streets of Belfast. 'That's just too bad,' he whispered to her brutally when he felt the wetness of her cheek. What cause had she for tears? He lay back, exhausted, but as he stared at the eerie lights on the ceiling, he realised that he had forgotten the brand name of Danny's cigarettes, and he assaulted her again, this time mistaking her distress for a shuddering of ecstasy.

The sensation was unbearable—would it never end? She could no longer go on living with this man! If only. . . . This was the one occasion when she had the courage to hope that Martin might really leave his wife and she could be with him forever. When John was asleep she got up and went outside in her dressing-gown and wellington boots and sobbed, idiotically, over the flowers that her mother-in-law had helped her to plant. She ground her fists into her streaming eyes, thinking that, if she were to go on crying like this, her spirit would leak away. . . .

She saw him watching from the window, then a little later opening the front door, fully dressed, walking towards her. The moon was sinking and the brief night was already pale with birds chattering in the trees. She went on ahead and he followed her down to the sea.

'It's the shortest night of the year,' he said, as he caught up with her. He should apologize, he should ask her forgiveness, comfort her. Instead he sat down on a rock. 'I had such a dream. . . .'

'Did you? What did you see?'

'I was in Donegall Place. It was the middle of the winter and the Christmas tree outside the City Hall was all lit up and snow was falling. It was pretty except that all the buildings were on fire. Women were running out of them, weeping and passing bunches of flowers to one another as they fled from the explosions. I just sat on the kerb with my feet in the gutter, hiding my face. . . .'

'Then what?'

'I woke up.' He blinked at her, as if only at that moment awake.

'That's not a dream, it's a vision.' She reached out and touched his face, thinking how little she understood her intimate companion. He looked as tired and lined as his father.

'There's another dream that I've had quite often—oh, for years, on and off—but I've always felt too ashamed to tell it to anyone. . . .'

'Won't you tell me?'

'You'll laugh—you, of all people!' He rubbed his eyes. The sky was rapidly lightening and there were a number of sea-birds swooping in long arcs across the water. 'I don't know when I first started to have it—perhaps when I used to come up to Castle Hardwicke when you had just left school—or it may have been even before that. But in it I have a sense of bliss that I've never experienced in waking life. You see,' he took her hand, 'I dream that I am being received into the Catholic Church! At first I feel a little guilty about it—after all, it's rather a shocking place to find oneself—then that passes away and I realise that this is what I have been longing for all my life and every problem seems to fall off me—unburdening of the soul and all that!'

Catherine did laugh. She put her arms round him: 'Only an Ulster Protestant could dream such a dream!'

He pulled her down on his knees and held her against him. 'I saw something yesterday evening. . . .' He hesitated: 'Never mind—I'll tell you about it another time.' From the foreshore they could hear stirrings of activity, dogs barking, lowing cattle and the head-lights of a car through the morning mist. 'Catherine,' he stroked her hair, smoothing it away from her forehead, 'if I really believed in something, would you back me?'

'Why should you ask?' she said, thinking how much more important he was to her than her lover and how ironic that her passion should have been aroused by another man. 'I'm your wife.'

It was Margaret who arranged that the twins should come

201

home for the weekend. There were now only a few months left before Martin's term in Ulster would end and, although he had not yet been told where he was being transferred, she was afraid that they might be sent to some distant place where they would see less of their children. She was very excited when she met them at the airport.

On the Saturday she persuaded Martin to take them up to Lough Erne for boating and water skiing. They passed Castle Hardwicke on the way and, when he told her he had once spent a night in the fine house above the water, she became curious to see the place and suggested they call in on his former hosts. It was with reluctance that he turned off up the bumpy drive; he felt uncomfortable arriving there with his wife and was nervous lest Desmond should say something indiscreet. The day was mild and overcast and it seemed to him that the landscape was oppressively green. Margaret commented on the nettles growing on either side of the drive, but she admired the setting of the house—from a distance it looked like an old print—and the handsome steps curving up to the open front door.

No one answered when they rang, so she walked in. It embarrassed Martin when Sonia discovered them looking up at the family portraits as if they were in a museum. The bear had disappeared from the hall. He thought at first that Sonia had forgotten who he was, but, when she peered at him more closely, she smiled to herself and he felt relieved to learn that Desmond was out. She gave them a drink and chatted for a while, mostly about her horses, then with a vague excuse left the room. While Margaret inspected the furniture trying to assess its value, Martin was thinking of his first meeting with Catherine, which now seemed a very long time ago, recalling her changing expression and the exact words she had used; the atmosphere was over-weighted by memories. He felt uncomfortable when his wife criticized the frayed carpets and the cracked mouldings on the ceiling.

'Well, she's obviously not going to come back.' Margaret looked at her watch. 'Very casual, I must admit! I suppose it's typically Irish to be hospitable one day and forget you the next?'

Would Catherine forget? He was gazing at a pastel that had

been done of her as a child; the resemblance was not very striking. He stood in front of it for so long that when he turned round he was put out to find his boys watching him; they were growing up, their eyes questioning, cynical.

'I suppose that's Catherine Mulholland? I'd forgotten she was his sister.' Margaret screwed up her eyes, trying to decipher the artist's signature. 'I don't care for those prettified society portraits.'

As they got back into the car, Margaret loudly complaining about the rudeness of their hostess, Martin felt so depressed he could hardly speak to her. Although they were lucky there was no rain, it seemed to him the afternoon, spent boating amid scenery he had once thought idyllic, would never end. In his abstraction he slipped and wet his shoes climbing onto the jetty, which gave him an excuse for bad temper on the long journey home.

Sunday was an anti-climax with nothing arranged and the sky so oppressively low that the far side of Belfast Lough was veiled in greyness. Margaret spent the morning cooking lunch for her hungry schoolboys and watched with satisfaction as they wolfed down their food. They had just passed their fifteenth birthday. Margaret, who had made herself well-informed on the subject, talked cricket with Roger, the more confident of the two, while his brother, Bill, stared moodily out of the window. They needed a hair-cut, Martin said, and told Bill to sit up straight and stop picking his nails. After lunch the boys slipped away to listen to pop records in their rooms, while he helped his wife with the washing up. This finished, she settled into an armchair with the Sunday papers.

'Your turn,' she smiled up at him, 'I reckon I've done my stuff.'

She took off her shoes and stretched out, absent-mindedly exercising her toes. He remembered admiring her legs when he had visited her in her room in Somerville. In those days she had been vivaciously intellectual, discussing the Italian poets as she poured out the tea, and he had been impressed by her self-assurance. Now, as he watched her raising her eyebrows, making faces at the newspaper, he thought: she always was complacent! He had eaten too much and the house still smelled of food, while the walls vibrated with pop music. If he were married to

Catherine, would he still find Sunday the worst day of the week?

The boys sulked when he suggested they go out for a walk. 'Good idea!' their mother backed him up. 'I'll have a smashing tea waiting for them before they catch their plane.' She turned her chair and switched on the television, leaning forward to watch the programme with a smile of eager interest, her chin on her fists.

'We'll do some climbing in the Mourne Mountains.' Martin held open the car door; but, before they had got inside, he ordered them back to the house to change out of their trendy shoes. While driving he lectured them on the beauty of the surroundings and it was not until he glanced in the mirror and saw their yawns that he realised he was talking to himself.

He drew the boys' attention to a barn with 'I am the Way, the Truth and the Life' painted immaculately across the corrugated roof; 'Jesus saves' was nailed to a gate. Roger sat up and looked out with indifference. Martin was irritated to see that he was chewing gum. He caught sight of a white-washed farm sunk down at the foot of a lane and thought: what a charming little place! But, almost at once, his delight changed to apprehension as he wondered what was going on behind those small darkened windows—who lurked within the ragged trees? It was the time of year when Lambeg drums were being played in back yards and alleyways in preparation for the Twelfth; he had heard the sound reverberating across the fields, muffled but insistent. At a bend in the road he saw 'I.R.A.' painted on the tarmac and he wondered if this was a Catholic area. He had been sceptical when Catherine had told him the locals could recognise one another. 'You think of this place,' she had said, 'as England gone wrong and you're irritated by the unreasonableness of the people. You don't understand that faith is more important to them than common sense and material things have less reality than the world which is unseen. The failure of the British in Ireland is due to lack of imagination.' Now, driving through the country-side, so quaintly pastoral with its little round hills, its patch-work of tiny fields, he thought of the baffling friendliness of the inhabitants and felt that the problem was beyond him. He would never understand.

The mountains loomed above, bluish-purple, their peaks

obscured by white, lambent clouds; there was a suggestion of sublimity as if some sort of peace was to be found up there, or just over the top on the other side. The boys grumbled at getting out of the car. As they tramped across the bogland, intensely aromatic, dank and windless, it depressed him to find that he could think of nothing to say to them. He was missing Catherine. And yet she was with him; he could no longer see the landscape through his own eyes. He thought how curious it was that this emotion should cut across his other interests and affections and that when she was absent he should feel so bored that his ordinary life had lost its savour.

They were walking along the banks of a stream where the path was flanked by gorse bushes, whose yellow flowers were only just beginning to fade. Their fragrance was so reminiscent that he surprised himself by thinking that at least in another country he would no longer be tormented by the scent of the gorse. But how long would it last, this painful emptiness? Would it continue once he had been transferred to a different place, or would he be cured by the stimulus of a new job? For Catherine there would be no such change and he reflected guiltily on the damage he must have done to her marriage. She was over-romantic. He even resented her for his own misery at the thought of leaving her behind.

The boys had lagged and were out of earshot, muttering to one another. How would they react if they knew that their father lived for secret meetings with a stranger? The air was very still, humming with insects. He felt as claustrophobic as in his own drawing-room with the stale smell of lunch, the scattered papers, his wife settling down in front of the television, cheerfully ignorant of his malaise. He had not taken it into account that he might find himself in conflict between the two women. Catherine he associated with his feelings for the country, poetic, other-worldly (he had been offended when she had once said: 'it's just sex, that's all!'); whereas his real life was with sensible Margaret who he had been relying on to save him if he became too ensnared. Catherine had said that the influence of Ireland was corrupting: it was not a place for the positive and the energetic, people who stayed there too long became as vague and easy-going as the natives.

He had not realised how fast he had walked. While he was

waiting for the boys to catch up, he noticed that the gorse bushes were full of tiny cobwebs. At first he was intrigued and peered into the complex of prickles where insects struggled in mesh after mesh—the whole bush was a trap! He remembered Catherine's child, Patrick, smiling with false innocence: 'I saw a spider wrapping up a fly to put away in its larder! The little boy was too golden, spoiled, and he had already acquired a swaggering, upper class arrogance. There were times when he had looked at his mother's friend as if he knew. Martin gazed at the tiny webs and was disturbed, when his sons, coming up unexpectedly, caught him groaning aloud. Catherine was rich, he reminded himself, and had a built-in advantage. His remorse about making her unhappy was exaggerated.

During the rest of the walk he made an effort to talk to the twins, questioning first one then the other. But they had sensed his estrangement from them and his bullying interest increased their hostility. It began to rain. As he ran out of conversation, Martin was oppressed by a need to relieve himself, which became more acute as he suddenly felt a prudish reluctance to turn away from them into the bushes. When they were back in the car and down in the village, he parked outside a public lavatory, saying uneasily, man-to-man: 'I must take a leak.'

He was followed down the steps. The stranger was middle-aged, not as tall as Martin and, wearing a raincoat and a shabby cap, his appearance nondescript apart from his glittering eyes. The place was empty. Although he remained at a discreet distance, Martin was conscious of those eyes upon him as he unbuttoned, thinking at first he was imagining the interest. Then the pervert's eyes became nightmarish and he began to sweat. Going over to the basin, he splashed cold water on his face to steady himself. When he turned to go the way was blocked. The man opened his raincoat to reveal a placard: 'See ye the Lord?' Martin edged away and he advanced, his fanatical eyes glaring as he caught hold of Martin's lapel. The whispering voice was curiously high-pitched:

'See ye Him?'

Martin pushed him aside and ran up the steps and continued running until he reached the car.

'Seen a ghost?' said Roger. 'Your hand's shaking.' They chatted to him quite amiably on the way home and, through his sons' friendliness, he became aware how much he longed for normality. The landscape with its shifting lights now seemed to him treacherous, melancholic. It would be a relief to get away from this country that was so bewilderingly enclosed, to be set free from his own confusion. Although he had dreaded leaving Ireland, he began to hope that the transfer to his new posting might come earlier than expected.

'It's you!' Felicity's large eyes seemed to protrude, showing their whites, as she opened the door to John.

'I'm not disturbing you?'

'Oh, not at all!' she closed the door and let him in and he squeezed past, careful to avoid touching her. 'No, as it happens,' there was a suggestiveness in her smile, 'tonight I am alone.' She went upstairs and led him into her living-room. 'It's a dreadful tip in here. You see, I sue this as my studio.'

John looked around, wondering where to sit. Catherine had spoken, it had seemed to him with envy, of her friend's bohemian life. Felicity continued to apologize for the mess. 'That's all right,' he said, adding ineptly, 'after all, you're an artist.' He was surprised that she should seem so nervous of him. 'There's something I wanted to talk to you about.'

'Ah, yes—of course.' Felicity smiled, suddenly more at her ease, thinking that he had found out about Catherine. With sympathy she laid her hand on his arm. 'Well, won't you sit down and make yourself comfortable?' He found a chair and she seated herself at his feet, looking up at him. Embarrassed by her manner, he found it hard to begin, and he asked her about other things, her job, her painting—she even raised the subject of her broken marriage. He had come to her for consolation, thought Felicity, looking at his lined, anxious face; although she had never liked John Mulholland, she was nonetheless gratified that it should have ended like this. 'I won't eat you,' her hand was resting on his knee, 'you needn't be so backward!'

It was only then that John realised she had thought his intentions were amorous, and he remembered the stories he had heard of her lovers, her emancipated views. 'I seem to have given you the wrong impression.' He had meant to push her hand away, but instead he found that he was holding it. 'I'm afraid I'm boringly monogamous.'

'Why naturally—I should have known!' Offended, she withdrew her hand. 'Married to a lovely girl like Catherine. . . .' There was an awkward silence. Then she glanced up at him slyly: 'But what about her—is she boringly monogamous?'

'Catherine?' he edged back his chair. Although it was quite late, there was a summer glow in the window. He began to notice that the room was very dirty and was repelled by the clotted paint rags lying on the floor. She was watching him, her eyebrows raised, laughing at him. 'I really wouldn't know,' his reply was cold. He had not come to talk about his wife. He frowned, trying to concentrate, but was distracted by her amiable smile, suddenly reminded of the popular saying: 'it's their eyes—something wrong with the eyes!' If she had been a Protestant he would have felt simply that the girl was unreliable, rather tedious. But, as it was, he thought: she's typical—you can't trust Them, and was depressed that, in spite of his theories, he should remain instinctively so prejudiced. He had not answered her question. When he looked up, he saw that she was now shrinking from him. Her social *faux pas* had become obscured by a deeper apprehension. 'I suppose to you,' he said, 'I'm a hard-faced Prod?'

At this she seemed relieved and uncoiled herself. 'Perhaps you'd like a drink?'

'If you're offering it? I'm not that good-living!'

She gave him a glass of beer. 'I suppose you drink whisky at home? This is all I can afford.'

'Beer is very pleasant at this time of year.' As she sat down opposite him, fussily patting her hair and pushing an old newspaper out of sight, he thought of Catherine: they were friends, had been at school together. He said: 'I came here to ask if you had any contacts within the Catholic business community?'

'In business?' she looked at him in amazement. Most of her friends were artists or connected with the University.

'It's a small place,' he persisted. 'Your father, for instance, Judge O'Keefe—he must know most people?'

After a pause, she said: 'I don't see much of him.'

John sipped his beer. He did not want to discuss her rebellion against her family. 'I gather from Catherine that you have an interest in politics?'

'Sure, I have an interest! Is there anyone in this country who's immune?'

'True enough—there's no one who doesn't talk about it, on whichever side they may be.' It took him some time to get over his inhibition about explaining his mission. 'It's the Catholics I want to win over,' he said. 'People in England might listen to them where they'd be deaf to the most eloquent appeal from the other side. Nothing can happen in this country—there can be no development at all until the violence ends. The English don't seem to believe in evil and perhaps because of this they can't face the reality. They manage somehow to ignore the carnage by talking politics—in the hope that the problem will miraculously fade away without them having to take any unpalatable decisions about dealing with it.' He glanced at her, expecting an adverse reaction, but she was staring at her hands, like a little girl being lectured by the headmaster. 'If the violence were brought to an end, of course, this would have to be followed by some attempt at better relations between the two communities. But the longer it goes on the more difficult it's going to be. And it's my opinion, as they're in the minority, that it's the Catholics, who will suffer the most.

Felicity murmured about internment.

'But this is a sophistry!' he heard himself shouting at her. 'Don't you understand the meaning of terror? Unless they leave the country the internees have no choice but to go back into action. You can't really be saying that you sympathise with the atrocities of the I.R.A.? I read in the paper today that they put a bomb in a pram and left the baby sitting on top. How long d'you want this to continue?'

'Oh, it's dreadful!' At the thought of the baby Felicity's eyes had filled with tears. 'I know people who have links with the I.R.A. and I've said to them: a united Ireland's one thing. But all this horror—can it be right?'

'You actually bother to ask,' John was incredulous, 'can it be right?' He thought of the hopeless impracticality of the Irish and the little boys from Catholic slums, who, interviewed on television about what they would like to do when they grew up, who would cheerfully reply: to die for Ireland! But the other side were no better. Catherine's daily had told her that the Troubles would soon be at an end because Bibles were being smuggled into convents in the South and that peace would come without a struggle as the Catholic population was getting ready to receive the Light.

'I just don't know,' Felicity twisted her hands. 'To tell you the truth, it's nearly driving me back to the Church. But then, the Churches, what are they doing about it?'

'Not a marvellous record,' John agreed, 'considering their common ideal of human charity.'

'I've been mean to you,' she took away his beer glass. 'I do have some whisky—but I only keep it,' she lowered her eyes, 'for specials.' When she sat down again, she asked him: 'You've got a good idea, but how far d'you expect to get with it?'

John held up his glass and looked beyond her to the window, where, through the amber liquid, the sunset was intensified as if the sky above Belfast was aflame. 'The only man I've spoken to so far was sympathetic, but he told me that trying to clear up the I.R.A. was like sowing dragon's teeth—remove all the men and their place will be taken by youths, or even girls.'

'And, he wouldn't commit himself?'

'No, unfortunately not—didn't see the point. I suppose the fact is that, although most will agree with me, very few would be prepared to act.'

'Then why d'you do it?'

'You mean why do I risk my neck over what would appear to be a quixotic exercise?'

'Yes,' she topped up his glass, 'why?'

'We live in a society which is no longer democratic and where the individual feels himself helpless and submerged. But, in spite of the frustrations of this time, certain freedoms still remain and, if enough people who feel as I do would take the trouble to make themselves heard, we could end up as a political force. You could ask: what can one person do? But you only have to look at the really tough Protestants to see that they have no inhibitions about stating their case. It will be an unhappy day for people like you if they end up running the country.' Sipping her whisky, he did not like to add that he had been brought up to believe that the privileged members of society had an obligation to play their part in terms of public service. Then it occurred to him that this attitude, with its emphasis on the responsibility of the individual, belonged specifically to the

Protestant ethic. 'I daresay you think I'm pig-headed ? A fool ?
But there comes a point when, if you believe there is something
you ought to do and you don't do it, you can't live with yourself.'

She wrote down some addresses. 'But you won't mention my
name ?' She leaned forward, and stroked his sleeve. 'You
promise that ? I can rely on you ?'

'Don't worry,' he put the piece of paper in his pocket. But
as he got up to go, he began to wonder why she should have
questioned him about his wife, and again he looked at her with
suspicion. 'I'm boringly reliable.'

Felicity blushed, thinking of Martin and Catherine's endless
telephone calls about whether or not he really cared for her. At
the door she impulsively kissed him on the cheek: 'John
Mulholland, I've misjudged you—you're not such a bad soul!'

Aunt Maude was momentarily popular with the children
because she arrived with chocolates.

'Very bad for their teeth,' said Aunt Sadie.

'Remember to say "thank-you",' Catherine whispered to
Patrick, but it was Edward who went up to his great-aunt and
dutifully kissed her when she inclined her stout frame.

The drive was blocked with a selection of cars belonging to
two generations of the Mulholland family; Aunt Sadie's chauf-
feur had retired to the kitchen.

'It's very good of you, Catherine, to have had us all,' Tom
looked around him, pleased to see his sons and his grand-
children gathered together. He frowned when he saw George
lifting a carry-cot into the house, thinking it must have been a
disappointment that his first child was a girl.

'I'm sure you're glad you've at last come round to having a
deep freeze,' said Alicia. 'Quite an effort to feed so many of us!'

Catherine received the compliment dully. She had arranged
the lunch party not out of friendliness for her in-laws but as a
cure for her own lethargy. The long hours at home had become
a torture. Although John was often out in the evenings, Martin
had told her that it would be quite unthinkable for him to get
away with Margaret still around. Her dependance on him would
not have been so abject if she went out to work, but she was so

unskilled that there was nothing she could do without a long period of training. If she were to take up some sort of career, John would not actually prevent her, but he would disapprove, feeling that she was neglecting her family; the only respectable occupation open to someone in her position was to join the charitable committees run by women like her mother-in-law.

Before going inside Alicia insisted that Catherine take her on a tour of the garden, where she scolded her for the aphids on the roses. 'Of course the winter was much too mild,' she complained. 'One thing to be said for a hard winter is that it really does deal with the bugs.' She rubbed her hands with sadistic relish, 'it kills them off!' It was a dark summer day, still dry, but smelling of rain. Catherine followed her mother-in-law keeping her eyes on her broad, vigorous back. The damp greenery seemed distilled in the air; it was like an element in itself, Catherine thought, one could swim in it—or drown. She envied the older woman her passion for plants.

In the drawing-room Liz fussed over her baby and Maude, peering into the carry-cot, enquired about her feeding habits and when she would be old enough to eat anything interesting. John poured out the drinks and, when his father objected that they were too strong, replied with an abruptness that was out of character, causing a moment of unease while people glanced from the one to the other, wondering what was the reason for the coolness between them. The silence was broken by Tom's younger brother, Arthur, white-haired but still curiously boyish, whose rosy face gleamed as he described a blast he had witnessed at the Europa hotel.

'You should have seen the plate glass windows,' he exclaimed delightedly, 'they were falling like leaves!'

'Is that their eighth bomb?' said Peter. 'It's a wonder the place is still standing.'

'It's mostly journalists who live there—they concoct their stories round the bar.' Sadie seated herself, clutching her hand-bag, and George could not resist teasing her:

'In which case it doesn't matter?'

'Oh, by the way,' Alicia tapped Sadie on the shoulder, 'have you heard about Brenda McTaggart?' Expecting gossip, Sadie's eyes brightened maliciously. 'Poor Brenda, she's lost her plumber—he had a lethal package in the boot of his car!'

To please her mother-in-law Carol tittered.

Tom stood in the centre of the room, glaring under his eye-brows: 'We will not discuss the Troubles!' He went over to the window and looked out at the garden with its water-logged vegetation and the low clouds overhanging the sea.

Before going in to lunch they went through to the kitchen to look at the children; Carol's little boy, Jonathan, was not old enough to sit up at the table.

'What's that you're eating, dear?' Maude asked Edward.

'Shepherd's pie.'

'Why's it called "shepherd's" pie?' said Patrick.

'I expect,' Arthur's eyes twinkled, 'it's because it's made of shepherds.' There was excessive, callous laughter at the weak joke.

Over lunch Alicia praised the flower arrangements and Carol asked for recipes. When Tom congratulated her, Catherine felt that she only had standing with him for her cooking. She was unable to swallow the tiny portion she had given herself, and listened to them talking about their summer holidays and food on the continent: Peter said the only point in going abroad was to eat and to lie in the sun. (Martin was due to leave in October and during part of the short time that was left he, too, would be away on holiday). George and Liz had found a little place in Corsica—very secluded, but expensive, frequented only by the most charming people from French and Italian society. Was he joining the Eurocracy? John sneered at his brother, finding the trivial conversation intolerable. Sadie complained that Tom had been wrong to send his boys to English public schools where they learned to give themselves airs and acquire a taste for lavish living. As Sadie was the richest person in the room this was a cause of discreet amusement to the younger generation.

It was George who rose to help her when Catherine began clearing the plates. 'I suppose I ought to be doing that?' John rested his hands on the arms of his chair as if preparing to stand up. George wheeled the trolley into the pantry and began stacking the dishes.

'You're being very domesticated,' said Catherine. She told him he looked much better now without his moustache.

He was pleased: 'You think so?' He glanced into the passage, then closed the door. But, when he tried to catch hold of her, she slipped out of his grasp and he said petulantly: 'It's hardly flattering to have been included in your duty lunch. I suppose you thought you'd get rid of the whole lot of us in one boring go?'

She eyed the door, but he was leaning against it. 'Well, if you want the truth, the answer is yes.'

'You've changed. I used to think you were a sweet little thing, but you've become a bitch. Doesn't make you any the less attractive—more so.' He advanced towards her, 'you get sexier every time I see you!' He pinned her against the wall and kissed her, slipping his hand inside her dress. 'I've always thought John was the lucky one of the family. . . . Why don't we meet for a drink sometime?' Catherine was so shocked to be pro-positioned by her brother-in-law that she submitted limply to his caresses, thinking: three years ago this not only would not, it could not have happened—their society was deteriorating. But, then, who was she to criticize? Ever since she had met Martin she had been pursued by other men as if the affair had marked her. 'Well, what about it?' George was squeezing her breasts with both hands: 'You're bursting for it—you're as keen as I am!' The door opened and he let go, clumsily backing into the trolley so that the cutlery rattled.

'I'm so sorry!' Ellen stared.

Catherine made a pretence at dignity: 'That's all right we'd come to get the next course. . . .'

They returned to the dining-room and John got up to carve. 'You've been out a long time—what's herself been up to?'

'I wish you'd stop calling me that!'

'What now?' he glanced at her, sharpening the knife. They stood side by side at the serving-table, piling up the plates, tensely opposed.

'The meat's too rare,' Maude poked at it with her fork.

'Not rare enough,' said George, 'you should see the blood!'

The door opened and Edward tip-toed into the room to whisper to his mother: 'Patrick's being naughty and hitting Jonathan—he won't do what Ellen tells him.' Carol looked up in alarm. Catherine frowned at the child, angry with him for telling tales.

'He's hitting someone younger than himself?' said his grand-father. He turned to Catherine: 'You've spoiled that boy!'

Patrick then entered, defiantly unrepentant. He pointed at Catherine's wine glass: 'I'd like some of that.'

'What a pretty suit,' Liz fingered the material. 'I bet Mummy didn't buy it in Belfast!'

'He's kept his curls,' Maude winked at him, holding out her own glass. 'He always was the bonny boy.' Patrick smiled at his great-aunt and strolled across to her, rapping his finger-nails against the backs of the chairs.

Tom caught him by the arm: 'What's this I hear about you bullying your young cousin?'

Patrick reddened and thrust out his jaw. 'Let me go,' he said, 'this is my house!'

John got up, flinging his napkin on the floor, and dragged the child outside where he smacked him viciously. At the sound of his screams Catherine laid her hands over her ears.

'That's what he needs,' said Tom, 'a father's influence.' John returned, followed by Patrick, who ran, sobbing, down the far end of the room. 'So now you come crying to mother, do you?'

He clung to Catherine, but she did not dare to comfort him.

'Get back to the kitchen,' John rounded up his children, 'both of you!'

Sadie raised her fork and sniffed at the meat as if it was contaminated: 'Garlic!'

'It's the modern taste,' Maude shook her head sadly. 'But the vegetables, Catherine, dear, they're really excellent, particularly the cabbage. It's not everyone who knows how to time the boiling of a cabbage.'

'I will say that for my little wife,' John's voice was too hearty, 'she can cook a good cabbage!'

'One down for Women's Lib!' Catherine rose from the table and left the room.

She must grow up! she tried to brace herself—it just didn't do to have the sulks in the middle of lunch. She ran into the bedroom and flung herself down on the unmade bed digging her fists into her eyes to stop her tears. Martin was being sent to Tokio. He seemed pleased by the posting: it would be an interesting change. Tokio! she had stared at him unbelieving. If it had been anywhere in Europe there might have been some chance of their meeting—but Japan! It's better that way, he had told her, it's pointless to cling to the past; nostalgia was the vice of the Irish—she was, he said, too Irish. Saying good-bye was merely part of the routine of service life.

She had been so upset that she had lacked the courage to suggest that if he was trying to offload her he could do it more tactfully. She could imagine him congratulating himself on having got over it sensibly, and might even turn it to advantage by confessing to his wife so that she tried harder, taking him less for granted, giving a boost to his marriage.

He had blamed her for her lack of reality. The choice was simple: either he went to Tokio with her or he went with his wife and his commitment was to his family—as hers, he reminded her, should be to her family. That was not the point, she had wanted to protest, but could find no way of expressing her anguish at his sudden coldness. But what else had she expected? Like John, he was treating her as if she were irresponsible. It was part of the system, she realized, that where women are protected in their marriages they remain immature. When he had complained that she made him feel guilty, she sensed that the guiltier he felt the worse he would treat her. It was part of the system, too, that women accept bad treatment and that, if sex enters a relationship, the man in the long run will automatically be abusive unless the woman happens to be his wife and his desires coincide with his conscience. Because Catherine felt herself to be in the wrong she saw no choice but to endure her wretchedness in secret.

She got up, dry-eyed, and looked out at the sea where a silver gleam in the greyness, suggesting change and hope, added an irony that she found unendurable. It was going to end and she would have to live without him. . . . But how? I will never be happy, she thought, unless I rid myself of a childish craving for love. Without really admitting to herself what she was doing, she walked slowly across the room and opened a cupboard door, went away again to fetch a chair so that she could stand on it, reaching up to the shelf where John kept his gun. I'm just looking at it, she said to herself, I'm not going to use it. She took it out and opened it to make sure it was unloaded; the bullets were at the back of the shelf wrapped up in a piece of cloth. Every day on the school run she passed a jetty, which was wide enough to take a car and she had often thought how simple it would be just to drive off. She could hear the children in the corridor, Patrick's voice. When Martin was gone, Patrick would still be there. Or she could have another child—Martin's child. . . . The stupidity of her thoughts aggravated her self-contempt and it was not her real distress but her embarrassment at having to return to the dining-room to face her bewildered in-laws that made her reach out for the bullets, undoing the cloth and rolling the small pieces of metal, obsessively, from hand to hand.

There was a knock on the door. Alicia entered without waiting for a reply and Catherine barely had time to push the things out of sight.

'Ah, there you are! Poor old John was getting worried about you.'

'Was he?' Catherine climbed down from the chair. 'Why didn't he come and find me himself?'

Alicia glanced at the unmade bed, then looked for somewhere else to sit down. 'Now that we're alone, my dear, there's a little point I've been wanting to discuss with you. Your girl, Ellen— oh, I know she may be satisfactory in other ways—but when it comes to disciplining the children she really hasn't a clue. . . .' She hesitated, seeing the peculiar light in Catherine's eyes. 'What were you doing? What have you got up there?' Her daughter-in-law stiffened and she realised she had over-stepped the bounds of privacy. 'Oh, never mind! I'm a bossy old creature—I can't help it. You ought to know me by now!' She rose to her feet, two spots of brightness colouring her sallow cheeks and, to Catherine's horror, she put her arm round her. 'You've worked very hard to prepare us a delicious lunch and we've all made pigs of ourselves. You're a good girl!' Half-embracing, half-shaking her, she said: 'Come on, now! I expect it was a handkerchief you came out to get and somehow got side-tracked?'

How had she guessed? Although this had never been her intention, Catherine had been so over-wrought that it would only have taken a moment, an impulse of desperation for her to have loaded the gun and used it. She thought of the children coming in to find their mother in a pool of blood and how terrible it would have been for John, especially with his parents in the house—terrible even for them. . . . Although she had never been very fond of her mother-in-law, Catherine was now subject to a

new distortion where she saw her as her guardian and saviour—
her jailer. For, due to Alicia's intervention, things were as they
had been before and would remain: she was in a trap, imprisoned
by her own feelings.

She said: 'Yes, that's right—it was a handkerchief that I was
looking for.' Ashamed that she had been caught with the bed
still unmade, it seemed to her that, although she lived for a
radiant illusion, it was through trivialities that she would survive..

Peter and Carol's new house was well-placed for a view of the
Orange parades and they decided to give a party on the Twelfth.
John was reluctant to enter Belfast on that day: the Protestant
masses, he said, were on the verge of revolt and it was expected
that an exceptional turn-out would be followed by riots. Catherine sulked at the idea of missing an outing and it was to humour
her that he agreed to accept. Because it was no longer safe to go
to public places, there had been many more parties than usual
during the summer where, under a facade of brittle gaiety,
everyone usually became very drunk and there were unpleasant
scenes; it was at these moments that the destructive effects of
frustration and despair became visible.

John was pleased when he woke up and saw the rain, thinking
that this would keep the crowds off the streets. But, when they
drove through the countryside, even the villages were full of
marchers with dripping children running alongside, waving
their flags. Soaked bunting did little to brighten the streets of
Belfast where they saw children rioting. The leaders were two
little girls who ran down the pavement with a flaming pram,
which they pushed through a doorway. Something caught fire
inside and the building began to smoke, but no one paid any
attention. They could hear helicopters whirring overhead and
sirens in the distance. Sinister graffiti all over the walls promised
death to informers, to Taigs, Prods, the Queen, the Pope, the
Army. The daubed message to all factions was: 'Beware!' The
barricades were up, the Protestants having been permitted by a
conciliating administration to set up no-go areas in competition
with their rivals, and large sections of the city were sealed off.
The streets were full of umbrellas as the populace hurried out

to see the bands, whose piping and drumming carried erratically above the noise of the traffic. Military vehicles added to the congestion and Carol was anxious because they arrived so late.

'We were wondering whether to go on without you—but then these days one wouldn't dare to leave the house open.' The house was still being furnished and she took Catherine upstairs to show her a new wall-paper. 'All sorts of people have turned up that we never invited. I don't know half their faces, let alone their names. Already Peter's had to go out to buy some more drink because at the rate they're going we won't have enough to last the day.' Although the windows were closed, they could hear music through the trees of the suburban gardens. 'Better than machine guns,' said Carol: 'We're kept awake at night by shooting in the Falls.'

Everyone gathered up their umbrellas and walked down to the end of the road, filing past a tidy barricade that had been put up by the Army. Catherine contrived to remain at the side of Walter Blackwell, one of the official guests, who worked for the Foreign Office. Tall and well-groomed, he picked his way with distaste between the puddles.

'We've met a number of F.O. types,' she said casually. 'I don't suppose you know Martin Evans?'

'Martin? Yes, I know him well. I had dinner with them a couple of nights ago.' She lowered her eyes, depressed by the thought of his normal life, the dinner party where he would be pouring the wine while Margaret served up. 'Have you met his wife? She's an interesting woman. Good linguist—which, of course, is a bonus for him. I was trying to persuade her,' he chuckled to himself, 'that it was time she learned a bit of Gaelic.'

'Does she know Swahili?'

Walter looked down at her. 'One thing I have noticed is that the Irish, in spite of their famous humour, seem remarkably unable to take a joke against themselves. Or perhaps this only applies to the North?'

'That's right,' said Catherine, 'we're a different breed—less sympathetic.' She edged away from him and joined Desmond, who had come up for the day with a group of people from Fermanagh. Ambrose, as usual, was alone. Sonia warned her not to question him about his wife: she had been eccentric before, but now she was so melancholic there was talk of committing her to an asylum. There had been a number of casualties among their friends, she observed, as if the Troubles had had an obliquely undermining effect, accentuating whatever weakness or vice was already there: the temperamental had become depressive and some of those who drank too much were sinking into alcoholism. It hadn't made much difference to her, said Desmond. When she laughed her breath smelled of gin: she was immune—having grown up in Poland at the end of the War, she had seen worse.

The marchers tramped past in a procession that would last throughout the day. A smart band with colourful banners would be followed by a ragged collection of long-haired youths, waving bottles and dancing in the street with sluttish girls; then a Temperance society or a group of respectable men wearing bowler hats, who jerked their elbows in time to the drumming. The leader of kilted pipers did spectacular things with his band stick and was applauded. Some marched past in silence, but often the music was quite professional—rousing and jolly— though the members of a few of the more unruly sections had already relapsed into drunken singing of Orange ballads.

Sonia said: 'That is Ulster walking past.'

'The *canaille*,' Desmond corrected her.

It was one thing for Desmond to criticize. But, when Walter turned up his handsome nose, exclaiming: 'Rubbish people!' the Ulstermen gathered round eyeing him with malevolence. 'My solution,' he was leaning elegantly on the umbrella, which, since it was now only drizzling, he had been reluctant to unroll,' to the problems of Belfast is two good football teams!'

John muttered to Ambrose: 'That man's lucky he doesn't get his nose punched!'

But, although there was a little cheering and flag-waving, the crowds on the pavement were mostly silent and it was noticeable that the festive character of the marches had disappeared, leaving their original menace as a show of force. John watched with dismay, thinking: what could the Army do with a mob like that? Under Direct Rule the Protestants had been allowed to mobilize and in their no-go areas they practised exactly the same brutalities as the I.R.A., intimidating the inhabitants and setting up 'kangaroo' courts with savage punishments. He had been disturbed to read that open-air services had been held in the streets. Was it divine inspiration that had given them the courage to confront the Army in such numbers that the generals had had to be called out to plead with them and television viewers had realized that, in spite of the efficiency of modern weapons, a popular revolution was still possible? Immediately afterwards Mr Whitelaw had tried to do a deal with the I.R.A. with an offer of peace on their own terms. With the further unrest that followed this, it seemed to be the opinion of the British Government, on seeing the violence spreading to the opposite camp, that some sort of balance had been achieved. While Protestants were now entering the detention centres, the I.R.A. were still being released, with a cry of open defiance: 'One more heave, boys, and we're there!' The two sides were murdering each other every day and it seemed that nothing could be done about it. In the middle of the morning a terrorist in the Falls had been watched by large numbers of people as he fired a machine gun into a body long after it was dead. A man had been found hanged by his tie from some railings, while others had been burned alive, locked into the boots of their cars. It was said that to speak with the wrong accent provided a sufficient motive. . . .

'There's a party going on,' said Desmond to acquaintances he met on the pavement: 'Why not come back and join us?'

'But there's not enough food!' Carol protested. On returning home she came near to tears when she saw how much cigarette ash had been stamped into her new carpets. Trying to be helpful Desmond went into the kitchen, opened a few tins and fried up all the eggs he could find. She had nothing to worry about— of course there would be enough food.

Over lunch people talked about the Alliance party. 'We've just joined,' said Carol. 'Nowadays all the nicest people are Alliance.'

'The Malone Road,' said Desmond, 'is good Alliance territory.'

John said: 'The "nicest" people have opted out.'

'And why not?' George paused, because his mouth was too full. 'What's the point in getting involved? The only thing to do is to keep going in the hope that one is still there when the thing blows over.'

'The cynicism of the privileged!' John turned from his brother with contempt.

'Not at all. Any other view is wasted idealism—or, to put it more bluntly, stupidity.' George wiped his mouth and reached out for a second helping. 'The Army are not allowed to clobber the yahoos any more than the old gang at Stormont. The important thing is that their presence here gives the appearance that measures are being taken. When the fact is that so long as the status quo is maintained they merely provide a front behind which anarchy rampages on all sides. With a bit of luck it could go on indefinitely!'

Walter seemed shocked by his language. 'We approve,' he turned to his hostess, 'of Alliance.'

'Because it's ineffectual?'

He ignored John's interruption. 'The Protestants had better behave themselves because when we have this referendum on the Border they're going to find that it contains a catch.' Walter laughed when he explained that, although it was obvious they were going to vote to a man for the continuing of the Union, in doing so they were committing themselves to the Westminster package, which was to include an opening of the doors to the South.

'And yet you seem surprised,' said John, 'that the "rubbish people", as you call them, have somehow got wind of your high-flown tricks? The average Prod is a law-abiding creature, but if they're thwarted and humiliated beyond a point they can endure and the dam breaks, they'd make a far more thorough job of it than any Mick. How come no one had the imagination to realize the effect it would have when the British Government were seen to be shaking hands with the I.R.A.?' In the papers Mr Whitelaw had been quoted as saying: 'I will surprise you gentlemen by the speed with which I shall act.' (However, the suspicions of the Ulster people were only guesswork; they were not, at that time, to know that the British had been prepared to offer all-Ireland elections on the future of the North and a place, after this event, for the I.R.A. at the conference table.)

'On, I say!' Walter's calm face showed animation when Carol offered him a choice of puddings: 'You've discovered my weakness!' He waited until she had piled up his plate before

222

objecting: 'What I can't understand is why everyone gets so excited about poor old Willie's efforts at peace-making. Granted it didn't work—and the sin, of course, is to be found out. But the general principle is perfectly sound. After all, dealing with terrorists is an accepted part of British diplomacy. We did it in Aden, we did it in Cyprus—there are plenty of precedents. And, as we pride ourselves on being a nation of empiricists, the precedent will tend to carry more weight than the principle.'

'Well, if you're as machiavellian as all that why did you miss an opportunity to scoop up the top members of the I.R.A's so-called "high command"?' Ambrose grimaced at him and he edged back his chair in alarm.

People had begun to leave the house, but not all of them took the trouble to say good-bye.

'We'll not bother with coffee,' said Desmond: 'Let's go straight to the liqueurs. What have you got?' He rummaged in the sideboard and brought out a bottle of green chartreuse. 'This'll do for a start.' Carol dabbed at the stains on her polished table. 'Don't worry about all that!' Desmond pulled her on to his knee, thinking she needed loosening up. 'Surely you Mulhollands are rich enough to afford servants?'

Ambrose eyed, through his small green glass, the other occupants of the room, his gaze fixing on Catherine. By now the remnants of the party were very drunk. They carried their glasses into the drawing-room where, in a moment of quiet, the continuing rumpus of the bands was audible and, to drown this, George put on a record. A few couples began to dance, but, when he made for Catherine, he was deftly intercepted by Walter.

'I thought we might resume our conversation,' he said, as they shuffled over the carpet. He had lost his neatness, she observed, and his speech was no longer so crisp. 'You've been avoiding me!' He took a firmer grip of her. 'Jolly good party, don't you think?'

'It's one way of filling in the time.' Although the afternoon was so dark, she could see lurid flashes beyond the window. It was the green chartreuse, she thought, but not even the drink was much help when she tried to pretend that this man was Martin. She was suffering from his absence. Walter startled her out of her reverie by asking:

223

'How did you come to know Martin?'

'Martin?' she stared at him, feeling persecuted. 'Martin who?'

'Martin Evans,' his hand was kneading her back. 'I thought you said you knew him?'

'Did I?' She saw Ambrose glaring at her. The other couples were stationary, hugging and kissing with abnormal abandon. She was astounded to see Carol with Desmond, his face jammy with lipstick.

Walter was annoyed when she refused to let him kiss her: 'I thought you were a friendly-looking girl!' On the excuse that she wanted a drink of water, she left him and went to the kitchen. Through the open door of the dining-room she saw her husband looking into Sonia's eyes, behind a blue haze, the room empty; she dug her nails into her fists, thinking that she would like to claw her sister-in-law's beautiful white face. Walter had followed her: 'Tell me about yourself?'

He had reminded her of her first meeting with Martin and she flared up at him: 'I'm not everybody's Irish colleen!'

John had found in Sonia an unexpected ally. 'In their attitude to terrorism,' he was saying, 'the British with their liberal traditions are as out of step with the times as the Catholic Church is on contraception.' He described his visit to Danny McQuade and she listened, fastidiously picking a speck off her black skirt. 'Afterwards, when I came home—' he hesitated; he was not a man who normally discussed his intimate feelings. The curious thing was that when I found Catherine lying asleep I felt quite vicious towards her.'

Sonia told him that the bear had been removed from the hall at Castle Hardwicke; Guy had taken it out and burned it after one of his colleagues in the U.D.R. had been murdered. 'But I expect it was just an excuse—he'd always had rather a thing against poor bear. I'd wondered for a moment if he was going to start generally smashing up the furniture.' She stretched out and yawned. 'People's standards have become degraded. I don't think anyone from outside could appreciate the dreariness of the Troubles—it's the poisoning effect of a submerged civil war where there isn't even the villainous satisfaction of having got something out of the system.' She fitted a cigarette to an ebony holder. 'The country's gone bitchy. Even for people like us, who're not in the thick of it. there's a sort of nerviness, as if your best friend might betray you.'

'Do you feel nervy?'

'I live behind walls,' she raised her glass, 'this.' The chartreuse was finished and people were drinking through the rest of the liqueurs.

'That wouldn't suit me,' said John, 'I'm too orthodox. But perhaps you have a recipe for sleep? If I sleep for too long I wake with the hallucination that I'm hearing a knock on the door.'

'And they've come for you?'

He nodded and she took his hand. Catherine appeared in the doorway, a dreadful expression in her eyes.

'Perhaps we'd better go through,' said Sonia. 'before we add to the bad blood.' Tightly holding his hand, she advanced towards Catherine, who fled as if she were seeing an infernal dream.

In the drawing-room the dancers were stamping their feet and singing to a popular record:

' "The people of Belfast are friendly and quiet
   It's just sometimes that they like a little riot
   Oh, Belfast, Belfast, wonderful town. . . ." '

Ambrose grabbed Catherine's arm: 'It's time we had a little talk. . . .' He pulled her towards him and began mauling her. 'You were always a pretty girl, but something's happened to you—you've come into your own!' He put his hand under her chin and jerked her face towards him. 'Who's been sexing you up? Is it a soldier?' She shook her head. 'Then one of those creeps in the Diplomatic—Walter, for instance?'

'No, Ambrose,' she whispered, 'it's not Walter.'

'But it is one of them, isn't it?' He shook her. 'D'you know what you are? You're a Quisling!' He picked her up and threw her across the room. The others watched and the needle could be heard scratching after the record had finished. No one, not even John, remonstrated with Ambrose, nor did they offer to help her as she slowly rose to her feet, her hand on the back of her neck, which felt as if it had been dislocated. Her brother sat down and buried his face in his hands.

225

'What's wrong with you?' Ambrose shouted at him: 'You blubbing?'

Desmond looked up, stupidly shaking his head. Then the dancing recommenced, and no attention was paid to Catherine when she left the room and went upstairs.

She lay down on the spare bed where the throbbing of dance music beneath her competed with the racket in the streets. She felt very sick and the room whirled: it was as if not only the material objects but also the spirit of the people around her were disintegrating. With desperate nostalgia she returned in memory to the time of Patrick's christening when, it now seemed to her, she had been perfectly content. She remembered John playing with the baby on the grass and the grass full of daisies. It seemed inconceivable that the country had then been at peace. The baby faded before an earlier image and, thinking of the days when John had first come up to Castle Hardwicke and he had told her that what he really liked was a quiet life, she fell into a stupor.

When she woke, the dance music had stopped, but she could still hear the bands, thumping and whistling and the wind slithering through the wet trees and, from somewhere not very far away, the familiar whine of sirens. In a few hours it would be dark and then the firing would start. Rain trickled in smears down the window. She saw John sitting at the end of the bed. She raised herself to speak to him—it was you I was thinking of, she had wanted to say—but she felt so ill that she sank down again on the pillow.

'I hadn't realized you were drunk,' he said. 'Is that why you were behaving so oddly?'

She reached out to him: 'Hold me!'

He got up and bent over her; then drew back. 'Well, I don't know that I will—your breath's awful!'

'That's John Mulholland!' A group of people turned to stare at him as John entered the television studio. He had persuaded an acquaintance on UTV to allow him to take part in a discussion group titled 'The Way Ahead'. There were three other men on the panel, a Republican, a social worker and Roger Banson, a member of the Alliance party, whom he had met before.

The interviewer, Joseph O'Brien, seeming to take it for granted that his face was well-known, shook them in turn by the hand without bothering to introduce himself. He had long hair, a straight black fringe and a drooping moustache and his modish clothes had been carefully chosen to look well in colour. It was the controversial programmes, he explained, that he enjoyed the most; the Troubles had made his job more exciting. Encouraging them not to feel inhibited when expressing their different views, he said that it was usual for people nearly to come to blows in front of the cameras and then to return to normal, joking and on good terms, as soon as the show was over. John looked round at the other members of the team, all of whom were wearing suits except Paddy Hennessy, the Republican, who had shown his contempt for the system by turning up in an open-necked shirt and a cardigan with a hole at the elbow; although he was already voluble, he was chain-smoking, while Roger Benson had begun furtively mopping his forehead.

'No need to be so nervous!' O'Brien seemed amused by their discomfiture in a scene where he, himself, was at ease. 'Just work out what it is that you want to get across. We've got fifteen minutes so that should give each of you time to have a fair crack of the whip.' He turned to John: 'You're being very quiet, but I suspect that you're the man who's really got the most to say. You asked to be put on this, didn't you?' John nodded. 'Well, perhaps you'd like to go over it with me—I understand you feel that the ruling caste in Ulster has become demoralized?' From the way he pronounced the word 'caste' John guessed that he had a chip on his shoulder. He was incensed to find himself being patted familiarly on the cheek: 'Watch it! You're the one I'm going to gun for!'

When they went into the make-up room John was surprised to find that the girls not only knew who he was but were competing to do his face. 'You've got presence—that's very important.' They laughed coquettishly when he grumbled that they had put mascara on his pale eyelashes: 'See how pretty we'll make you!' He noticed that O'Brien spent a long time in front of the mirror and was snappish with the assistants.

In the studio, in spite of the powdering, their faces began to shine while they waited under the heat of the arc lights and

227

large drops of moisture appeared on Roger Benson's forehead; he was so agitated he was unable to keep still. John leaned forward, thinking that O'Brien wished to speak to him; it took him a time to realise that he was talking to himself, rehearsing aloud his introduction: 'In Ulster today. . . .' Gesturing and raising his eyebrows, he was actually practising his expression. When the warning light came on he hissed at them: 'When I ask you a question you must answer at once—say anything you like—but keep talking!' Then they were on and, using exactly the same expressions, even the hand movements, he was explaining to the viewers that, joining him in the studio to discuss the problems of Ulster today were members of two political minority parties and, from the social and economic sphere, Gordon McMahon, who had first hand knowledge of the troubled areas and John Mulholland, representing industry—and the interests of the privileged sector. From this John suspected that whatever he tried to say would be misinterpreted. Whispering under his breath, 'Call me, Joe!' the interviewer started with Benson: 'Well, Roger, now what's the main obstacle as you see it?'

Stammering pitifully, the Alliance man began a speech about the need for conciliation and a better spirit of harmony between the two communities.

Obviously bored by his timid sincerity O'Brien turned to the social worker to ask with a facetious grin: 'What hope of harmony, Gordon, in Sandy Row?'

His cheeriness had misfired: Gordon solemnly described the bitter prejudices of people brought up on legends. 'The irony of it,' he said, 'is that the working classes in the Falls and Shankill have a great deal in common with one another in their general way of life.' He scratched his head, correcting himself without a smile; 'Though it's misleading to refer to them as the working classes when so many of them are unemployed. . . .'

'And now, John, you're the man with a positive solution to offer!' Confronted by his suave smile, John shifted uneasily. 'I take it you follow the Faulkner line that there's no sense in talking politics until the violence has been stamped out?' He frowned, as if in an effort to present fairly his own version of John's views. 'And to achieve this you would like to see a ruthless deployment of the armed forces—quite regardless of

the casualties among innocent civilians that this would involve?'
When John did not reply, he prompted: 'Have I got it right?'

'That's one way of putting it.' John knew he must commit himself, but he could feel his hands becoming clammy through a fear of being tripped up by his own words. 'Yes, that is right,' he looked firmly into the camera: 'I think the violence must be stopped—and, of course, the only people who can do this are the Army. As our politicians have been dismissed it is my hope that members of the business community will join together to put pressure on the British Government to see that a determined—and final—effort is made.

'Your hope, John?' the interviewer had dropped his voice, his eyes crafty. 'This is wishful thinking?'

John refused to address him by his Christian name. 'No, it is my intention to try to bring it about. The reason for my coming here this evening. . . .'

'It's people like the Mulhollands,' Paddy interrupted, 'who are the cause of the disturbances in this country. Everyone knows they're partisan—they've never employed a Catholic! It's because of him,' he pointed accusingly, 'that the boys are in the camps. . . . And it is my hope that they shall be set free as soon as possible! There can be no justice while internment lasts and no peace until the Army is withdrawn.'

Now it was John's turn to interrupt: 'Those are the demands of the I.R.A.!'

'The I.R.A?' Derisively Paddy tossed back his hair. 'Who's wasting their breath on them when the real danger comes from the gangs of Prods marching about wearing,' he circled his fingers over his eyes, 'goggles and stocking masks and frightening the populace out of their wits!'

'If the I.R.A had been dealt with they'd be off the streets. They're only there because the security forces give them no protection.'

Paddy slammed his hands down on the table, shaking the glasses of water. But, before he could object, O'Brien intervened: 'Gentlemen, please!' Delighted that the show was progressing stormily, he returned to John: 'Perhaps we could hear your views on the Protestant menace—or don't you see it as a menace?'

'I do indeed! It is one of my main complaints against the new

229

regime that it should have been allowed to take shape. The U.D.A. ought to have been proscribed!' The camera rested on John's face.

'Those are forceful words,' O'Brien drawled, playing for time: this he had not expected. 'A provocative statement at the very least in these days. . . .' He managed to insinuate a sense of danger. 'So I would be correct in quoting you—a member of the Protestant establishment—as saying that in your opinion the U.D.A. ought to be outlawed?'

'You would.' John glanced at Paddy who was lighting a cigarette from a stub. 'When Whitelaw first came over here he seemed somehow to close his eyes to the fact that there was a problem of law and order—it was nearly three months before he visited the Army Headquarters in Lisburn!'

'Is that so?' O'Brien was interested. Trying to catch him out, he asked: 'So it's on Mr Whitelaw that you lay the blame?'

Again the camera lingered on John while he paused, clearing his throat before replying in the affirmative. One of his golfing friends, a surgeon in the city's principal hospital, had written to the Secretary of State, sending him a photograph of a heap of severed limbs, in order to bring home to him the urgency of the situation; in reply he had received a note from a girl in the office informing him his communication had been filed. 'Yes,' said John, 'I do personally blame him for the worsening of the Troubles.'

The others glared at him in astonishment. The Alliance member stammered a defence of the Supremo, but the interviewer cut him short and turned to the Republican:

'Well, Paddy, as a representative of Catholic opinion could you be said to share this view?'

'Ah, now,' Paddy tilted his head to one side, 'you pose me a ticklish one.' He leaned his elbows on the table, resting his chin on his hands, and stared moodily into the camera. 'No, it couldn't be said that I was satisfied—but for the opposite reason. Mr Whitelaw, he seems to me to be far too slow and grudging—he's not been liberal enough, not by a long way. When the internees. . . .'

'How can you describe that man as a representative of Catholic opinion when he's a known sympathiser with the I.R.A?' John refrained from adding that, as such, his presence in the studio was an affront. 'The bulk of the Catholic population is as desperate for peace as anyone else. The only trouble is that many law-abiding Catholics, while they deplore the violence, are reluctant to raise their voices against it because of a whimsical nationalist sentiment that they knew perfectly well had nothing to do with the reality.' As the camera closed in on him, John became aware that the nearer he came to the truth the more unacceptable his views would be. He tried to fix his gaze on the centre of the lens: 'And it is to those people, you who are watching this programme now, that I appeal. . . .'

'I must remind you, Mr Mulholland,' the camera shifted to the stern face of the interviewer, 'that this is a discussion, not a political platform!' The camera travelled slowly over the members of the panel, ending with John. Then the programme was over. 'That was great!' O'Brien jumped up from his chair: 'What timing!' The others rose to their feet, blinking now that they were no longer under the lights, and Benson wiped his moist brow. 'I pride myself on producing something lively. It's when the insults start flying that the thing makes an impact— that was a fun show!' O'Brien shook John warmly by the hand: 'A very good first performance! We'll see you here—' his sharp eyes were asking beyond the question: 'You may have cause to visit us again, I hope?'

John tried not to appear too uncivil as he made his escape before he could be further interrogated. He had taken such a dislike to the man, with his fancy hair-cut and tricky manner, that he felt humiliated to discover how nervous he had been when he clasped his fingers. He went to the wash-room and scrubbed his hands as if they had been contaminated. A clown's face looked out at him from the mirror. He found the make-up girl and asked brusquely:

'Can you get this muck off me?'

'Sure,' she simpered at him. 'Just sit you down and lean back your head. Now close your eyes. . . .'

'No, no! I'll do it myself!' Feeling suddenly that he could not bear to be touched, he dabbed at his face, thinking fleetingly of the corpses that had had their eyes torn out. But the girl seemed unaware of his aversion. Her friends clustered round his chair with teasing offers of help and compliments on the way he had stood up to O'Brien: 'He'd said he was going to make it hot

231

for you before you came in!' Flattered by their attentiveness, he left feeling less dissatisfied.

But, once he was in his car, he felt ashamed at losing his temper and for allowing himself to be manipulated into saying things that were indiscreet: he had attacked the man whose influence was all-powerful and, by his criticism, had probably antagonized the people he hoped to woo. He had behaved with the lack of sophistication typical of Protestant politicians who showed themselves at their worst when harried by hostile interviewers. When it came to publicity, would it be best to leave it to the professionals—presumably they, or their advice, could be hired? As he drove through Belfast and saw the grim messages scrawled all over the boarded windows, he wondered if it would be worth investing in posters, propaganda on the walls. . . .

His agitation lessened and he felt more optimistic after he had left the city and was driving through the countryside with its long shadows. He re-enacted the interview, wording it with greater eloquence and planning how he would restate his case given another opportunity. For a moment he felt elated by the limelight, the sense of power; even the little girls, flirting with him as they applied the cosmetics, had made him feel important. Perhaps his regret at having been so outspoken was merely a loss of nerve. . . .

I'm becoming an exhibitionist, he thought, as his car rose over the crest of a hill and a wide view of the landscape was spread out for him: is it egotism that deludes me into leading a one-man crusade? So far his efforts had been discouraging, his main support coming from a group of Jewish businessmen; some Presbyterians, whose views were hard-line but who did not want to be associated with formal politics, had promised to back him, and one exuberant Catholic who had made his own fortune. But he had failed to attract the moderates from either side. A couple of large concerns had offered to help financially provided their names remained anonymous and there were others who, while sympathetic, preferred to wait till he was seen to succeed. More often, however, his plans would be greeted with coldness and it seemed to him that those who could be most effective were more interested in their summer holidays. Such is the force of rumour in a small place that nowadays when he entered the Ulster Club he would find himself being regarded with antagonism by Protestant and Catholic alike and, when he sat down at a table, his companions would appear uncomfortable; he had overheard complaints that he was a meddlesome fool heading for trouble.

The sun was slanting towards the horizon and the loneliness of the golden land oppressed him. His father had told him he was being selfish and that he was putting his family at risk. Approaching his house, as he drove across the causeway, he thought he saw them, but it was only a trick, the glittering sea or a flash in the mirror. The image, however, was so vivid that it was as if he really had glimpsed his wife, silhouetted against the evening light, their little sons on either side of her clinging to her hands. She, too, was alone as she walked away from him. The mirage remained in his mind, within a frame—like something on television—and, for no reason, saddened him unbearably: it seemed as if he had been looking at her from another dimension and that no matter how much he might yearn to reach her he would never get through the screen.

The countryside had ripened and changed colour, with creamy patches in among the small green fields and the lanes sweetened by honeysuckle flowering in the hedgerows. At the beginning of the summer holidays Margaret had returned to England; the sound of explosions echoing down Belfast Lough and the masked, hooded gangs marching the streets had become too much for her. She had told Martin that the boys were not to come back to Ireland. Catherine had returned from taking Patrick to school and was walking along the shore with Edward, pointing out to him the little yachts whose sails were perfectly reflected in the water. Behind her the island was yellow with ragwort; they would have to cut it down, she thought, before the seeds fluffed and blew into the garden. Edward peered into holes between the rocks and she was surprised at the tiny creatures he discovered. She watched him frowning as he concentrated on the contents of his bucket, the mild sunshine whitening his pale eyebrows, and, as if she were looking at him for the first time, she wondered what was going on inside his head. Would he be a scientist? She bent over him and he

233

smiled at her affectionately but the inner world was locked away and, as soon as she had left him, his brows again contracted over his findings.

She looked at her watch, calculating the hours: John would be back late and she was expecting Martin. Trying to calm herself she looked up at the flight streamers arching over the sky's dome whose blueness was still faint with haze. . . . It was because of her affair that she could no longer enjoy the simple things, the beauty of a landscape, without restlessness.

John was out so often and Martin had become such a regular visitor that it was almost as if she had acquired a second husband, the routine remaining in that, instead of cooking for John in the evening, she prepared the same meal for Martin. Once, to tease him, she asked: 'Well, darling, had a tiring day at the office?' To which he replied rather irritably: 'Yes, as a matter of fact I have!' But, although they now met so often, they had become curiously formal and, instead of the ease of familiarity, there was greater constraint. There were too many subjects to be avoided: never once did they discuss what would happen after he left. This is it, she told herself, this is all; but, however extravagant their love-making she still clung to him when the time came to say good-bye. Once John spent the night with his brother, Peter, and he was able to stay until dawn; this time it was Martin who was reluctant to let her go. He entwined their arms as she walked down the garden with him under the early brilliance of a day that would later become overcast, and he held on to her hand through the car window. 'It's no good,' she said, 'we can't live inside one another.' When she pulled away he became bitter: 'You've drugged me. I'm addicted to you—you're a bad habit!'

Turning from Edward, Catherine pulled up her skirt to examine a bruise on her thigh. He had become much rougher and she was so covered with bruises that in the morning she would get out of bed as soon as she woke so that John would not see her dressing. She left traces everywhere. She had given no explanation to Ellen when she had told her she could extend her holidays by a fortnight. A sailing-boat veered in close to the shore and Edward waved to the crew. At the weekend, if the weather were fine, Martin would accompany them when they went out for a picnic on the lough. Although she despised herself for arranging this and Martin for accepting, she so longed to be with him that she was ready to sacrifice all her scruples. He had come with them once already. John had told her he had an aversion to him, but was prepared to put up with his company because he had influence. 'Doesn't he suspect?' Martin had asked her anxiously. Observing his nervousness before her husband's cooler manner, she had felt that he was not only an opportunist but a coward. Throughout the afternoon he conversed with a facile charm that had aroused John's antagonism and his mistrust of the English.

'Can't you appreciate that you're putting me in a dreadful position?' Martin said to her later; but he became moodily withdrawn when she replied:

'Well, you don't have to come!'

He resolved his discomfort by a show of concern: 'Anyway where is John? Where does he go to when he's out, night after night?' He tugged her hair and pulled her towards him. 'Are you sure he's not at the U.D.R?'

As he looked accusingly into her eyes, she thought: he believes I'm lying—he's like John who thinks that all women are by nature deceitful. 'I don't know,' she said. 'Martin, I really don't know where he goes.'

The evening was dull but very mild and the shadows of basking sharks could be seen near the surface of the water. 'It's stuffy in here,' he complained. 'Let's go out for a walk? We've got plenty of time—or at least,' it angered her that he should choose this moment to finger her nipple, 'time enough.'

'You mean so long as you get it?'

'Oh, come on!' Fraternally he kissed her on the cheek; he had his reasons for wanting to cheer her up. 'We can't spend all our time in bed!' They went out into the garden and he held her hand, walking slightly ahead of her as she had seen him with Margaret in the art gallery. He spent a long time inspecting the roses: 'You really ought to do something about this greenfly!' He picked up one of the insects and squashed it, leaving a small, green stain, then hastily wiped his fingers when he saw that she was looking at him with disgust. 'Tell me,' he linked her arm, 'what is it that John's up to?'

'What d'you mean?'

He made her sit down on the grass and played with her hand,

lightly kissing her finger-tips. 'There are rumours. . . .'

'What rumours?'

'You don't know?' He had lost his abstracted expression and was looking at her sharply. 'Oh, I suppose it's only right that you should be covering up for him.'

'But I don't know what you're talking about!'

'That's a pity!' He shifted his legs. 'You must, surely, be aware that he's got himself involved in some sort of movement?'

He slapped a fly off his leg. 'He's openly critical of the way we're handling things. . . .'

'You mean that television programme? I thought he spoke well—I admired him for it!'

'He certainly managed to exploit the thing. He was trying to turn it into a political broadcast.' Martin touched her cheek, twisting her face towards him so that he could see into her eyes. 'What exactly is he aiming at?'

'One of his workers was badly injured in a blast and I know that upset him. I think he feels pressure ought to be brought to bear on the British to make them do something more effective about it.'

'Is that all?'

Catherine knew so little of the detail of his plans that, unnerved by Martin's questioning, she began to wonder if her husband was organizing an armed rebellion against the Government. She shrank from her lover. She could see him arranging for John's arrest—with regret, of course, but nonetheless congratulating himself on having had the strength to place his duty above personal ties.

'You're asking me to spy on him!'

'Oh, no, no!' He flushed, embarrassed. 'It's just that I wouldn't like to see him getting into trouble. . . .'

Where does John go? Catherine asked herself. She could not imagine him associated with anything that was illegal. And yet the doubt had been planted in her mind—a fear for his safety. When he came home late and Martin had been with her, she would pretend to be asleep. Perhaps it was then that he would have liked to talk to her? A greyness fell over her vision. Edward tugged at her skirt: 'Look Mummy!' But her eyes had blurred and she could not see what it was that he was holding out in his hand. The sailing boat that had curved out to sea now circled back so that the crew could take another look at the girl on the stones. 'Like a turn on the water?' they shouted. 'Why not come and join us?' She shook her head, pointing at Edward: 'He can't swim.' She watched the boat grow smaller as it glided away over the smooth surface. When the white sails had gone from her sight she felt that to look out had become unbearable and, lifting Edward in her arms, she carried him back over the rocks, while he clutched at his bucket.

In the evening Martin rang to say that he would have to go to an official cocktail party: 'I'll try to get away,' he said, 'I'll ring you back.'

'You could have let me know earlier—I've been waiting for you all day!'

'I didn't know that this was going to happen—you're being unreasonable. I did say I'd do my best not to get tied up later on. . . .'

Without waiting to reply, Catherine slammed down the receiver. She looked at her mirror reflection, angry with herself for having changed and for spending such a long time brushing her hair. She read stories to the children till they fell asleep, then went into the drawing-room and tried to settle down with a book. The house was so silent that she even missed the sound of Ellen's transistor. When she switched on the television, she was unable to rectify the stripes that flickered across the screen and she realised how dependent she was on John for dealing with mechanical problems.

Her mother-in-law rang and a friend asked them to dinner. Each time she heard the bell she reached for the telephone in such agitation that she had difficulty in answering. He had definitely said he would ring back. . . . Had she offended him? She had heard the noise of the party in the background—he had been too preoccupied with his own affairs to get in touch with her before he went out. She imagined him ingratiating himself with the appropriate officials, unable to miss an opportunity when they invited him on to dinner. Or perhaps he had met a girl? Was it Anne, the young woman she had met at his house with whom she had argued with such venom? She thought of her long nails and immaculate make-up, a look in her eyes. . . . Was he forming a new liaison to counteract her influence so that the parting would be less painful? It was more simple than that—he was bored! The reason why he had not rung was that he was at home with her now. He was touching her fingers as he handed her a glass; he was talking about his drawings. . . .

She poured a drink for herself and rehearsed the phrases, getting it word-perfect. Then she dialled. The phone rang six times before she panicked in case she really should find him at home. She gulped her drink, poured herself another. When she looked at her watch, she realized that for five hours (even while reading to her children) she had thought continuously of Martin.

The front door-bell rang. In terror she shrank back from the windows and crept into the hall, edging very carefully along the walls, not daring to look out in case she was spotted. The ringing persisted, followed by a loud hammering on the door. When she forced herself to peep, she saw a couple of policemen shuffling their feet and looking round into the shadows.

She let them in, but, to her shame, was stammering so badly she could hardly speak. They apologised for making such a noise: the outside light had been left on and they had felt exposed, standing there, out in the open. She led them into the drawing-room and the more senior of the two asked her to sit down before he told her that her husband's hooded body had been dumped in a quarry up in the hills behind Belfast.

There was a high wind on the morning of the funeral, but the rain kept off until after the cortege had left the house. Obeying a call from Mrs Mulholland, Sonia arrived early to help with Catherine, who was so doped that she was unable to make up her face. The morning papers had been kept out of her way so that she should not see the photographs as the funeral was headline news. John's murder had hit the international Press and her in-laws were taking it in turns to stay with her as a protection against the journalists who came sneaking through the garden in spite of the barrier that had been put across the gate to prevent them from driving their cars up to the house.

While Catherine was being dressed, her relations stood in the hall, shuffling their feet, not looking at one another. Aged and shrunken, Tom Mulholland seated himself beside the coffin, as if keeping watch. No one had been allowed to see the body.

238

The reason given to Catherine was that he had been shot through the head, but the rumour was that he had been tortured. The police had not yet discovered clues to the murderers but, although they were popularly assumed to have been members of the I.R.A., another story was that, because of his public condemnation of Protestant violence, he had been dispatched by 'his own'.

There had been a quarrel about where he should be buried, his parents insisting that he should be laid in the family vault in a cemetery outside Belfast, while Catherine was adamant that where he would have wanted to be was in the little graveyard above the lough belonging to the church where Patrick had been christened. In the end Alicia gave in to her. There had been trouble, too, when Catherine had said she wanted to be present during the burial service. She had stood at her father's grave; it was only women of the middle classes, she had exclaimed offensively, who remained in cars outside the gates in case they fainted at the sight of a coffin being lowered into the ground. On this point, however, (handing her a tranquilizer) her mother-in-law had been firm.

Desmond came upstairs and waited outside the bedroom door. He looked very smart in his morning suit, clutching his top hat. When Catherine emerged he put his arms round her and the other women drew back.

'Don't be too nice to me,' she said, 'You'll start me off. . . . I've taken so many pills I can hardly see.' Her face had been turned into an immaculate mask with plenty of rouge to brighten her white cheeks.

Mrs Mulholland waited in the car with her daughters-in-law while the cortege set off; she made Catherine sit with her back to the driver so that she should not have to watch the coffin. The disadvantage of having the burial in the country church-yard became apparent in the congestion of the roads; in addition to hundreds of civilian cars there were vehicles belonging to the Army and the police, who were keeping an eye on the immense crowd of mourners. The U.D.R. had turned out in force, along with the employees from the family firm, many of whom were wearing bowler hats and Orange sashes; even Danny McQuade had been lifted into a car by his work-mates. Placed prominently on the huge pile by the graveside was a

239

wreath from the workers, bearing the message: 'He shall be avenged!' As people were forced to park their cars and make their way on foot through the lanes, the procession became a march.

Because of the rain, television viewers would receive a blurred image, cluttered by umbrellas and garments being blown about by the wind. The picture was further confused by the glare of many flash-lights. A close-up of the coffin-bearers lingered on the faces of the brothers and brother-in-law and a scoop for one photographer was a shot of the murdered man's father breaking down in tears beside the grave. On Ulster television a funeral was a familiar sight: on the whole the mourners would appear restrained, walking along in silence, their eyes lowered, with only the very poor abandoning themselves to public demonstrations of grief. Where the crowds were large enough to need an Army guard there were often shooting incidents and a new casualty. To the I.R.A., dressed up in uniform and stamping their feet, death was a pageant. But the most spectacular funerals of all, for the Irish with their love of children, showed processions headed by a weeping father with a tiny coffin on his shoulders. On this inclement day the attention of cameramen and the Press was so taken up with people of importance and the fact that there were Catholics among them that they failed to notice one ominous feature, the grim expressions on the faces of the Protestant workers.

Most of the men from Fermanagh were dressed like Desmond in morning suits, except for Guy, who looked like a tinker, unshaven and in filthy denims, his matted hair straggling over his shoulders. Although he still retained a depraved beauty, his gaze was vacant; in a few months he had become a heroin addict. When Catherine saw Davina and Sonia entering the churchyard, she stirred, reaching out for the handle of the car door; she felt like a child that has been excluded from a party. But, once they had gone, she sank back again and stared, unseeing, at the people endlessly filing past. Liz and Carol fidgetted with their gloves and even her mother-in-law avoided her eyes. Catherine had appeared so impassive that they were unprepared for her sudden collapse, sobbing as if demented. She had seen Martin. There was a struggle while she tried to escape from the car.

'John! John!' over and over she repeated her husband's name. She wanted to throw herself into the grave beside him.

Alicia, who had come prepared, took a flask of brandy out of her bag and forced her to drink. 'You're having hysterics,' she held her firmly in her arms and rocked her: 'We can't have you behaving like this!' John's mother's cheeks were bright red, but, in spite of the glitter in her eyes, her mouth was set and determined. Passersby looked in through the window, then turned away, ashamed at having peeped at this spectacle of desolation.

While the burial was taking place, a local band stood at the gates playing hymns; the doleful music fluctuated with the wind, now loud, now vague, and was carried away above the crowds shivering in their mackintoshes.

So many turned up to the reception that there were cars parked all along the causeway to the island. It was Alicia who had made arrangements with the caterers. While the guests were being received, she stationed herself beside her daughter-in-law, keeping her eyes on her glazed, smiling face; Catherine had been given another pill and her mother-in-law's anxiety was not that she might be unable to bear the strain but that she might faint from too many drugs. Felicity wept on her shoulder and Alicia moved her on. Although when they entered the house and removed their damp coats people were very quiet, the atmosphere, slowly and discreetly, as voices were raised and bottles were opened, became almost festive; even the young women, who had arrived red-eyed, sniffing into their handkerchiefs, became more cheerful after a few drinks. Sonia was surprisingly upset, her nose red like a clown's in her white face.

Catherine appeared to have no idea who was embracing her or whose hand she was shaking. It was with vapid radiance that she greeted Martin and it was not until she felt his lips on her cheek that she remembered who he was. The kiss was sloppy, maudlin, his mouth very wet. She was amazed that he should have done this out in the open in front of so many people—she had been touched that he had turned up to the funeral at all. It was only when she watched him shaking hands with her parents-in-law, then with George and Peter, that she realised he had kissed her good-bye and that he would be unable to manage his own guilt unless he could persuade himself that he

241

had at least had the decency not to pester the widow.

Arthur Mulholland was ticked off by his sister, Sadie, for telling a story about some Americans visiting a famous graveside who had knelt mistakenly at a flower bed. Teresa helped hand round the refreshments. Uncle Hugo, shaking his fist in the air, regardless of any embarrassment to his listeners, was declaiming against the murderers:

'Those damned butchers! Those vermin—just look what they've done now!' He caught sight of Guy, who was smoking a marijuana cigarette, and put his glass away: 'Can't drink any more—even champagne tastes like vinegar! My liver's gone, old age of course. Old wretch, that's what I am!' He turned to Davina for sympathy: 'It's a damnable thing to have out-lived one's time. . . .'

Davina teased him about his digestion and laughed till the tears ran down her cheeks. Although they had made an appearance together, she was no longer on speaking terms with her husband, Julian, who was flirting with a pretty girl on the other side of the room.

Sonia looked around, thinking of the man who had been buried: 'This makes one realize how very careless we are of our lives.'

Catherine sat in a corner with John's aunts, still smiling and holding an untouched cup of tea. Not knowing what to say to her, Martin decided to leave, finding the noise of the party unendurable. But she saw him sidling out of the door. She went over to the window and watched him hurrying away, his head bowed and his collar turned up against the rain. Although the figure was familiar, she was looking at a stranger. Why is he so miserable? she wondered: that man is unhappier than I, who can't feel a thing. . . . She was vexed by her bewilderment. My husband is dead, she thought; he has been murdered. Why? What can this mean? She remembered a newspaper article and a woman's reply to a journalist: 'You ask why a man has died? In Belfast nobody knows why. . . .'

The men and women had segregated and some of the older people were already preparing to leave. George, Desmond and Ambrose were re-filling their glasses before the supply ran out. 'Any suggestions,' Desmond asked them, 'as to who we should get to take John's rod in the fishing syndicate?'

242

1973

Alicia was in the green-house with her gardener, trying to decide which pot-plant to select for a fund-raising sale for the Unionists. An azalea would be the obvious choice, but she was pleased to see that, although they were flowering outside in the garden, the potted varieties were past their best.

'The camellias are over. And, of course, there's no question of the scented rhododendrons—I mean, one can't allow oneself to be carried away. . . .'

'Aye,' Nathaniel breathed heavily, resting his knuckles on his hips, 'it's not the best time of year for indoors.' Ranged along the shelves were begonias, fuchsias, a collection of lilies and a few exotic plants much too rare to be relinquished. Knowing that she disliked it, he determined that he would fight for the enormous aspodistra that had come from the original family home. He pointed accusingly: 'You're not going to give them that?'

'Good heavens, no—it's far too big!' Alicia frowned: 'I was wondering about some geraniums—they're no great loss as it's so easy to take cuttings from them. . . .' She sighed as she inhaled their fragrance, but was careful not to look at the freesias. The morning sun beat down on the glass roof. It irked her that because of her son she would be expected to give of her best. 'I'll tell you what—we'll let Catherine choose. . . . Ah!' She looked up, shielding her eyes: 'She must have arrived, I thought I saw the children.'

245

Compassion mingled with anger in Nathaniel's lined face. Catherine was his heroine. If he could have got his hands on the murderers. . . . He took pride in being connected with the family of one of the most famous of the victims.

The garden was at its showiest with the rhododendrons in flower. They could see her walking down the path, holding her two little boys by the hand, telling Patrick not to wet his shoes on the grass. She had become very strict with them and they were spotlessly clean. Her hair had been tightly scraped back and her full lips seemed to have contracted, but there was no sadness in her closed face.

'You know, Nathaniel, she worries me. 'Alicia screwed up her eyes, wrinkling the crows' feet. 'I'd always thought she was a highly-strung girl who would have taken it very badly. But now I sometimes wonder if it wouldn't have been better if she had made more of a fuss.' She went out and kissed her daughter-in-law, then bent down to present her cheek to the grand-children. 'Just a moment and I'll get Grandpa for you. Thomas!' she called out. She found him in a secluded corner hiding behind a newspaper. 'It's Catherine. . . . Come on, dear,' she helped him up, 'do come and say hello to them!'

'Oh, very well!' He rose reluctantly and smiled at Catherine, trying to think of something to say; but, after patting his grandsons on the head, he retreated to his paper. His hair had turned white. He had never got over John's death and dreaded meeting his widow as he was no longer capable of sympathy. He could not bear to look at Edward because of his resemblance to his father.

'Well, it's a powerful spell of fine weather we're having!' Nathaniel beamed at Catherine, rubbing his hands. He took some sweets out of his pocket and gave them to the boys. Edward smiled, but Patrick thanked him sullenly, annoying his mother by kicking the pebbles and taking the polish off his toes. He was still a handsome child, but his former flamboyance had turned inwards as if he had developed a precocious contempt for the world.

Her mother-in-law linked Catherine's arm and talked about the day when the garden would be opened to the public and the possibility that she might be visited by someone important. . . . In spite of his many errors, the Secretary of State (no longer referred to as the Supremo) had replaced the Governor as the butt of social aspiration.

Catherine listened, praised the flowers, but kept discreetly silent her disapproval of the British. In an attempt to pursue what she had mistakenly imagined were John's aims, she had become a hard-line Unionist and bitterly anti-Catholic. She had not seen Felicity since the day of the funeral. She·gave ladies' lunches and worked tirelessly for political committees. Although she appeared to be without emotion, she would become unnecessarily flustered over small set-backs because in the past she had been so dependent on her husband. The people they had known in various services were now scattered to other postings in different parts of the world.

Alicia tried to distract her when she mentioned the elections that were about to take place. She shared the opinion of her son, George, who felt that the whole thing was a farce, the English having destroyed the existing political forces in the country without creating or stimulating anything new to take their place. Although they lived under a form of dictatorship, the fact that the economy was booming showed that people could manage perfectly well without democracy. They had become adjusted to the inconvenience of the Troubles, the searches in every shop, and the problem of finding somewhere to park; being held up by security road blocks was still not as tedious as the traffic jams in more crowded places, nor the irritation of Army helicopters compared with the noise of jets over important cities. When the centre of Belfast had been sealed off and turned into a pedestrian area filled with flowers, the effect had been so agreeable that planners were wondering if the experiment might not be tried elsewhere. Although the numbers of dead had almost doubled since the beginning of Direct Rule and the hospitals were over-crowded with patients learning to use the limbs that remained to them, the I.R.A. had been clever enough to strike at the poor and insignificant whose disappearance left no trace. The Protestant gangs had been cleared off the streets, but they, too, were active after dark and extremists in the slums still murdered one another, causing little stir as many of the victims were themselves involved in terrorism and it was felt that they had received their deserts. As the violence dragged on with nothing effective being done

247

about it, the population, inversely, became anaesthetized, so that thirteen deaths in 1969 had been more shocking than the hundreds of fatalities and the thousands injured the previous year.

'Now, dear, we won't talk about the elections—that's your ploy.' Alicia peered into Catherine's face. 'Though I wish I could persuade you to give it up! You look so strained. . . . I'm sure you've been over-doing it?'

Catherine's face appeared calmer than ever; she did not reply that she had to have something to live for.

Her mother-in-law guided her towards the green-house: 'I want you to help me make up my mind—I've got to do my bit for this confounded sale!' But she wrung her hands when Catherine admired the freesias, the potted rhododendrons, the lilies. She paused before coming to a decision:

'They're superb, but they won't do. They'd be far too expensive for the ordinary buyer.' Knowing exactly what she was expected to say, she pointed at the geraniums: 'I think those would be suitable. Everyone likes a splash of colour and,' she turned to include Nathaniel in her smile, 'you grow them so cleverly!'

Nathaniel glanced at his employer: 'What's the use,' he said harshly, 'in wasting good stuff? Unionism's finished!' It was his opinion that the I.R.A. had triumphed. Had he been given a gun, he would have used it in the Name of the Lord.

'Well, that settles it!' Not wanting to appear too mean, Alicia chose the three healthiest specimens, handing one each to her companions.. Holding their plants in front of them, they walked uphill through the garden under a bland sun that spread a haze over the Province as the dew melted. Before entering the house, Catherine complimented her mother-in-law yet again on the outlook to the blue sea.